To my Todd, the best of husbands with the most twisted of plot ideas.

To Lynda, the best of cousins and cruelest of editors.

To my Irish expert Christy, and clever Laura, who came up with the title.

And to you...
A sincere and whole-hearted thank you for reading Hellion.
Proceeds from this book benefit the two crisis nurseries in my city.
The crisis nurseries here are non-profits that help families who are
overwhelmed and in desperate need of help. Their little ones can be
lovingly and safely cared for while their parents are hooked up with
services for anything from housing, to employment, to mental health and
substance abuse treatment programs.

Thanks to your kindness, I've had the chance to purchase much-needed
items, like cases of diapers, industrial-sized boxes of goldfish crackers,
books, formula, toys, and more.

And socks. Those kiddos can never hold on to a pair of socks.

Contents

Title Page

Copyright

Dedication

Free Books!

Preface

Chapter One   1

Chapter Two   7

Chapter Three   14

Chapter Four   22

Chapter Five   32

Chapter Six   40

Chapter Seven   48

Chapter Eight   54

Chapter Nine   64

Chapter Ten   74

Chapter Eleven   85

Chapter Twelve   92

Chapter Thirteen   107

Chapter Fourteen   113

Chapter Fifteen   122

Chapter Sixteen   129

Chapter Seventeen   137

Chapter Eighteen   143

Chapter Nineteen   156

Chapter Twenty   168

Chapter Twenty-One   177

Chapter Twenty-Two   186

Chapter Twenty-Three   194

Chapter Twenty-Four   203

Chapter Twenty-Five   214

Chapter Twenty-Six   222

Epilogue   232

What happens after Happily Ever After?   239

A Favor, Please?   241

The Morozov Bratva Saga   243

Books By This Author   245

About The Author   249

Hellion

An Arranged Marriage Bratva Romance

Arianna Fraser

STA, LLC

Free Books!

Join my email list and I'll shamelessly bribe you with a free book! You can download your copy of my dark Mafia Romance *The Reluctant Spy here.*

I'm too lazy to spam you, so you'll only see an email pop up when there's giveaways or a new release - like **Deceptive,** Book Four in the Morozov Bratva Saga - which will be released in July 2023.

Preface

Hellion - An Arranged Marriage Bratva Romance is set in the brutal world of organized crime. Those Russians were not messing around, and as you'll see, the Irish Mobs are just as outrageous.

As such, there is violence, torture, consensual explicit sexual activity between a husband and wife, kidnapping, forced marriage, memories of child abuse, and human trafficking.

If these things are not to your taste, I thank you for stopping by, but please find something that will make for more comfortable reading.

Still here? Excellent! Grab a glass of wine or a bag of Cheetos and let's get started. As always, thank you for reading and supporting my books.

Warmly, Arianna

Chapter One

In which Aisling discovers that her grandfather is just as vile as she thinks he is.

Aisling...

Just look casual. I'm almost out the door and out of here and-

"Your grandfather is looking for you."

Damn. IT. I was *so* close to the front door, close enough to reach out and touch the copper doorknob.

I froze, hating myself for it. No one wanted Padraic O'Connell looking for them. I'd seen the meanest, most brutal clan thugs who worked for my *daideó* abruptly turn the other way when he bellowed for them. *Daideó* was a word too warm to describe my grandfather, but he insisted we address him with the endearment. I don't know if he thought it would somehow force us to actually love him, not that he would care.

Trying to smooth down my hair with suddenly sweaty hands, I sucked in a deep breath. There was never good news when I went into that room. The only question was how bad it was going to get. I knocked on the tall, hand-carved door to his study.

"Come in."

His study was designed to make everyone who entered it feel lower than dirt. It was a two-story monstrosity with imposing bookcases soaring up behind my grandfather. He was sitting behind his desk; the thing was heavy African ironwood and massive enough that if you tipped it over you could have used it as an ark. There were no chairs in front of the desk; he preferred to keep visitors standing.

"You were asking for me, *daideó*?" I said, despising myself for the tremor in my voice.

He looked up long enough to frown. "Why do you look like you've been dragged backward through a bush?" His look of disappointment was very familiar.

"Oh," my hands went to my hair again. It was thick and curly and a dark auburn, not the bright red of the O'Connell side and it was never tidy. "I was out playing with Mickey and Bridget's kids." His grandchildren, in fact, but I doubted he could have successfully remembered their names, even if I held a gun to his head. Fighting down the brief surge of satisfaction the image granted me, I tried to divert him.

"Are- are you looking forward to the distillery opening tonight?"

Padraic O'Connell was far too powerful, important, and too much of a sociopath to bother with small talk.

"I've spoken with Michael Kelly," he charged ahead, ignoring me, "we've decided on a match between you and his son Cillian. You'll be getting married next month."

"Wh- are you serious?" I gasped.

Within seconds he was in front of me and backhanding me hard enough to split my lip. "This is how you talk to me?" His hand swung back and up to hit me again, but this time, it felt like it was in slow motion. I should have begged for his forgiveness for questioning him, I should have cringed and cried, he liked that.

That small, furious voice in my head hissed, *fuck you, you fekkin' bastard!* I straightened my spine, staring at him.

My moment of courage didn't impress Padraic O'Connell, my cursed grandfather and the head of the most vicious Irish mob on two continents. He still slapped me hard enough to knock me off my feet.

Standing over me, he shouted, "You useless cow! You should have died with your whore Ma-"

"She was not a whore!" I shouted. This was insane. I must be insane because no one back-talked this man.

Yanking me up by my dress, he shook me hard. "I should strap you for talking like that to me, but you're going to be the Kelly boy's problem startin' in four weeks. You stay the fuck out of my way until then. This is the only thing you're good for." I stared at him until he let go of my dress, pushing me back. "Get out."

"You talked back to him?" Bridget's warm brown eyes were wide with horror. "What were you thinking?"

"I don't care!" I snapped back, which opened the cut on my lip again and I dabbed at it with my bloody tissue. "He told me I was marrying Michael Kelly's son next month. Just like that. Like I was property, like one of his shipments of guns."

She brightened, "Cillian Kelly, then? Honey, this is good news. He's in his early thirties, I think and he's good-looking. At least he's not sticking you with one of those creepy oldsters he's always bringing to the house."

I looked at the picture of Cillian she pulled up on her mobile. He was attractive, but with a smirking sort of grin that screamed, "I know I'm hot and so do you." But at least he wasn't sixty and hadn't murdered any of his wives.

Wait.

"Has he murdered any wives?" I asked Bridget, "Being hot doesn't keep him from being a monster like everyone else we know."

"He's never been married," she said absently, flicking through his bio on his family company's website. "He's the CFO, so he's smart, he's educated. Maybe he's not on that side of the business."

That side of the business. Every Irish mob family had some kind of "respectable" business that was flashy and impressive and drew attention away from their sleazy doings. To my eternal shame, the O'Connell Mob went far past sleazy, diving into the soulless pitch-black of Hell's deepest circle under the malevolent leadership of my *daideó.*

It meant I grew up without friends - unless you counted the offspring from the other mob families, which I didn't - because no sane parent would allow their child to hang out with the granddaughter of Padraic O'Connell.

I couldn't blame them.

On the bright side, I was very close to my sister-in-law Bridget and my niece and nephew. My brother Mickey was too obsessed with trying to live up to the murderous reputation set by our Da.

"Where is Mickey?" I asked, trying to keep my bloody lip from staining the white couch Bridget insisted on buying when she decorated their wing of the house. It's a neoclassical monstrosity and testament to excess and was, I was pretty sure, the biggest house in Dublin. Certainly, the grandest and if you were an O'Connell, you were born, lived, and died here.

"He's already at the distillery, getting ready for tonight and no doubt following your father around and repeating all the same orders," she answered dryly. Bridget was a classic example of an arraigned mob marriage. She didn't much like my brother, but once she'd given birth to Zoe and Finn, she knew she had to make the best of it.

"Maaaa! Maaaa! Zoe smacked me!" The outraged shriek of my nephew was getting closer and I rushed into a bathroom to hide.

"Won't be the first time I've hidden a fat lip or a black eye from the kids," I mumbled, "but God willin' that if Cillian's not a complete bastard, it will be the last."

It was after midnight when I heard the commotion downstairs, frantic voices and doors slamming. Hauling myself out of bed, I groaned. It was probably my idiot brother and our Da. Bad enough sober, worse hammered. I can only imagine how much whiskey they sucked down tonight.

But it wasn't any of the men in the family, it was police detectives talking to a sobbing Bridget.

"What the hell's going on?" I snapped, putting a protective arm around her, "what did you say to her?" The *gardai* were never welcome here, the ones on *daideó's* payroll never showed up here at the house.

"Aisling O'Connell?" The man was older, with graying hair and a bit of a paunch. He was going for a kindly uncle look when he tried to smile, "I'm Detective Ryan. We have some hard news. Your..." he hesitated, "there was violence at the O'Connell Distillery tonight."

Of course there was, I thought sourly, *get a bunch of O'Connell Mob men together and they'll be celebrating like they're the kings of Ireland.*

"Yes?" I asked, confused about why Bridget was crying so hard that she couldn't speak except for little, hitching breaths.

"Your Da... they were all killed. Every one of them shot. It only took minutes, no one was alive by the time we got the call." Detective Ryan reached out his hand when I swayed, still holding up Bridget.

"You're- that's ridiculous," I said hoarsely, "you're talkin' about *Padraic O'Connell.* There's no way."

"I'm sorry," and he almost sounded it, "it's true. Every man there is dead."

"M- my Da? Mickey, my brother, they're..." My mouth opened and closed like a goldfish's; I couldn't seem to shape the right words to form a sentence.

Part of me was terrified and heartsick that all the men in our family were gone. But there was a dark, cautious little corner in my brain that was cheering, dancing, and laughing like a mad thing and the feeling that came over me wasn't grief.

It felt like freedom.

Chapter Two

In which the only thing better than revenge is success.

That evening at the O'Connell Distillery...

Patrick...

Killing every adult male O'Connell didn't give me the pleasure I could see on Maksim and Yuri's faces. But the *Pakhan* and the *Sovietnik* of the Morozov Bratva had as much desire for revenge as I did on the O'Connell Mob, and unless we wiped them all out, this feud would never be over.

I gritted my teeth and picked off a man aiming his gun at Yuri, and shot another O'Connell soldier making a run for it.

Chickenshite.

Firefights are never how they look in the movies- all guns blazing and men roaring. They're mostly color and movement, the yellow blaze of a gunshot, splashes of red, shadows of bodies turned black and gray.

Once the first shot was taken, it was over in minutes and we were surrounded by one hundred of the most influential men in the O'Connell Mob, and every one of those bastards was dead.

I held back the monster raging inside me until we made it back to the warehouse. The ugly, vicious part that remembered what this evil fuck did to my family. To my little sisters. Until I stood in front of Padraic O'Connell.

"Do you know who I am?"

He looked up at me, his eye was already blackening and the wounds in his side and leg soaked his expensive suit with blood. "Another Russian piece of shite," he hissed, trying to spit blood at me.

I gave a humorless little chuckle, "I'm proud to be the Morozov *Obshchak*, but I'm also proud to be a Doyle. The last of that line, thanks to you." Squatting to his level, I grinned at his look of horror. "Frustrating, aye? Never sure if you murdered all your enemies? Wondering if there's another grandma to kill, another little girl to- to hurt?" Rising up, I punched him in the face as hard as I could, enjoying how his chair flew back, crashing against the floor.

Putting my boot on his chest, I pushed down on the wound, enjoying his bellow of pain. "I'll be taking over your empire and running it as the Doyle Mob, just as it should have been. I'll be paying tribute to the Morozov Bratva, the family you hate most in the world." Leaning closer, I grinned, "And I'll be marrying your sweet little granddaughter to cement the deal with your associates."

The old man's eyes bulged and his beet-red face turned nearly purple with rage.

"You've tortured and killed enough people, likely including your own family," I said. "I'm not gonna kill you, but there's definitely a line forming behind me." I pulled him upright by his tie, settling the chair again. "What's left of your miserable life is going to be spent feelin' everything you did to the innocent. Rot in hell."

I turned and walked away, a grim little smile on my face as I listened to his shouting and then, screaming.

"Are you all right?" Maksim asked. "This is... a great deal to handle, Patrick." He was frowning as he put his hand on my shoulder.

I stared at him. The *Pakhan* of the Morozov Bratva, talking to me like I was a brother?

Taking a deep breath, I let it out slowly and nodded. "It is. But I will be."

The next morning…

Bracing my hands against the wall of the shower, I let the hot water beat down against my skin. I hadn't slept, despite the comfortable bed. There was too much to do, too much to think about.

Thinking about the woman I was about to enrage made me drop my head and groan. By all accounts, Padraic O'Connell's granddaughter Aisling had been kept secure in her family's compound, not allowed to go to college or get a job. She would be some hothouse flower, likely to collapse at the first sign of bad news.

Finding out we just wiped out the entire leadership of the O'Connell Mob would be bad news.

Dressed and pulling on my suit jacket, I met Yuri in the living room. "Are you sure you don't want me to come with you?" he asked.

Straightening my shirt cuffs, I shook my head. "No. If I'm going to be the head of the clan, I have to show my authority. Dragging my *Sovietnik* along doesn't exactly inspire confidence."

He shook his head. "Ah, but I am no longer your *Sovietnik*, and you are no longer our *Obshchak*," he said with a wry smile. "You are your own man now, Patrick. Head of your organization and *Ceann Fine.* You are correct, you must do this on your own."

"Since I'm about to go in front of the Irish Council, this Ted Talk is much appreciated," I said dryly, "maybe they won't shoot me the minute I walk through the door."

"They all hated Padraic O'Connell as much as we do," Maksim joined us in the front hall, "they were just too spineless to do anything about it." The Six Families here in Ireland are just as dogmatic and obsessed with bloodlines as the Russian Six. They will validate your claim." The cold, controlled Pakhan that I've rarely seen crack a smile, did now as he reached out his hand to shake mine. "Vengeance is good, Patrick. But success is even better."

"Thank you, boss." He raised a brow at me and I chuckled, shaking my head. "Thank you, Maksim." I looked at an openly grinning Yuri and shook his hand, too. There's so much more I wanted to say, to thank them, but we are stoic men and I was pretty sure they already knew what I would tell them.

Liam was leaning against my black Range Rover, smoking a cigarette, and he brightened when he spotted me. "Hey, brother! Ready to go get our asses kicked, then?"

"Very inspiring, dickhead," I said sourly. Liam Fitzpatrick was my first cousin on my mother's side, which was the only reason he and his family survived the O'Connell slaughter of my father's people, the Doyle's. "I'm questioning if you have the ability to keep your smart mouth shut as my Second."

"You're lookin' fancy," he said, "that watch alone will impress those old bastards." He looked pretty good too, in an expensive Armani suit, his dark hair cut short. I could see his neck tattoos crawling out from under his dress shirt, and he'd put on about twenty pounds of muscle since I'd seen him last.

"Money and power," I sighed, "the only things that interest this bunch." I slid into the car as he took the wheel, and two discreet SUVs pulled out to follow us.

"Borrowed muscle?" Liam asked, looking in the rearview mirror.

"A gift from the Morozovs until we build our ranks," I said. "I've worked with most of these men for ten years. Maksim and Yuri sent us some of their best."

He shrugged, keeping his eyes on the road. "You're gonna make them a shite tonne of money."

My cousin was fighting his natural antipathy toward the Bratva, and it made sense. The Russians came in and took over swathes of London, Toronto, and Montreal and pushed out the Irish, or shrunk their reach to a tenth of what they had. But the O'Connells did much worse to the other Irish families- to their own people.

Now their territory is mine.

We were meeting the Council at a fancy restaurant owned by the Kelly Mob. There was a massive back room built like a proper library, all wood paneling and expensive leather furniture, and enough Cuban cigars to give everyone within a block radius lung cancer by association. The security men at the private entrance give me a respectful nod.

"Mr. Doyle, welcome. You're expected, may I take you back?" I recognize the man speaking, he's one of Kelly's men.

"Thank you," I answered, looking back to see my Bratva backups stepping out of their SUVs. I gave them a slight head-shake, and they stayed put, aside from Liam.

The meeting room was just as I remembered, the five expensively dressed men sitting around the huge table, a blaze crackling in the fireplace and reeking clouds of cigar smoke. They all stand to greet me and shake my hand, slapping me on the shoulder and offering congratulations.

After I'm served a drink and the pleasantries were over, the interrogation began.

"What makes you think you're up to this, Doyle? Most of your people are dead and gone. How many men are loyal to you?"

Declan Flanagan is first out of the gate with a hard question. He's a giant of a man even at sixty, with shrewd brown eyes.

"The O'Connells murdered my family, it's true, but we have a large network of extended family and other professionals ready to join with me," I said blandly, keeping my hate in check. All these powerful men sat by when my people were obliterated.

"You've got a heavy Russian presence," pursued Rian Dwyer, he's in his seventies and I know his two sons are counting the days until he keels over from a heart attack. Based on how he was plowing through that roast beef, it would be sooner than later.

"For now," I allowed, "the Morozov Bratva has an interest here." Better to lay this out on the table now. "But this organization is mine."

The questions volley back and forth, but they're nothing I didn't expect. The only man who doesn't look pleased is Michael Kelly, who spent the entire meeting glaring at me, but as long as the others agreed it doesn't matter what Kelly's got stuck up his ass, the territory was mine. In the end, the rest of the most powerful Irish names in organized crime rose to their feet again.

"Welcome to the Six," Flanagan intoned, and they all raise a glass.

I drank to their health; they drank to mine and I leave as soon as is respectful.

"Where to now?" Liam said, back behind the wheel.

Running my hand through my hair, which was getting grayer by the day, I said, "To the O'Connell compound. Time to introduce myself to my future wife."

Liam started laughing, which is never good. "I know Aisling," he chuckled, "she went to school with my sister. She beat the shite out of one of the rugby boys for pinching her arse. You got a battle coming, brother."

"You know, so far you're not the most inspiring Second,

arsehole," I said.

He shrugged, keeping his eyes on the road. "I know you didn't hire me to massage your tiny dick and call you sweetheart. You're a big boy."

"You can still do your job with a black eye and a couple of missing teeth," I said, scrolling through my mobile.

The irritating bastard was still laughing, but at least he shut up.

Chapter Three

In which Aisling discovers that yes, things can always get worse.

Aisling...

I had my arm around Bridget, who was sobbing hard enough to make the front of her shirt wet. I know it's not the grief of a wife who lost her husband, it was the same terror I'm feeling. Who killed all the men in our family? Who could possibly have that kind of power? More importantly, what would happen to us now?

There had been some hope that *daideó* was still alive, he was missing from the carnage at the distillery. But then, his body was found today, dumped on the road in front of the iron gates blocking our driveway from the street.

What was left of him, at any rate.

The only person I could think to call was our family solicitor as no one was telling us anything. The detectives had nothing for me, other than wanting someone to ID the bodies.

"Why the hell do they need anyone to identify the bodies?" I hissed to Bridget, "They all have that same disgusting brand, it's not like anyone's going to question if they're O'Connell's for god's sake!"

"Aye," she took a deep breath, trying to pull herself back together. "But which branded O'Connell bastard in particular is what they're wanting."

I shuddered.

"Aisling! Bridget! Girls, I'm so sorry I took so long to get here." It was Darragh Griffin, our family solicitor who was - finally - here to hopefully tell us what was going to happen now. He was closer to our age, inheriting the firm from his Da, with expensive suits and an expensive haircut and it was all paid for with our family money. Given how many times he'd kept the O'Connell men out of prison, he was worth every Euro we paid him.

"What's going on?" Bridget wailed, "How are we supposed to keep things running if we don't-"

Darragh took her hands squeezing them anxiously. "Here, let's go sit in the study, all right?"

"Not in there," we said together.

I added, "The sitting room. It's much more comfortable." Neither Bridget nor I would ever step willingly into the room where *daideó* held court. As I was recently reminded, nothing good ever happened there.

The sitting room was one of my favorite places in the mansion. There were a series of French doors that led out to the stone terrace, overlooking the ocean. The bright white walls and colorful paintings made this room so much brighter and happier than most of the house.

"Would you like some tea?" Bridget offered, ever the attentive hostess.

Darragh loosened his tie, eyes darting nervously between us both and I said, "It sounds like whiskey all around might be a better idea."

"Aye," he agreed, heartfelt. I poured a hefty portion for him and smaller ones for Bridget and me. It was one of the new O'Connell brands the distillery had been about to roll out.

Bitterly toasting myself in the mirror, I whispered, "Sláinte."

Taking a deep breath and gathering my courage, I sat back down and pointed at Darragh. "Tell us what's going on."

This was a man who'd managed to keep some of the most vicious men in the O'Connell Mob out of jail, but he looked shaken. Rubbing his hands down his face, Darragh said, "All of the men in your family are gone. Every one of them over the age of eighteen."

Bridget wept hopelessly and I put my arm around her as he explained what happened the night before.

"It may not surprise you to know that the Irish Council from the Six Families is not demanding retribution," he explained. "Your father and grandfather's behavior has been considered unacceptable - even by the other families - for some time."

I knew the families agreed on territory and certain - limited - standards of behavior to keep the law from coming down on everyone. Standards I knew my *daideó* violated, repeatedly.

"So, what happens now?" I asked, rubbing my forehead. I could feel a migraine building. "How do we take care of the families who lost their men? How do we protect them?"

He looked pale, this man who was used to defending monsters. "I need you to be brave. The Morozov Bratva killed everyone in the distillery. They have an Irish representative who is taking over all the O'Connell business interests and assets."

"Who?" I asked, trying to imagine what Irishman would work for the Russians.

"His name is Patrick Doyle," he said heavily. "His family was one of the Six before your grandfather had them all killed."

"All the men?" I wheezed, trying to comprehend it.

"No," he reached out and squeezed my shaking hand. "Everyone. From the oldest to the youngest, it was how Padraic built his empire. No one dared cross him after that."

"E- everyone? You mean… my grandfather killed…" My lips were still moving but nothing else came out. I knew the old man was evil. I knew he'd done horrible things. But… I covered my mouth, trying not to vomit. He'd killed children, grandparents, mothers… just to cement his reputation as a monster. All those people.

"Our family is a curse," Bridget sobbed, "everyone's going to come after us and we deserve it, but not my kids, they didn't-"

"Shh, hey. Hush. It's all right," he said urgently. "Unlike your grandfather's reign, the Doyles don't hold the sins of the father against the children. He'll be taking over everything, he has the council's full support. But all the families will be cared for. Men who worked for the O'Connell Mob who wish to stay alive will pledge loyalty to him."

"Are there any left?" I laughed, a high, hysterical sound that made me wince.

"They would all be lower level or very young," he admitted. "But with the Council's backing, no one will go against him."

"Okay, okay…" I nodded mindlessly, trying to process this. "What about us? Bridget and the kids and me?" I never thought I'd be grateful for not having any other brothers or sisters - alive, at any rate. This mess was bad enough.

This question seemed to affect our solicitor more than the other horrible news.

"Well, Aisling," he stammered, "you need to understand, that-"

"You'll be marrying me."

There was a tall man standing on the terrace just outside the sitting room, the white French doors framing him.

He wore an expensive suit like he was born with a silver spoon shoved up his arse, hands in his pockets and legs spread.

"Where did you come from?" Bridget gasped.

"More important," I snapped, "who the *fuck* are you?"

His brilliant blue eyes narrowed as he tilted his head, looking me up and down with an alarming level of thoroughness. "Patrick Doyle," he finally answered me. "I'm going to be your husband."

Patrick...

Aisling... I thought, *this must be her.*

The woman stalking angrily toward me with her hands clenched into fists was beautiful and, thank God, didn't look anything like her bastard father or the old man. She was petite and too lean, unlike the stubby, barrel-chested O'Connell men, and with pale green eyes alight like the fires of hell.

I had intended to come through the front, but I could hear women's voices - high and agitated - through open doors to the terrace. Strolling over silently, I listened long enough to know their solicitor was coming to the toughest part of the conversation.

"You..." she hissed, teeth clenched, "I'll kill you, you bastard! I'm going to-"

"Ah, ah!" I chastised her, grabbing her around the waist and swinging her off her feet when she tried to punch me. "I've never hit a woman but there's always a first time. Lock it down and listen before ya' fly off again."

"To *you?*" Aisling said incredulously. She raised her hand to slap me and I grabbed her wrist, twisting it behind her back and caging her in with my other arm across her chest.

"You do not hit me," I growled into her ear, feeling her shudder. "I left your innocents alive, unlike old man O'Connell and what he did to my people." The fight seemed to go out of her with that and she slumped against me.

Pulling herself free, she smoothed down her dress with shaking hands, trying to calm down. "I am sincerely sorry for what my *daideó* did to your… your people," she said formally, "it was evil. But *you* murdered our men! You must be an eejit if you think I'm marrying your sorry arse!"

Sighing irritably, I hoisted her up by the waist, ignoring her outraged yelp and carried her into the room, dumping her into a chair and putting my hands on the armrests, blocking her in. "Shut yer mouth and listen. You think I'm the only one who wanted the O'Connell men dead? There's plenty of others - most recently the Chinese Triad and the Italians - who were crossed by the old man. And unlike me, they're happy to tear a strip off the O'Connell women instead to get their revenge."

Aisling angrily tried to pull loose and I pushed her back against the chair.

"Let me be clear," I snarled. "The vultures are circling, and your chances - and those of your brother's wife and kids - of surviving longer than a week are slim to none if we are not married and you're all under my protection. So put the crazy away and pay attention."

I was close enough to appreciate how beautiful she was; her porcelain skin, heaving breaths through her pretty pink mouth…

You're thinking the granddaughter of that murderous fuck is beautiful? I was instantly disgusted with myself.

"Mr. Doyle? Darragh Griffen, former family solicitor for the O'Connell clan. A pleasure to meet you." The fancy-dressed weasel was up with his hand held out to shake in an instant. I noticed Aisling's eyes narrowed as he specified "former" family attorney, distancing himself with an impressive speed.

Nonetheless, I straightened up and shook his hand. "I heard you were explaining what is about to happen to the ladies?"

"We ah, just got to the part where we were discussing Miss

O'Connell's marriage to you to cement-"

"Oh, hell no!" Aisling bounced up and I gently pushed her back onto her seat.

"Let the grownups talk, lass," I said, enjoying the almost audible grinding of her teeth. "But yes, counselor, why don't you explain it to her?"

"Aisling," Darragh said, crouching next to her chair, "he's telling the truth. There's a horde of very, very bad men who want to take what belongs to your family - to the Doyle family -" he corrected hastily, with a nod to me. "People who want revenge. They're perfectly happy to take your life to get it, Bridget's, even her children's. *This* is how you protect your people. This is why anyone left from the O'Connell mob will fall in line instead of trying to kill more people and leaving you in the crossfire."

"This is-" she was shaking her head mindlessly, her pale skin going impossibly paler, "this can't be- he's- I can't! I won't *do* this-"

"You were going to have to marry Cillian Kelly next month," Bridget spoke up. "It's not like you were getting out of an arranged marriage any more than I was. *I'd* marry him-" she nodded at me, smiling weakly, "but I'm pretty sure he doesn't want to be raising Colm's offspring."

A muscle ticked in my jaw at the mention of that bastard, who nearly cut Yuri's arm off. I forced myself to smile and nod politely back. "Bridget, correct? This is an awkward meeting, but you have my promise to protect you and your children like you were-" The memory of my little sisters nearly derailed me with grief, but I kept talking, "like you were my own family."

Bridget was five or ten years older than Aisling, but it was clear the fragile-looking blonde had more experience with the reality of mob family obligations. She smiled back at me tiredly. "Thank you, Mr. Doyle."

"Patrick, please," I said.

Aisling was apparently done with these little pleasantries. "Cillian Kelly didn't murder the men in my family!" she shouted.

Ah, Kelly… I thought, *that explains why the old bastard was glaring at me during the meeting with the council.*

"If we're racking up a body count, I believe your family's ledger is far more in the red than mine, little witch." I said sharply. I nodded to Liam, still waiting patiently by the door and he brought in two of the Bratva guards. "You're going to have security until the wedding."

"You're bringing *Russians* into our house?" Aisling yelled.

"You might want to be more polite. They're prepared to lose their lives to protect yours," I said coldly. "I'll be back tomorrow."

The last thing I heard as I walked out the door was her shouting, "And I'm not a witch, you arsehole!"

Chapter Four

In which Aisling witnesses the Duel of the Fiancés.

Aisling...

It was early enough in the morning that I could see the first streaks of pink and yellow mellowing the dark sky. Pacing in front of my windows, I eyed my untouched bed. There was no sleep for me. Not with the horror of marrying that murderous prick hanging over my head.

"I could run..." It took me a minute to realize I said that out loud and I groaned. Sure, yeah. Sure, I could run. Leave Bridget and the kids on their own? Would she be willing to run with me? I had some money stashed away where my Da could never find it, but with Zoe and Finn, could we do it?

Looking around my room, I wondered what I could take with us and sell for getaway money. I'm twenty-two, but my bed still had the white silk comforter from my teenage years and the mountain of pillows. Excessive pillows, as Bridget teased me. There were the ridiculous little trophies from tennis and golf, back from when I pretended I was a normal human being and not the daughter and granddaughter of, apparently, the most evil bastards in Ireland.

Even so, I felt guilty for not feeling worse about their deaths. There were too many times I hid from them, too many times I took a beating if they found me. I never had any value aside as collateral for some match that would be advantageous for the family "business."

I could sell my jewelry, the only piece I cared about was the locket Ma had given me. Thinking of my mother made me tear up again. She was trapped with my Da in an arranged marriage, too. What would she do in this situation? Would she have taken me and run?

Pulling the comforter off my bed, I walked outside onto my balcony and settled myself in a big chair to watch the sunrise. This wouldn't be so difficult but for who Patrick was, and what he did to my family. I thought about how he looked, striding into our sitting room like he owned it, the arrogant ass.

He looked so good in that suit with those wide shoulders and that stupid smoldering male model look. Shouldn't he be uglier? He should definitely be uglier. And just picking me up and hauling me around like that? Like I'm a toddler propped on his hip?

Screw you, Patrick Doyle, I thought bitterly. *Screw you and screw your stolen empire. Like you will be any better than my grandfather was.*

As he had threatened, Patrick showed up later that day, though not before I had another visitor.

"Miss O'Connell, your solicitor is here," grunted one of the Russian guards Patrick had stationed here.

"Thank you, uh… Kirill?" I said, hoping that was correct.

He nodded, so I supposed that was a yes.

When I entered the sitting room, it wasn't Darragh waiting for me. The man pacing in front of the marble fireplace was familiar, though. "I thought my solicitor was here," I said cautiously, wondering if he was dangerous.

"Forgive me for the lie, Aisling," he smiled warmly, stepping closer. It clicked then, this was Cillian Kelly, I recognized him from the photo Bridget showed me. "I'm-"

"Cillian Kelly," I nodded, "but... why are you here, then? I'm sure you know that our engagement is off." I chuckled weakly, not sure how this could be more awkward.

He had another warm smile ready to go. "I'm barging in, I know. What's happening to you is wrong. My condolences for your father and grandfather, but this move by Doyle to snap you up..." he shook his head angrily, "the Council should never have agreed to his claim."

"I'm... thank you?" I said, "I'm not sure how to respond." He really was handsome with warm brown eyes and short-cropped hair. He wasn't much taller than me but he exuded confidence.

"I just want you to know," he said earnestly, "that you still have friends on the Council. People who can help you."

"Why are you doing this?" I frowned, confused by his intensity and apparent sincerity. "You don't even know me."

Cillian smiled bashfully. "You won't remember this, but I saw you at your family's Christmas party last year."

I nodded, another one of *daideó's* grand events to show off how powerful he was. His Christmas parties were legendary, all the local politicians would show, the other crime families, even the Garda Commissioner would be there, toasting the O'Connell clan. So, it made sense.

"When talk rose about marrying you to someone high-ranking in one of the Six Families, I pressured my father into requesting our arrangement," he smiled, "I think we could be a good fit, Aisling."

"Wh- I-" Floundering, I tried to think of what to say. "Cillian, you are lovely and it was very nice to meet you, but I'm stuck with that man. The Council gave their blessing and I-" I swallowed down my bitterness, "I have people I have to protect, here."

"The person you need protection from is Patrick Doyle," he

interrupted me urgently, taking my hands. "I believe that he's acting as a tool for the Russians. They're really running the show and he's just the face of the operation. They're going to dismantle the O'Connell legacy, bit by bit until there's nothing left and he'll leave you here, defenseless."

"I know he's been serving in the Morozov Bratva," I said, shaking my head, "and they've given him some men while he's building up his ranks, but-"

"You've lost everyone you love, all the men who were meant to protect you," he said. "I know it's too soon to be saying this, but I care about you. I want to keep you safe and I'm willing to wait until you feel the same way about me."

I stared at him, speechless. I didn't know anything about this man, but he did seem sincere, and concerned. "This is… you're very kind. There is still a very large mobster-shaped roadblock in the middle of this."

Squeezing my hands, Cillian smiled at me. "As I said, there's those on the Council not liking this current development. If we can give them proof that Doyle's just a plant working for the Russians, they will withdraw their support. Has he said anything, have you heard anything that would help us-"

"Take your hands off my fiancée."

Patrick walked through the open doors to the terrace. Again.

"Do you never walk through the front door, then?" I snapped. He ignored me as he stalked toward Cillian.

"Did you hear me?" Patrick snarled, "I told you to take your hands off of her."

Cillian laughed contemptuously, a mistake in my opinion, and said, "Aisling is *my* fiancée. You're a puppet for the Russians. You don't deserve her."

Surprisingly, Patrick didn't seem unduly upset by this, "I can guarantee that you don't either, Kelly. Now let go of her hands before I make you."

Embarrassed, I pulled my hands free and stepped back from both of them. "So much bristling. So much testosterone, isn't it? Cillian was just here to make his condolences about my Da and grandfather. You know, the men you shot?" Patrick didn't even flinch. "He was just about to leave. No need for more of this."

Reluctantly, Cillian nodded and smiled at me. "Goodbye for now, Aisling. If you need anything, I'm a mobile call away."

"She won't," Patrick said sharply. "On your way now while you can still walk."

Ignoring him, Cillian left, giving me one last smile.

"Now then," Patrick said from behind me, "let's have a talk about why I walked in to see another man holding hands with my fiancée?"

"Will you stop calling me that?" I shouted.

Patrick...

I knew the Kellys were underhanded weasels, every one of them, but to come in and find one of them snuggling my bride-to-be made me livid. Aisling having the nerve to be angry with me was not helping my mood.

"As Cillian said, we were engaged to be married, an alliance between the O'Connells and the Kellys," she said defensively, putting her hands on her hips and attempting to look haughty.

"Sure, yeah," I chuckled derisively, "for less than twelve hours before the old man's end dissolved that arrangement." Her face flushed a furious crimson at my ridicule.

"It may give you pleasure to gloat over slaughtering my Da and every other man in my family," she said quietly, "but you're just making me hate you more."

Letting out a long sigh, I nodded reluctantly. "You're right. I will avoid bringing it up again."

"Did you just… apologize?" Aisling asked incredulously.

"I did. Now, let's go back to my earlier question. Why was he here and holding your hand?"

"I told you," she protested, "he was just offering his condolences. He seemed concerned about me marrying you."

That was the least interesting thing I'd overheard, and her little evasion tactics would not go unanswered. But not now.

Christ Almighty, this girl was beautiful. The sunlight streaming into the room lit the gold strands in her auburn hair, flowing down to her waist, and her eyes were a translucent green, the color of the tidepools I used to play in as a kid. Then I remembered that my little sisters had played there with me, until her grandfather…

Forcing my thoughts back to the present, I said coldly, "Did you discuss anything else?"

Frowning angrily, she shook her head. "No! Do you think any of you men offer sensitive information to a *mere* woman? What are you doing here, then? Don't you have a day full of meetings or murders or whatever you do?"

"That was this morning," I said, giving her a chilly smile. Cocking my head, I saw the dark circles under her eyes. She wasn't sleeping any more than I was. "I will be questioning the guards about why they allowed a feckin' Kelly in here-"

"It's not their fault." She was defending them? "He told them he was my solicitor."

"That's no excuse," I said, "I'll be relocating you to my house today. Apparently, I need to keep a closer eye on you."

"You already have a house?" Aisling blurted.

"Sure, yeah. Did you think we would be living here, then?" My gut twisted at the thought of living in that evil old bastard's hell hole.

"I…" she shrugged awkwardly. "I've avoided thinking about you at all. I can't leave Bridget and the kids here unprotected! There's no reason to leave just because you want to be all autocratic and-and *unreasonable.*"

"It's my decision to make," I said coldly. "Get your maids to pack your things and I'll have them brought over. But I'm taking you with me now."

"No! I'm not going anywhere with you, you feckin'-"

"You're heading in the right way for a spanking," I interrupted her, "so you should be very careful about the next thing that comes out of your mouth."

"Are you taking Auntie away?"

Groaning silently, I turned to see a teary-eyed little girl standing in the doorway. Walking over to her, I crouched down. "You must be Zoe. What do you have there, then?"

She held up something brown and wiggling. "It's Miso, my rat."

I nearly fell on my arse. *Rats.*

I controlled a shudder, remembering a class in torture at the Ares Academy where they forced us to watch a video of a man being eaten alive by a starving rat tearing into his stomach. Swallowing hard against my breakfast threatening to make its way back up my throat, I said, "Well, it's a… handsome one."

"It's a she," she corrected, thrusting it at me.

I stared at it. Its beady little eyes stared back.

"I can see you take very good care of it- her." I managed, "As for your auntie, she's going to stay with me because we're getting married. That means I'll be your Uncle Patrick."

I heard an unladylike snort from Aisling but I ignored her. "You can see her anytime you like."

Bridget hurried into the room as I was trying to avoid the rat her daughter was enthusiastically shoving at me. "Patrick! Hello. I see you've met Zoe and her... friend." She gestured to the smaller boy hiding behind her. "This is Finn, my youngest."

I stayed on one knee. "Heya Finn. Nice to meet you, I'm Patrick."

He didn't come any closer, but I saw his little fingers wave. Rising to my feet, I glanced back at Aisling, who seemed to have dialed her rage down a couple of paces. In fact, she was examining me with some surprise.

"Bridget," I said without taking my eyes off Aisling, "would you pack an overnight bag for your sister? I'm taking her back to my house for some additional security. Don't worry, I'm also bringing in my guards here for you and your kids."

"Uh..." she faltered, looking between me and a newly enraged Aisling. "All right."

My lovely bride-to-be sat next to me in the back seat of my armored Range Rover. I may have the blessing of the Council, but not everyone was happy about the transfer of power, so bulletproof glass it is. Aisling refused to look at me, staring out the window with her arms folded. That was fine, I had plenty of calls to make.

When Liam turned into the long driveway leading to the house, she leaned forward, eyes wide. "*This* is your house?"

I looked up from my mobile, "Yes. My family's. It's been vacant for a few years, no one can seem to stay longer than a year or so." I leaned closer, "It's said to be haunted." My bitterness rose before I could stop it. "So many Doyles butchered, it seems likely."

Aisling flinched, and when her gaze met mine, I saw shame.

I must stop driving this home, yeah? I thought, *she didn't kill my people, her piece of shite grandfather did. She's probably been abused plenty by him as well.*

Her eyes narrowed and she tightened her lips, ignoring Liam when he opened her door and stomped up the granite steps to the house.

It was one of the most beautiful houses in Ireland, a huge stone mansion with towers on either side, and the back overlooked our private beach. Nothing was as calming as the watching the waves roll up on the rocks, or on the rare occasions where I had time and the waves were big enough, surfing.

Aisling was standing in the two-story entryway, eyeing the ancient tapestries on the walls and the massive iron chandelier hovering over her like the sword of Damocles.

"I'll show you the bedroom," I said, herding her toward the sweeping staircase that led to the second and third floors. "Most of the house is closed off for renovations. The guards have a separate building in the back."

"I'm not sleeping in the same room as you!" Aisling snapped.

"Protecting your virtue until the wedding then?" I smiled indifferently. "I must warn you that there's only two bedrooms open on this floor, the master bedroom and Doris's."

Now she was good and mad. "Who's Doris? You're keeping your mistress in the same house as your wife?"

A jingling interrupted her righteous fury as Doris came around the corner, skidding a bit on the polished wood floor and barreling into me.

"There's a good girl," I crooned, stroking her silky red coat. She attempted to lick my face and I raised my head just in time.

"Doris is a *dog?*" Aisling shook her head, glaring at me.

"She is," I answered, "and the second bedroom is her's. She's lived here for the last few years with the old caretaker who recently passed away. So, you can share a bed with Doris, or share a bed with me."

Doris sat on her haunches, long pink tongue hanging out and looking between Aisling and me.

"I don't like dogs," she snapped. "Why isn't she sleeping on a dog bed downstairs or in the backyard in a kennel? That's where my family's dogs slept."

"Because she is a valued member of this household," I answered, "and you are the newcomer." I checked my mobile. "I have meetings. Or murders, as you've said, so I'll take my leave. If you get hungry, the housekeeper's name is Maeve. Don't get on her bad side."

I left her there, standing in the hallway between the two bedroom doors, fuming.

"I hate you!" Aisling shouted after me.

Chuckling unkindly, I assured her, "The feeling is mutual."

Chapter Five

In which Aisling encounters unwelcome roommates, and Patrick utilizes violence to select his leadership.

Aisling...

That rat bastard.

Really? He was just going to leave me here, standing in the hall? Doris was looking up at me, long pink tongue hanging out of her mouth, like she was grinning at me.

"I'm not sharing a bedroom with you," I said, attempting to look stern. Doris wagged her tail. "I mean it!" She wagged her tail harder.

With a sigh, I walked into the bedroom, worried that there would be nothing but a dog bed. But thank the Lord, there was a regular, human bed, neatly made with a beautiful tapestry-style quilt in reds and blues, and an abundance of pillows. "Pillows, so many pillows," I sighed.

I didn't know the state of the rest of the mansion, but this room was beautiful, with more of the floor-to-ceiling windows I'd seen through my short tour with a sweeping view of Sandycove Beach. I watched the swimmers and surfers and for a moment, it felt like a fist was squeezing my heart. I was trapped in the Doyle house with a man who had every reason to hate me as much as I hated him. How could this possibly work?

First things first, I thought grimly, *making Patrick and Doris roomies.*

Seizing the massive dog bed, I began hauling it out of the room, Doris following alongside me, looking as concerned as her doggie face would allow.

"Not to worry," I assured her, nudging the master bedroom door open with my shoulder, "just giving you a lovely new roommate. I'm sure you two will be very happy together."

Dragging the dog bed over by a window, I straightened up, brushing my hair out of my eyes. "See? You have a great view. Look at that ocean!"

Looking around the room, I noticed it looked barely lived-in. The master bedroom was twice the size of mine with an even more spectacular view and doors that led out to a terrace. There were all kinds of flowering plants in the urns lining the granite wall and big, comfortable chairs. Like the bedroom, the expansive stone terrace looked like it had never been used, with no book forgotten on the low table or flower petals scattered by the sea breeze.

Doris followed happily at my heels as I went snooping in the master bath. There was a magnificent marble shower and in front of another window, a massive porcelain bathtub. The double sink was spotless, no random bits of toothpaste. Even the slightly wet towel was neatly folded over the warming rack with military precision.

Who *was* this guy?

"You must be Miss O'Connell."

I gave an unladylike yelp and spun around to find a middle-aged woman eyeing me. Her red hair was fading nicely into a gray-blonde mix and she had a wide mouth that looked like it was usually fixed in a smile. It wasn't now as she looked me up and down.

"You must be Maeve, then?" I offered weakly.

"Yes," she agreed.

"I'm Aisling, it's nice to meet you. Please don't call me Miss O'Connell."

"Good," she said, "your last name is a bit of a dirty word around here."

I cringed for a moment, then felt all my thwarted rage come barreling back. "So I hear. Just so you know, since your boss murdered all the men in my family, Doyle's not my favorite right now either."

Her eyes narrowed and I remembered Patrick's warning to not get on her bad side. Was she going to poison my food?

To my relief, she chuckled, all those smile lines deepening and proving my theory that a grin was her usual expression. "Sounds fair. You hungry, then?"

To my surprise, I was. "Yes, thank you," I said.

"So, tell me more about the house."

We were sitting in the breakfast nook off the enormous kitchen that looked like it was equipped for feeding an army, rather than just a newly-crowned mob boss.

With a shudder, I had refused Maeve's offer to eat in the formal dining room. Dinners at my house were horrible affairs, where if my *daideó* didn't go after one of us, yelling and screaming, my Da would. Mickey, my brother would usually get the worst of it, but there was always plenty of abuse for Meghan and me. I was always grateful Zoe and Finn were too young to be included.

I scooted in my chair a bit to follow the sun's rays streaming through the windows. It felt glorious to be warm.

Maeve laughed, "You look like a cat, trying to soak up the sunshine."

"I am," I agreed. "My house – the O'Conn- uh, other house - was always freezing."

"Fortunately, a nice big furnace was the first thing Patrick had installed here, he's certainly Americanized, wanting to be *warm* and such. He bought the house under a shell corporation when he was here last year. The renovations will take a good long time because he's so cautious about vetting the construction crews, but at least we'll be comfortable," she said, eyeing the other half of my sandwich. "Is there a problem with your lunch?"

"Oh, no." I shook my head, "It's delicious, but…" I didn't want to admit that my Da shamed me if I ever finished my meal, calling me a pig. Bridget and I took to hiding snacks in our bedrooms to eat after dinner. Taking in a deep breath, I picked up the other half of the sandwich. "In fact, I could eat half a dozen of these."

Taking a big bite, I smiled, giving his departed soul the middle finger. "So, about the house? When did they add the towers and turn this place into a castle?"

"Ah, that would be Cathal Doyle's time, about 150 years ago. He had delusions of grandeur, but he was an utter scoundrel who charged "fees" for traveling on public roads and created the first protection racket in Dublin. The house had suffered some neglect and a couple of terrible attempts at remodeling in the ten years it had been out of the family. Now that your fiancé has bought it back, I know he intends to bring it back to its true glory."

She eyed my sudden scowl. "Very few arranged marriages in the Six Families are happy, and I reckon you're looking at a harder start than most, but Patrick Doyle is a good man. Well," she allowed, catching my sour expression, "as good a man as you'll find in the Six, eh?"

I nodded, keeping my gaze on my sandwich. "I hope you're right."

Patrick…

"How many are genuinely ready for this, and how many are just afraid I'm going to shoot them?"

Liam and I were walking into a meeting with fifty or so of the toughest men in Dublin, men we thought were a good fit for this new empire.

He thought about it, "I'm guessing seventy percent for the former, thirty percent to the latter. You're gonna have to kick the shite out of one or two of the arseholes who are there to test you."

"To be expected," I agreed, watching the home security video feed on my mobile. I had to smother a laugh when I watched Aisling angrily dragging Doris's dog bed out of her bedroom and into mine. If she keeps this up, she's going to be the one sleeping on that thing, and Doris sheds. Fortunately, she's an Irish Setter and her coat was almost the same color as my intended's auburn hair.

The meeting was at a pub that was an old Doyle hangout. I was not starting my new dynasty at an O'Connell pub, even if I now owned it. I recognized most of the faces there, and it warmed me to see the old guard step up and join us, even after my family was wiped off the face of the earth.

"I'll make this quick," I said. "You're the men we hand-picked as leaders. I know where you've been. Who you served under. Who you refused to work with. Your history makes you valuable in this new clan."

My gaze fell on Cormac and Dylan Fitzgerald, Liam's massive and boisterous uncles. They were also the men who dug me out of the wreckage of the warehouse where Padraic O'Connell shot and killed my father and older brother, pumped five bullets into me, and set the place on fire. They'd bandaged my wounds and kept me hidden until Yuri got me out of the country. They would be named my Bosuns and run their own groups under the clan.

"For those of you who worked with my father, you know you're welcome here in this clan. You are family. I reward loyalty with loyalty and protection in return. Your people will always be taken care of should anything happen to you."

Sweeping the room, I caught the glares and whispers from two of the younger men. I knew one of them; Cian Murphy. He was an excellent smuggler of goods but an arrogant arsehole. The other prick had a skull tattoo on his neck. I despised him immediately.

I spoke in a voice cold enough to send a chill over the room. "If there are any questions or you've got something to say, this is the time. Because from now on, pushbacks will be met with a beating. Or a bullet."

Naturally, Neck Tattoo stood up.

"We heard you're workin' for the Russians. How are you gonna stand for our interests when you're kissin' Bratva arse?"

Liam leaned forward menacingly, but I shook my head. "What's your name?"

"Tommy O'Brien," he said, smirking.

"Keegan's boy?" I asked.

"Yeah, sure," he said, the stupid bastard was still smirking.

"C'mere, Tommy," I said.

When he strutted up to the front of the room and grinned at me, I pleasantly smiled back before punching him in the mouth hard enough that one of his front teeth was embedded in the skin of my fist. Shaking it off, I stared down at him, rolling on the beer-soaked floor, wailing, and spitting out more teeth and blood.

I looked up at Cian. "Anyone else have a question?"

He shook his head vigorously. I'll still have to keep an eye on him.

On the way home, Declan Finnegan called me. "How is it going, building your new army?"

Thinking back on Tommy O'Brien's ruined face, I smile. "It's going well. What can I do for you?"

"I'm calling on behalf of my wife. She's quite skilled in organizing large events, she wanted to offer her help with your wedding if needed."

Frowning, I said, "Tell her 'thank you' from me, of course. My priorities are more focused on putting my clan together right now."

"You haven't set a date for your marriage?" I could hear his voice deepen, concerned.

"I wasn't aware I had a deadline." I chuckle to soften the sting, but who did he think he was?

"Patrick, you took over the O'Connell empire-"

"It was the Doyle's first," I interrupted sharply.

"This is well known," he said patiently, "and it's the reason we all accepted you into the Six so quickly. However, there are moves you must make to solidify your claim, and marrying the O'Connell girl is one of them. The longer you wait, the less secure your claim becomes."

Rubbing my forehead, I pictured Aisling's enraged expression when I left her in the hallway with her new canine roommate. "What sort of timeline does the Council expect for this blessed event?"

Now, there was amusement tingeing his voice. "A week or two, no longer. Book a church, throw a party, invite the families, and solidify the deal."

"And the wedding night? Should that be a public event, then?" I snapped. Unwise, given who I was speaking to.

He sighed. "Don't suggest that to the others, not even as a joke. They would attempt to make it a tradition."

I rolled my eyes. Of course, they would, the old perverts. "Thank you for the suggestion, Declan. I will attend to it."

"Of course," he said, "the offer of assistance still stands."

Liam was watching me in the rearview mirror, "The glamorous life of the *Ceann Fine,* eh?"

Scowling, I look out the window. "I thought I'd have more than seventy-two hours to put together my organization. Seems that my days as a single man are numbered."

Of course, the idiot laughs.

Chapter Six

In which Patrick discovers that those in his inner circle are not all on the same page. Some are complete arseholes.

Aisling...

The sound of my mobile buzzing angrily woke me early the next morning but when I lunged for it, I nearly fell off the bed because something heavy was on top of my feet.

"What the hell is- *Doris!*"

That mangy bag of fur was lying on my legs and she was surprisingly heavy.

"Get off me, you mutt!" I struggled to get my top half back on the bed while trying to make her move. She had the nerve to look up at me with a deeply wounded expression. "I mean it!" I snarled, "Ever heard of *101 Dalmatians?* I'm sure I can recreate that with Irish Setters and you'd make a fine coat!" She finally got to her feet and jumped off the bed, slinking toward the door, and looking sadly back at me. After opening the door just enough to let her out, I seized my mobile. It was Bridget.

"Morning," she trilled cheerfully, "ready to get to work?"

"What are you talking about?" I groaned, flopping back on my pillow. I didn't get a lot of sleep last night, even after I locked my bedroom door. Speaking of that, how did that rotten beast get in here?

"*Patrick.*" I hissed.

"Yes, he called me last night and asked me to help the wedding planner put your ceremony together. We're meeting with her at ten, so you should hurry up and get dressed. I know how long it takes you to get going in the morning," she said, sounding bright and alert even though it was the butt crack of dawn.

"You seem very happy about this," I groaned, rolling over to discover the other pillow had dog hair on it. "That damn Doris!"

"Who?"

"Oh, it's the house's resident dog and she's the worst," I complained, "she seems to think we're roommates."

As usual, Bridget's optimistic nature shines through. "A dog? That's lovely! You're always wanted a dog."

"No, Bridge, I have never wanted a pet, ever since Da... you know."

"I know," she agreed sadly, "but you can't let the past rule you. Those men are gone, God rest their-"

"Don't bother," I interrupted, "and we both know where the Almighty sent them. There's no rest there."

"True, it just seems so strange to not be sorry they're gone," she admitted, "I feel like I should at least feel bad about Mickey."

"No, no you shouldn't," I said, "we both know he was cheating on you with half the household staff. We're just lucky Finn was still too young for Mickey to start torturing him the way Da did with him. It's okay to be happy. One of us should be," I finished dismally.

"I know Patrick seems cold," she said hesitantly, "but he was so nice to Zoe and Finn. I think he's going to be kind once he's established his authority."

"Are you sure you don't want to marry him?" I asked.

She laughed, "Are you daft? Now I don't have to dread being the

Ceann Fine's wife and handling all the boring social events for the clan."

I knocked my head gently against the headboard. "Thank you, sis. This just gets better and better, then."

"Get dressed," she said unsympathetically, "I'll be picking you up in an hour."

"It's beautiful!"

Maureen - the horrifyingly perky wedding planner Patrick saddled us with - jumped a little and clapped her hands like an excitable bunny. I was standing in front of the mirror, wearing the fifth wedding dress from the endless rack of gowns the boutique had rolled into the dressing area. I was buried under a mass of ruffles and chiffon.

"I look like the top of a wedding cake," I said, already trying to get the thing unzipped.

"Well, hold on," Bridget said, "let me just straighten-"

"No!" I could feel sweat breaking out on my back. "It's itchy. What's this made of, stinging nettles?" She hustled me out of the gown before I ripped it.

"That's fine then," Maureen said, her giant smile getting more strained with each dress. "Is there a different style you'd like to try? There're some very nice gowns from the Vivienne Westwood spring line..."

The reality of what was about to happen hit me, sucking all the air out of the room and making me slump down on the white-covered pedestal I'd been standing on for the last two hours.

I was going to marry the mobster who killed all the men in my family. I was going to be the wife of the Doyle clan's *Ceann Fine* and this was going to be my life. All those business classes I'd been secretly taking online with the faint hope that I could earn a degree, then disappear from Ireland and make my own way were gone.

"Aisling? Dear one?" Bridget was forcing a bottle of water into my hand. When I looked up, the room was empty but for the two of us. "Drink. Come on, then."

"Where's Maureen?" I asked, wincing at my scratchy voice.

"I made her leave," she said, "she's off checking on flowers or some nonsense." She pushed the bottle and I drank, trying to focus on the simple sensation of the cold water. "It's going to be okay, really-"

"Don't," I managed, "don't say it's going to be okay. I'm the granddaughter of the man who killed his entire family. Everyone. He's going to remember that every time he looks at me."

Bridget sat down next to me, pulling a flask out of her purse. "Here. I keep this for emergencies."

I seized it, wincing at the burn as the alcohol went down my throat. "What the bloody hell is this? Lighter fluid?"

"No, it's vodka." She took the flask back. "I thought you should get used to it, what with all your new Russian associates."

"Cillian said something about that," I frowned, "that some of the families on the Council thought Patrick was just a puppet for the Russians to give them a foothold. Do you think that's possible?"

Bridget shrugged. "Well, I was talking to Yevgeniy yesterday and he said-"

"You were having a cozy chat with one of his Russian hitmen?" I leaned back to stare at her. "You? You hate tattooed thug types!"

"He's nice," she snapped defensively, "at any rate, he told me they could all hardly wait to go home, they just needed to be here as backup muscle until Patrick had his feet under him. He's paying a tribute to the Morozov Bratva, but that makes sense. Anyone else who'd had help taking down a rival would have to do the same."

"Taking down a rival? Listen to you," I teased, "so gangster."

"Shut it," she sighed. "Can you pick a gown so we can go home?"

"Do they have one in black?" I asked sourly.

Patrick...

"What else do you have for me?"

I looked down the long, gleaming table I'd ordered moved into my office at the house. Ten of the men I'd hand-picked for the key roles in the clan had prepared reports on the O'Connell assets and the transfers to our holdings.

"Some of the men are questioning the move away from the Red Trade that old man O'Connell established," Niall said. He was my new Counselor, primarily because he had advised my father in the same position. The past ten years had not been kind to him; he was a much angrier, harsher man than I remembered.

The past ten years had been hard on all of us.

"I made it clear from the beginning that we would not buy or sell flesh," I said coldly, "the strip clubs bring in enough money."

"If we don't, the Kelly's or the Campbell clan will," he argued, "why dismantle a system that-"

I slammed my glass down on the table, cracking the crystal. "Did you hear me? I said no. The two main suppliers for the Red Trade for the O'Connells were in the distillery that night and we took great pleasure in exterminating the vermin. I'm not a piece of shite slaver, so don't ever bring this up again."

"Does that mean we get to put a few bullet holes in the bastards that are still in business, then?"

I have ten men as my top advisors and one woman, Lydia

Fitzgerald, Liam's sister and a terrifying force of nature, with dark hair streaked with silver and piercing blue eyes, the color of a glacier. She preferred to wear stern-looking horn-rimmed glasses and told me once that her fashion sense was based entirely on what didn't itch. She was also the smartest member of her family and they all readily admitted it. When she announced that she was taking over banking fraud, bitcoin, and ransomware for the clan, there was not a man at this table who dared argue with her.

I had to hide my smile. I was the stern, authoritative leader here. "Certainly, Lydia. You find them, you can kill them."

"Thanks, boss," she said pleasantly, but her eyes were already narrowing in concentration. I almost felt sorry for the poor sods.

It took another hour of negotiation regarding designer drugs and rising production costs, and everyone finally rose from the table with relief.

"You've all done good work," I said, rising with them. "We'll be able to wipe the stain of the O'Connell mob clean in no time."

Liam and Lydia held back as the rest of the men filed out. The last was Niall, who said, "I would like a time to speak with you privately, *Ceann Fine.*"

"If it's to rehash the discussion about the Red Trade, you're wasting your time." I was disappointed in him, when he'd served under my father there was no talk about imprisoning humans and selling them as sex slaves. For Christ's sake, the man had two daughters of his own; granddaughters, even.

Niall's mouth tightened. "If you'd give me a chance to show how much profit we could clear from-"

"Stop right there," I interrupted him sharply. "I appointed you Counselor to the Doyle clan because of your good work and loyalty to my family. If you're intending to argue against my decisions already, I might have to reconsider this, then."

His eyes darted over to the Fitzgerald siblings, who both glared back before Niall nodded and took his leave.

"He's going to be a problem, that one," Lydia mused.

"We'll see," I said, rubbing my eyes. I'd had maybe four hours of sleep in the last three days, and tonight - after I unlocked Aisling's bedroom door and let Doris back in - I was going to sleep as if I didn't carry the weight of a thousand sins.

Aisling...

I'd almost drifted off to sleep when my mobile rang. Blindly reaching for it, I moaned, "Bridge, can we talk about this wedding shite tomorrow, please?"

"It's ah... it's actually Cillian."

"Oh!" I sat up in bed, "Oh... hello. Um... how are you?"

"I'm well," he said warmly before his tone switched to concern. "Are you all right? I heard Doyle kidnapped you. Did he hurt you?"

"No. I'm not sure you could call it kidnapping, I mean, I'm living here at the Doyle house," I said awkwardly. I wasn't abducted, even though I'm not happy with the change in venue or my new housemates.

"I feel responsible," he lamented, "if he'd not barged in when we were talking..."

"It's fine," I said, "I was going to end up here, sooner than later at any rate."

"It's still wrong," he persisted, "I'm going to get you out of there. Has Doyle said anything that we could use, anything that would help us reverse the Council's decision?"

I frowned, it felt strange to have Cillian talking like we were in this conspiracy together. I hadn't agreed to anything, Patrick could change the clan's name to the Doyle Bratva, and it still wouldn't count as proof that he was actually in collusion with the Russians.

"Patrick doesn't even speak to me. He dumped me here in the house and I haven't really seen him since," I admitted. "I don't have anything to share."

"Please look and listen for any information you can," he urged, "I'm going to get you out of there, I promise."

"Cillian, I don't want you to get into trouble with the Council over this. Please, just... it's not worth it."

"I'm not giving up on you, *cailín álainn,*" he said. "I'll speak with you soon. Good night."

"Good night," I echoed blankly, putting the mobile back on the bedside table. The whole conversation seemed odd to me, especially when he called me his "sweet girl."

"Presumptuous..." I mumbled, finally falling asleep.

Chapter Seven

In which Aisling encounters the mountainous Jack, and Patrick strips down.

Patrick...

I listened to the conversation between Aisling and that slimy prick Cillian, my fury growing with every minute. By the time he called her his *cailín álainn,* I threw my glass out the open window, hearing it shatter on the stone terrace.

I had, of course, put a tracker on Aisling's mobile and an app to record all her calls, and apparently, it had been a good idea.

Liam frowned, "It doesn't really prove that she's colluding with him."

"It sounded pretty clear to me," I said. I used to get hot-headed when I got angry, I'd lose my head and just start swinging until everyone around me was bloody and usually unconscious. Ten years with the Bratva taught me self-control, but I felt those old demons rising up again. I wanted to beat the shit out of that smug daddy's boy.

Did Aisling know the Kelly mob dealt in the flesh trade? Would she care? Her piece of shite grandfather had bought and sold women; it was very lucrative for him. According to numerous sources, the old man bragged when he was in his cups that the Red Trade made him a billionaire.

Maybe she did, and she just didn't care? As long as her expensive lifestyle was maintained, she likely just pretended not to know where the money came from that supported her lavish lifestyle. I didn't know what to believe about her.

"I'm just sayin'," Liam suggested, "don't assume she's spying for the Kellys. She hasn't heard a single thing that he could use against us."

I ran my finger over my upper lip. "Put Jack on her. She's not allowed to leave the house for any reason. Disable her mobile."

He eyed me for a minute before nodding. "It's done."

Aisling...

"What the...?" I turned my mobile off and on again. It lit up like always, but when I tried to call Bridget, the line was dead. "Trust this place to have terrible cell service," I mumbled, opening the window and leaning out a bit. "Maybe there's better reception if...?"

Nope.

I tried texting her until I realized there was no Wi-Fi. Fine, I will just go find a coffeehouse nearby and-

"Can I help you, Miss O'Connell?"

There was a mountain of a man standing in front of my bedroom door, wearing a dark suit with his hands folded in front of him. Based on the tattoos on every knuckle, he must be one of the Doyle enforcers.

"Who the hell are you?" I blurted.

He raised an eyebrow with a scar slicing through it. There were a couple of others I could see and several more, I suspected, under his big red beard.

"Jack. I'm your bodyguard."

I shifted uneasily. He gave me the barest of smiles, and he had big square teeth that looked like he ate small children for breakfast

because nothing else was chewy enough.

"Uh... sure, yeah. I need caffeine and Wi-Fi, Jack. There's a couple of coffeehouses over on Kildare Street, so if you could-"

"I'm sorry. Mr. Doyle said you were not to leave the house."

"I beg your pardon?"

"Mr. Doyle has instructed me that you may not leave the house," he repeated politely, just standing there like a massive musk ox, blocking my access to the front door.

Grinding my teeth, in my most snobbish English accent I asked, "Is the master of the house in residence?"

If Jack caught my sarcasm, he didn't seem too shaken up about it. "I don't believe so. Can I accompany you down to breakfast?"

"Wh- what the hell is going on here? Are you really going to just follow me around the house, then?"

He showed those big, creepy teeth again in what he likely considered a smile. "Yes, ma'am."

And he did.

He sat next to me in the kitchen as I ate my oatmeal, then followed me to the back door, stepping in front of me when I tried to walk out.

"Seriously now? Am I under house arrest?"

Jack smiled and shrugged politely. "I've been instructed to-"

"I know!" I snapped, "Keep me in the house."

Since he was clearly not going to be of assistance, I went looking for Patrick. He wasn't in his office, though Doris was snoring happily on the lovely oriental rug and likely getting hair everywhere.

I headed into the master bedroom with Jack following me at

three paces. Patrick wasn't there, either. Walking out onto the terrace, I spotted the Range Rover and Liam, who was smoking and joking around with a couple of the guards.

"He's here somewhere," I hissed.

Looking out at the beach, my eyes widened to see the man himself walking out of the water, wearing a wetsuit and carrying a surfboard. The murderous new head of the Doyle mob was a *surfer?* Seriously?

Folding my arms angrily, I stayed right where I was. This autocratic sod was going to have to come upstairs to change. His wet hair was hanging in his eyes, the silver streaks gleaming under the rare sun. He ran a hand through his hair like he was a model on a photo shoot. The view from the master bedroom terrace was good, so I could see him greet the two guards by the back gate as he walked through, handing one of them his surfboard and pulling his wetsuit down to his waist.

The man was *built,* with sharply defined muscles and while he was lean, those broad shoulders and overly generous biceps definitely added to this whole surfer boy look he had going on right now. I shifted uneasily, why was this making me so uncomfortably warm? He disappeared into the house and I listened for his footsteps on the staircase.

By the time he appeared in the doorway of the master bedroom, Patrick was down to a towel wrapped around his wet board shorts.

"Why is that walking tank following me around and why am I a prisoner in this house?"

Patrick shot a glance at Jack, nodding and I felt the bodyguard's footsteps shake the floor as he thudded down the hallway.

"You're going to need full, round-the-clock protection in your position. I'm sure you expected that," he said, heading for the master bathroom.

"That doesn't explain why I'm not allowed to leave the house. This place has shite cell service, I wanted to go to a coffeehouse and call-"

A thought occurs to me and I stalk over to the bathroom. "Did you do something to my mobile?"

Patrick pulled the towel off his hips, dropping it to the tiled floor. "You don't want to get yourself into more trouble."

"What are you talking about? If you've got some kind of mental health diagnosis, this is the time to share it because you are making no sense at all," I said, just wanting to crack him right over the head with the big vase of flowers sitting on the double vanity.

He paused long enough to look over at me, and his blue eyes were like polar ice caps. "You're not marrying that Kelly bastard, stop wasting your time kissing his arse. This-" he gestured between us, "is going to happen."

"Wait- did you put a bug on my *mobile?*" I gasped, stomping up to him. "You're trapping me here and taking away my only means of outside communication just because Cillian called me?"

We engaged in a round of hate-staring as he pulled his board shorts off. I knew he was naked but I stood my ground, refusing to look down.

"You're marrying me. You aren't my first choice. In fact, you would be my last choice if there was one," he said, his voice lacking any kind of emotion. "But if you attempt to communicate with him again, I will keep you locked in your room. It's not just my people you're endangering, it's yours as well."

"I didn't- what are you even- How did I become the evil super-spy here? I have met the man *once!*" I shouted, infuriated and close to tears. "You don't have the right to punish me for something I didn't do. I didn't tell Cillian anything! I don't even *know* anything!"

Patrick looked down at me indifferently. "And you never will," he said, turning on the water. "I'm taking a shower. Strip down and join me or get out."

"I hate you so much!" I knew I was yelling and I sounded completely mental but he made me this way.

Patrick turned so fast that I gave out a little yelp before he grabbed my upper arms and pinned me against the wall. "I don't care how much you hate me. I don't care that you don't want this union. I will marry you. I will fuck you. And I will keep you."

I stared at him, inches from my face and the heat from his hands on me, the scent of the sea salt... I couldn't think of what to say next, I fought an impulse to lean over and lick the skin of his shoulder, see if he tasted as good as he smelled.

He released my arms with a contemptuous flick of his fingers. "Now get out."

Whirling around, I stormed down the hallway to my room, slamming the door and sliding down it, bursting into tears.

Doris was on my bed again, a puzzled, anxious look on her doggie face as I sobbed. Jumping off the bed, she came over to lie down on my legs. I was too tired to try to get her heavy arse off me, so I cried, petting her soft fur. That cautious sense of freedom I'd felt when I found out about the end of the O'Connell reign of terror was slipping away, leaving me feeling trapped again.

Chapter Eight

In which Aisling discovers planning a wedding is much like a slow-motion car crash: not even remotely enjoyable.

Aisling...

When I was fourteen, I was in a car accident. My driver was stopped at a light when a car going too fast for a rainy day skidded through the intersection.

"Aw, bloody hell..." my driver groaned. We were trapped between two other cars and could only watch as the eejit slammed on his brakes and slid into a spin, rotating with an odd sort of grace right at us. It was almost in slow motion and we could do nothing but watch the disaster head toward us until he crashed into our car.

My wedding was just like that.

Since my rat bastard of a fiancé decided I was a spy for Cillian Kelly, I had been trapped in the Doyle House. Jack, my bodyguard trailed behind me like a mountain with legs, blocking out the light and casting me into shadow wherever I went.

As the days dragged by, all the wedding planning went on without me. Maureen pleasantly updated Bridget about how everything was going after I had hung up on her twice. Now that I knew Patrick was listening in on my calls, I spent a lot of time talking to Bridget and using every foul term I could think of to call him.

"Did you look at the pictures of the wedding dress I picked out for you?" Bridget asked hopefully, "It's really quite lovely."

"Sure, yeah," I said listlessly, "I'll look at it later."

"There has to be something else happening for Patrick to be locking you up like this," she said fretfully. "You've only met Cillian Kelly once! This was all from that single mobile call, then?"

"I am apparently a master spy who can read minds and use my X-ray vision to look through walls," I said, "because the phrase, 'I don't know a bloody thing about your business' means nothing to him."

"I know you must be so angry and frustrated," she said kindly, "but he'll surely give up this nonsense after you're married and he sees you're not conspiring with the Kellys."

"Oh, you never know, I might be sending classified information by sheer psychic power. Maybe he'll have to make me wear a tinfoil hat to block my brainwaves!" I shouted the last part because I knew Jack was standing outside my bedroom door and likely listening in.

"I know you won't agree with this right now but Yevgeniy says Patrick was their head of security - the Morozov *Obshchak*, I think is the right designation - and he was always the level-headed one. Yevgeniy says that-"

"How much *are* you talking to your Bratva bodyguard?" I interrupted, "Are you two up to a little something?"

"No," she said defensively, "he's just… nice. I like talking to him."

Uh, huh…" I said. "Nice. A Russian Bratva enforcer who's high up enough in the organization to be assigned here is no cupcake, Bridge. He's done some pretty terrible things."

She was completely unrepentant. "So have- so *did* our men. He's nice to the kids, he even held Zoe's rats."

"That's true love right there," I said dryly, but also a little impressed. My niece's rats were huge, with long, scaly tails that gave me the creeps. Even Patrick - the oh, so manly *Ceann Fine* of the Doyle Mob - flinched when Zoe tried to hand him her rat.

"I know this is hard," she said, "but just get through the wedding. As the wife of the head of the Doyle clan, you must have some freedom to move around and do your part. I know you hate it, but being Patrick's wife will give you your own power, too."

I rubbed my forehead, looking out onto the ocean. The waves were rough and no one was out surfing. "Did you know Patrick surfs?" I asked, "I thought he was stationed in Russia, not Malibu."

Bridget laughed, "How does he look in a wetsuit, then?"

"I don't objectify the bodies of men I hate," I answered primly.

"I asked Patrick if I could take you out for a Hen Party, and he said no," she said regretfully. "I'm sorry."

"It's all right," I sighed, "it's not like there's anything to celebrate."

I sat on the terrace, watching the waves and marinating in my hatred until I heard the thunderous footsteps of Jack.

"Mr. Doyle would like you to join him," he intoned, hunching his massive shoulders in his suit jacket.

"Where would he like me to join him?" I asked suspiciously. Aside from that disastrous encounter in his bedroom, I'd not seen or spoken to Patrick in nearly a week.

"He's at a Doyle pub called Lydia's, it's a nice place."

I frowned at him, confused. That heartless sod was inviting me out somewhere on the eve of our wedding via Jack?

"Uh... I guess?" I said, "Give me a minute."

I threw on a dark green dress, sleeveless and a bit tight. I wasn't dressing up for him, but I wasn't going to go cowering into Doyle territory in my sports bra and yoga pants.

Lydia's was actually a very nice pub, as Jack had promised. It was tucked into a cute, cobblestone street just off the upscale shopping area in downtown Dublin, but there were no well-dressed women with Prada purses here. This was definitely a Doyle hangout. The brick walls and exposed wood beams were weathered but beautiful, along with a magnificent mahogany bar that gleamed from years of polish. There was a tiny stage where a roadie was tuning instruments, hurrying from the drum kit to the guitars and patching all the snaking cables into the sound system.

"Surprise!" Bridget bounced up to me with a huge grin, "I really did try to convince Patrick to let me take you out, but Liam had already set up a party. This is going to be so much fun!"

My head tilted as I stared at her. Was Bridget drinking the Kool-Aid, then? She was excited to have a pint with the people who wiped out half our family? Her little grin faded a bit so I forced myself to nod and smile. It's not like she'd been allowed to do anything fun, either.

A very large man came up to us, and his whole look screamed Russian mobster. Maybe it was the knuckles heavily inked with Cyrillic letters or the scar down the left side of his face.

"You must be Yevgeniy," I said.

My sweet sister-in-law gave him a huge smile, which allowed me maybe three seconds to roll my eyes so far back in my head that it was a miracle they didn't get stuck there.

"Yes, it's good to see you again, Miss O'Connell," he said in only slightly accented English. He had one of those deep voices that sounded like boulders rolling down a mountain.

"Thank you for keeping Bridget and my niece and nephew safe," I said politely. Who cares if he was doing it to chat up my sister? The kids were safe and she was happy.

At least one of us was.

"With my life," he said sincerely and it was so sweet that I could feel a cavity blooming in my molar just from hearing it. Especially as Bridget looked at him like he was Ryan Reynolds and Tom Hiddleston combined.

"Aisling! Come to me now." It was Patrick, and he was far too happy. He had to be half-scuttered already. The crowd parted for him like the Red Sea and I watched him with narrowed eyes.

"I'm going to need a lot of drinks," I hissed to Bridget, "if I'm going to get through this night without stabbing him."

"I'll be back shortly." It was Yevgeniy who knifed through the crowd, clearly understanding what would be needed to halt the hostilities.

"Bridget, you're looking lovely tonight," Patrick said warmly before sparing me a chilly glance. "Aisling."

Naturally, the manky git sucked up to Bridget first as the weak link here. Her trouble was, she always saw the best in people. How she could still think that way after a decade in the O'Connell hellscape is something I would never understand.

"Hi Patrick," she beamed, "thanks for the invitation. This looks like a grand pub."

"It's Lydia's," he said, "you'll meet her soon enough. She's one of the top men - ah, people - in my organization."

My brow rose. A woman? Most Irish mobs were ruthlessly misogynistic.

"Speak of the devil..." A woman stepped up next to Patrick, and gave us both an assessing stare before turning to me. "I'm Lydia, and you must be the happy bride."

"That's one way of putting it," I said.

To my surprise, she started laughing. "Oh, I'm looking forward to this match already. Come over to the bar, I'll get you a drink and outline all of Patrick's shortcomings for you."

The man himself actually looked alarmed. "Lydia..." he said warningly. She smiled at him innocently as she led me away.

"I like your pub," I offered as she seated me at the end of the bar. One of the brick walls near the big bank of windows had a vertical garden structure filled with all kinds of plants and herbs.

"Thank you," Lydia said. "The garden was originally all catnip, meant for Bathsheba, there." She pointed at a massive tabby dozing under the display of some impressively top-shelf liquor. "I planted some catnip to relax her because she can make a complete haymes of the place when she's in a bad mood. See those scratches?" She gestured up at one of the oak beams where there were deep furrows dug into the old wood, "She decided she didn't like the ceiling and hung from it for five hours, ripping out the lighting system until the fire brigade found a ladder and someone stout enough to bring her down." She put a glass in front of me. "He needed sixteen stitches."

I stared at the innocent-looking feline. "The holistic approach, then. A sound plan." Looking more closely, I could see a sprig of catnip cuddled between her paws like a lover.

Lydia nodded at my glass. "You look like a vodka drinker."

"Last month, I would have told you I drank nothing but whiskey," I shuddered slightly. "That was before..."

Her pale blue eyes were studying me, but they softened slightly as she nodded. "I understand. Try it out, it's a new brand I'm carrying."

A hand reached for the glass and she slapped it away with a bar towel. "Manners!" Lydia snapped, "Wait for your own."

Patrick drew back his hand like she'd been a wasp who stung him. "I thought you made it for me, you harpy!"

"Of course, you're a vodka drinker," I sneered. "You can take the man out of the Bratva but can't take the Bratva out of the man?"

His gaze went from warm as he looked at Lydia to polar when he glanced at me. "I thought a good Irish girl such as yourself wouldn't touch vodka."

"That was true before my family's distillery got shot up," I snapped.

Patrick dismissed me, tapping on the bar with two fingers. "Make that a double, Lydia."

She slid his glass over without comment and he nodded, tossing half of it back before leaving.

"I see the engagement's going swimmingly," she said dryly.

Shrugging, I tried to shove down my anger and resentment. "So, I've never heard of a female... what's your title, then?"

"I'm the Arbiter," she explained, pouring two whiskeys for one of the servers, and sliding the glasses over onto their tray without looking at them. "I'm a bit of an advisor, though I've noticed I'm primarily settling disputes and shutting down the bickering."

I laughed, "In any Irish group, that's 90% of the meeting."

"You would be correct," she agreed.

Bridget and Yevgeniy joined us and after three more vodkas, I was giggling like a schoolgirl and Bathsheba was resting heavily on my lap as I gingerly stroked her fur. I met a few more of Patrick's "co-workers" from the Morozov family who'd apparently come down for the wedding, and even the Doyle gang was being respectful, if not friendly.

A shriek of feedback echoed from one of the mics on the little stage, and a collective howl went up from the group. Putting my hand to my ringing ear I turned around, ready to throw my glass at the stage until I realized the guys strapping on their guitars were from the band Flogging Molly.

"Get the feck out!" I shrieked.

Patrick…

"I don't know how you pulled this off, brother, but I'm impressed," I shouted to Liam, who was grinning big enough to show off his back molars.

"Your favorite band," he said, tapping his glass to mine. "You deserve it."

"How the feck are ya?" roared the lead singer, and a shout went up from the pub's crowd that rattled the windows. The band launched into "Drunken Lullabies" and the time for talking was over.

I watched Aisling throw herself into the mess of writhing, flailing bodies. "I should go pluck her out," I said reluctantly, "she's gonna get a black eye and that will go just grand with her wedding dress."

"You don't know Aisling," Bridget was next to me, bouncing on her toes. "We used to sneak out and go dancing. She can throw a mean elbow. How did you know this was her favorite band?"

"I didn't," I said, "Liam set this up." Glancing at Jack, I said, "Just hover. Make sure she doesn't get hurt."

"More like the other way," Bridget chuckled as he waded into the crowd.

Yevgeniy offered his hand to her. "May I have this dance?"

"Who's watching the kids tonight?" I said.

He stiffened a bit. "Stepan and Lev, boss."

I slapped his shoulder. "Just fecking with you."

He grinned, relieved, and headed out onto the crowded floor with a beaming Bridget.

"You coming?" Liam asked.

Shaking my head, I settled against the bar. "I'm just going to keep an eye out. Go on, then." We both knew that the pub was better protected than Buckingham Palace right now, but more than a decade after I'd lost my family, letting down my guard was still something I could never do.

Watching my bride-to-be let loose was a revelation. I'd only seen her at two speeds, enraged and actively murderous. Here, she was laughing, her flushed face bright and happy. Bridget had been right about her elbows; I winced in sympathy as one of my soldiers stumbled sideways with a groan as she twirled around.

"Where's the Skipper!" I looked up as the lead singer yelled into the mic, setting off a chorus of cheers.

"Better answer him," Lydia advised, brushing by with a massive pitcher of beer and a round of shots for the band.

With a sigh, I raised my hand.

"And where is the lovely bride?" he continued.

I watched Aisling frown as she hesitantly put her hand up.

"I reckon you two are mighty far apart," he grinned, "why don't you treat your missus to a dance, I got a special request for you."

I glared at Liam, who blinked at me innocently. Moving through the crowd, I offered my hand to a suspicious Aisling. "May I have this dance?"

Looking around at the eager faces, she sighed and took it as the band launched into "Death Valley Queen."

Swaying back and forth, I looked down at the top of her auburn head. That tight dress of hers was sparking my imagination in a direction I was against in every way. Finding this woman beautiful was never the problem. It was questioning if she'd slit my throat at the first opportunity that held me back. She loosened up slowly as we moved together, the feel and fit of her tucked in my arms felt much better than I wanted it to. When her head dipped against my shoulder, she pulled back abruptly.

"Hey," I said, "you have to let yourself enjoy the good moments. There's no guarantee we'll live long enough to see them again."

"You're a terrible motivational speaker," she said, but she didn't pull away. Without thinking, I kissed the top of her head and we swayed through two more ballads until the band kicked it up again.

Driving home, Aisling huddled on her side in the backseat, but she seemed more thoughtful than angry, looking out the window.

"Maksim and Yuri Morozov will be at the wedding tomorrow," I said, checking the confirmation on my mobile, "they will be bringing their wives, Ella and Tania."

"The *Pakhan* and *Sovietnik* for their Bratva, right?" Aisling's pronunciation was a bit off, but I was impressed.

"You've been doing your research, then."

She shrugged, "Just trying to understand this… mess."

"It is that," I agreed, rubbing the back of my neck.

The SUV pulled into the circular driveway of the house, and as Jack opened her door, she turned to me. "Thank you. For tonight, I mean. I haven't had that much fun in…" Her pretty smile died. "In a long time."

"Get some rest," I said gently, "tomorrow's going to be a long day."

Chapter Nine

In which there is rain, attempted murder, and unwelcome guests.

Aisling...

It's my wedding day.

The weather is matching my mood with a fierce downpour and God bless Bridget and the wedding planner for trying to make this beautiful. The only thing I could focus on was what I was losing. I mentally said goodbye to everything I'd worked for.

My college degree.

A chance to travel and see the world.

The dream of having children who wouldn't have to grow up surrounded by bodyguards and under constant risk of being kidnapped or even murdered before they make it to adulthood.

In the end, even if the man wasn't the one he'd chosen, Padraic O'Connell got his way. I was still collateral. A bargaining chip.

Bridget bustled into the bride's dressing room at St. Patrick's Cathedral, a beautiful, soaring church that was far too good for the likes of us.

"Time to put on your dress!" She forced me into the gown, fussed with it a bit, and stood back, putting her hand to her lips. "Oh, dear one. It's perfect. I had a seamstress come just in case, but... you look beautiful."

Forcing myself to look in the mirror, I had to agree. It was an exquisite ivory gown with a scoop neck and off-shoulder straps, a tightly fitting bodice, and a skirt that spread out in a silken lake of fabric. Maybe something I would have picked for myself if I were choosing the man I was marrying. Someone I loved, and who loved me back. I never dared to dream much about married life, but somewhere in my silly, romantic heart I'd hoped the walk down the aisle to meet my husband would be a joyful thing, that he would be smiling at me, so eager to say our vows.

"Oh, and for something old…" She reverently opened a box and held up an Irish lace veil. "The Sisters at the Holy Faith convent made this for your mother's wedding." Bridget's happy expression clouded, "I know your father said he burned everything of hers, but I managed to hide this." I ran my fingertips over the intricate needlework of the lace, admiring the flowers and vines twining over the slightly yellowed fabric, picturing the nuns bent over the delicate fabric, stitching away.

She carefully lifted the veil over my hair, swept up into some insanely complicated updo of swoops and curls, "Your mother was twenty-two when she got married, too. Did you know that?"

"I didn't." I shook my head, wishing so much that Ma was here. "I guess she and I are practically old maids when it comes to Mob brides, aren't we?" My mother had been gone now for ten years, and there were so many things I wanted to ask her. Bridget had been so kind about trying to tell me bits and pieces about her that I'd been too young to understand while she was alive.

"Well…" Bridget fussed with the veil a bit. "Any questions?"

"Yes," I said earnestly, "what happens on the wedding night?"

Her head shot up, eyes wide and shocked and for a moment, I had her.

"I'm just fecking with you, sis." I giggled helplessly, "I'm sorry, but you should have seen your face!"

"You heartless cow!" She slapped my arm. "Take a deep breath, then. You're going to sail down that aisle and make every man in that cathedral bitter that they're not the one getting married to you today, you hear me now?"

"Uh-huh?" I said skeptically.

"Declan is waiting for you by the entrance to the chapel," she continued, still fussing with my veil, and if she kept it up she was going to tear it off my head.

"Are you all right, then?" I searched her face.

Bridget nodded, even though her eyes were suspiciously shiny. "Yes. I just... even though I knew what a bastard your brother was - no offense -"

"Believe me, none taken," I murmured.

"I remember walking down that aisle and hoping that maybe we could... be happy?" She finished sadly, "We weren't, needless to say, but I have a feeling about this one. I think he could be good to you if you give him a chance to be."

I stared at her sweet, hopeful face. All my whining and complaining about Patrick must have brought up so many sad memories for her. I was a horrible person. "I love you," I said, risking a hug with all my wedding gear on. "I'll do my best, all right?"

Declan Finnegan gave me a kind smile as I walked over to him. He was a long-time family friend. He managed to be a fairly decent person, even if he was one of the Six. "You look grand," he said. "Take a deep breath, yeah?"

I sucked in a deep gulp of air and blew a strand of hair out of my eyes. "Let's give it a lash."

Walking down the aisle, my head held high, I recalled Bridget's words and tried to smile. Maybe she was right. Maybe Patrick wasn't the cold-hearted bastard I thought he was. Maybe...

I could see him standing at the altar, next to the priest on one side and a man I didn't know on the other. He was tall, with blonde hair and a scar that ran down his face. He must be one of the Morozov men.

Patrick looked amazing, damn him. The tux fitted him perfectly, jacket running smoothly over those broad shoulders and his silvering hair combed back and looking distinguished. The silvering hair... how old was he? I'd tried to look him up online, but apparently, an *Obshchak* for a Russian organized crime organization doesn't have a TikTok account. Or birth records. Or anything in between.

I don't know how old he is. His favorite color or meal. I don't know if he leaves his socks on the floor. Does he murder his enemies in the house or keep his work offsite?

My steps must have been slowing down because Declan pulled me slightly by my arm. Patrick's best man leaned over and whispered something to him with a chuckle, and he grinned at him. When my about-to-be husband looked back at me though, his expression was cold and composed and I thought Bridget, God bless her, was a hopeless romantic without a single clue about this man.

Patrick...

Through the veil, I could see Aisling's pretty pink lips were frozen in an odd little smile, like someone's fingers were pulling the corners of her mouth up for her. When her steps slowed and she nearly halted, I watched Declan tug gently on her arm to get her moving again.

Yuri leaned in, "This is exactly what happened at Maksim's wedding, and Tania not-so-subtly punched Ella in the back when she stopped halfway down the aisle. Why are all our brides so unhappy about marrying us?"

I grinned at him, an action I instantly regretted. Responding to Yuri when he was being an arsehole only encouraged him.

Aisling's body was stiff, she moved like she was being propelled to her own execution. When I took her hand, it was shaking. I squeezed it gently, trying to communicate comfort that I wasn't sure she'd be willing to accept.

The priest began the Celebration of Matrimony, and she swayed when he asked her, "Have you come here to enter into Marriage without coercion, freely and wholeheartedly?"

Her lovely face was pale, and her eyes darted from me to the priest to the side exit door from the chapel, as if she was trying to gauge the possibility of a successful escape. Taking her other hand, I bent to look into her eyes and nodded.

Clearing her throat, she managed a weak, "Yes."

We got through the rest of the ceremony, I slid the ring on her shaking hand and watched her mouth finally shape the words, "I do."

When I leaned down to kiss her, I hesitated. I'd never once forced a woman in any way physically, and when her head moved back slightly, I angled mine to look like we might have kissed and led her down the steps from the altar and out of the church.

The wedding planner and Bridget had done a fine job with the reception, held on the grounds of the Doyle House. It was easier to control security there, and the gardens were beautiful; the decorators made the best of all the blooming flowers, along with stringing garlands and twinkling lights around the big white tent.

The rain from this morning had given way to a rare early evening of sunshine and the breeze coming in off the ocean dried the grass enough to keep the guests from getting covered in mud. These fancy souls in their expensive shoes would melt like sugar in hot water if they came in contact with the earth in any way.

"Pity I couldn't get Flogging Molly for your reception, eh?" Liam leaned closer and offered me his flask, which I took gratefully. The champagne might be expensive, but it wasn't cutting it. I needed something stronger and the whiskey from the flask burned down my throat.

Looking across the garden, I watched Ella and Tania approach Aisling. The Morozov wives were good matches for Maksim and Yuri. Both women were surprisingly tough after everything they'd been through. Aisling was younger, sheltered, and while she grew up in this world, I didn't know if she had their kind of resilience and strength. She was tentative at first as they started chatting, but she was laughing along with them in no time.

"They are likely arming her with ammunition about all your weak points," Yuri volunteered helpfully, handing me a double vodka.

"Thank you, my friend," I said dryly, "I can always count on you for support."

"Of course," he said graciously.

Watching Yuri and Maksim approach us, Liam snorted quietly and headed out to circle the perimeter. I knew he was still put off by the Morozov men and while I didn't blame him, he'd learn to trust them soon enough.

Maksim moved to stand on the other side of me. "What's happening with your sister-in-law and Yevgeniy? Am I going to get him back after this?"

I shrugged, watching him dance with a blushing Bridget. "Maybe not. You took a chance on a transplanted Irishman in the Bratva, would it be so bad if I had a transplanted Bratva soldier in my clan?"

The *Pakhan* sighed. "Being married has made me soft," he said sourly, "but since we have this alliance, I wouldn't refuse his request to stay here."

My bride was still talking to Ella and Tana, and based on the frequent glances in our direction, it was obvious what they were discussing. "I don't know, Yuri," I said. "It's possible they're both telling Aisling how terrible Bratva men are and that she should run for her life."

"I am a model husband," Yuri proclaimed, "Tania tells me this daily."

"Is she laughing when she says this?" Maksim inquired, "Because that means something quite different."

"You are just jealous of my charm, brother," Yuri retorted serenely.

Maksim laughed, nearly choking on the swallow of vodka he'd just taken. "The fact remains that while we have all had to drag our brides to the altar, I choose to believe that Patrick's union will turn out as well as ours have."

The mild hope that gave me - that perhaps my marriage too, could grow into something more, something better - was instantly crushed when Aisling moved on from Ella and Tania, only to be intercepted by Cillian fucking Kelly. "That fecking gobshite," I growled.

They followed my line of sight. "Who is that *Tupoy ublyudok?*" Maksim asked.

"He is indeed a stupid bastard, and he's from the Kelly clan. He's been sniffing around Aisling and I'm going to shoot him in the face if he-"

Yuri grabbed my arm as I headed in their direction. "I know this goes against the tradition of Irish weddings, but let's not start a gun fight with a rival mob."

I ground my teeth and nodded. Tilting my head to one of my people that Aisling didn't know I said, "Marty, go listen in to what that bastard Kelly is telling my wife."

He nodded and slid off into the crowd.

"If that fecking weasel kisses her, I'm going to finish him," I hissed.

"Let's find out what he's telling her first," Maksim said, looking casually over the crowd.

I had picked the right man. Marty was pale and unassuming-looking. He blended into crowds well, which made him highly useful for tasks like these. Watching over Yuri's shoulder, I saw Aisling's body language change, she stepped away from Cillian and he moved closer again, trying to take her arm. His face was red and sweaty, he must be scuttered already. Every Irish wedding turned into a rager, but the son of the head of the Kelly Mob should be keeping his head.

When he grabbed her arm, I'd had enough. Cutting through the crowd, I snarled, "Take your hand off my wife or I'll cut it off."

"I was just wishing her good luck," Cillian blustered.

"And now you've done it. Fuck off." I stared him down until he turned, disappearing into the crowd. I turned to Aisling, who was surprisingly quiet. "Are you all right?"

"He's an arsehole," she said angrily. "Who starts pawing at the bride at her own wedding?"

"I'll kill him." I turned to head after him and pummel his skull flat with my fists, and she pulled on my sleeve.

"It's all right. He just grabbed my arm. He's not important," she assured me, looking up at me for the first time since the ceremony. "If you're going get into it at our wedding, wait for someone to do something really insulting."

I chuckled, "So I can beat the shite out of someone, they just have to be more outrageous than Kelly, then?"

"That'd be it," she nodded.

We smiled at each other cautiously. For the first time, I felt like we were in this mess together. The moment of warmth was interrupted by Yuri, who raised his glass and shouted, "I do believe it's time for the bride and groom to kiss!"

A cheer went up as I glared at him. The shite head grinned shamelessly back at me. He was the only one during the ceremony close enough to know that I hadn't really kissed Aisling.

"Kiss her!"

"C'mon, show her some love, Doyle!"

"Girl, grab your man!"

Aisling was fidgeting uncomfortably, eyes narrowed at Yuri, too. With a sigh, I leaned closer. "He won't shut up until we do this."

She looked up at me for a moment, so beautiful in the soft lights surrounding the tent, nodding briefly before her gaze darted away. I slid one hand around her waist, cupping her cheek with the other. Running my thumb along her cheekbone, feeling her soft skin- why *hadn't* I kissed her before?

I pressed my lips against hers gently, groaning inwardly at the feel of her lips, made slick by her lipstick and smooth, lush. The sounds of the cheers and catcalling faded as I ran my tongue along the seam of her lips, growling slightly when she finally opened her mouth and allowed me in. She tasted of champagne and berries, her soft little tongue hesitantly tangling with mine. I angled her head, kissing her more deeply.

The shouting suddenly grew louder again and Aisling pulled away from me, just enough that her breath mingled with mine and we could hear the raucous shouting. I reluctantly let go of her and scowled at Yuri, who was still wearing his infuriating grin.

Before Aisling could escape, we heard the wedding planner clear her throat behind us. "It's time for the new Mr. and Mrs. Doyle to drink from the Quaich!" A cheer went up from the crowd, and I groaned inwardly as the priest began to bless the wine as we stepped up to the small, raised stage where the band was taking a break.

"The years of life are as a cup of wine poured out for you to drink. This Loving Cup contains within it a wine with certain properties that are sweet and symbolic of happiness, joy, hope, peace, love, and delight," the priest intoned.

"This same wine also holds some bitter properties that are symbolic of disappointment, sorrow, grief, despair, and life's trials and tribulations."

The expression on my bride's face told me that she was thinking of the latter part of the speech, but when the two-handled silver cup was presented to us, she reluctantly took one handle as I took the other. It was a beautiful Quaich, heavy silver with beautifully etched designs and my family's crest engraved on the side. When I looked at the deep red Nebbiolo inside, my hand tightened, holding it still.

There was an odd, oily-looking sheen on the top of the wine. Aisling's head was bent, she looked up at me, puzzled when I pulled the silver cup away.

A slight murmur went through the crowd like an ill wind.

"Who poured this wine?" I asked sharply. I could hear the faint clicks as weapons were yanked from holsters around us, Yuri and Maksim pulled their wives closer as our men circled us. I put Aisling behind me, looking out over the shocked crowd.

"I- I don't know," the priest stammered, "it was given to me by the wedding planner?"

"Where's Maureen?" I roared, "Find her!"

Chapter Ten

In which Aisling encounters abandonment, dog hair, and leftover wedding cake.

Patrick...

"Is this the woman you are looking for?"

A surge of fury rose up my throat and nearly choked me. I recognized that voice. I could never forget it. Two dark-suited men dragged a body between them, dumping it on the dance floor. I heard shrieking from some of the guests as the third man strolled over, hand in his pockets.

"*Fu Shan Chu* Zhèng," I said evenly, "This is a surprise."

"A happy one I hope, *Ceann Fine*," he replied with a perfect, upper-crust British accent. Zhèng was a man nearly obsessed with his desire to appear perfect in every way. The toe of his polished shoe nudged the body over, garnering more gasps. Aisling, still behind me, sucked in a harsh breath but remained completely still.

It was Maureen, the wedding planner, her sightless eyes were open, staring blankly up into the night sky as blood still bubbled from the bullet hole in her chest. The smirking bastard stood over her, "I am happy we were here and able to stop her for you. Something with the wine?"

"A shame that she's dead," I gritted out, "it makes it so much harder to question her."

"Well," he shrugged elegantly, "I fear my main concern was

for your safety and thought stopping her was best. It seemed disrespectful to allow one's host to be killed at their own wedding."

"I must admit to being surprised you're here, *Fu Shan Chu* Zhèng," I said coldly, "I was unaware you were in Dublin, or I would of course have sent a proper invitation."

"Of course, you would have." Nolan O'Rourke strolled over to stand next to Zhèng, "This is why I invited our friend to join me as your wedding guest."

Nolan fecking O'Rourke. Well, this night just gets better and better.

"Why is the second in command of a Chinese Triad here!" I roared, pounding on the table, "How did he manage to shoot that woman before we found out who sent her to poison us!"

"Not just you and your lovely bride," O'Rourke said with a credible tone of concern, which I knew was completely false. "As the Quaich was passed around the wedding guests to drink to your union, we all would have been poisoned." His head cocked thoughtfully and I wanted to knock it off his shoulders. "Though there is a certain grim symmetry, given our activities just ten days ago at the former O'Connell Distillery, isn't it?" He chuckled heartily, as if he'd just delivered the punchline to the world's funniest joke.

"Do we know what the wine contained yet?" Yuri's jaw was clenched, and I know he wanted to lunge across the table and stab O'Rourke. The man may have helped us put together the bloody ambush that finally ended O'Connell's hellish reign, but for his own amusement, he'd put Yuri's wife Tania right in the middle of the shootout. Risking her life to "make a point."

"Ella's talking to the poison control expert as we speak," Maksim said, his voice cold and even. He rarely showed his anger, but the frigid sheen in his eyes told me he was ready to kill the next man who appeared to be even the slightest possible threat.

"Why did you bring Zhèng with you, Nolan?" I said, "What are you playing at?"

The door to my study opened before he could reply, not that I expected him to give me a straight answer. It was Ella, and then Tania who stopped short when she spotted O'Rourke.

"What are you doing here?" Tania said, "Shouldn't you be out somewhere playing polo with the heads of your enemies?"

He chuckled again, as if she had just said something adorable. "Tania dear. Lovely to see you again. And Ella, always a pleasure."

Ella linked her arm with Tania's, glaring at him.

Maksim cleared his throat. "Ella, what did you find out from Poison Control?"

"We didn't get a chance to make a UIV-detection after the solid phase extraction, but…"

I smothered a grin despite the seriousness of the moment, knowing the only person that understood any of the complicated jargon in this room full of rich, powerful crime lords was, in fact, Ella.

"The wine sample was put through capillary electrophoresis and the results were clear. It was made a little easier because the dose was huge. It's Strychnine."

"Ah, Strychnine," O'Rourke said reflectively. "A powerful poison, very fast-acting. A few minutes after exposure, the muscle twitches start and then turn into waves of spasms, they usually last around three or four minutes. The victims wear a huge grin as the facial muscles tighten and the back muscles convulse. It causes the victim to contort into an agonizing U shape, balancing on the top of their heads and their heels. Death only comes when the diaphragm then refuses to contract."

The room was silent. Tania looked a little green under her tan, though Ella was nodding along seriously - like the scientist she was - as he gave his nauseating little speech. "What's worse?" O'Rourke continued, "Victims are fully aware of their inability to breathe, the strychnine actually heightens the sensation of every inhale and exhale."

"You can stop," I said sharply, "we all understand."

"Of course," he said pleasantly.

"Now that we know what was in the wine, let's go back to the most obvious suspects," I said. "Why is Zhèng here? It's convenient that he 'caught' the culprit for us and killed Maureen before we could question her."

O'Rourke got up, strolling around the big, oak-paneled room before posing elegantly by one of the tall windows, where the lights in the tent for the hastily ended reception were still glowing. "I know the Morozov Bratva's last... interaction with the Zhèng Triad was not a pleasant one-"

"They torched three of our warehouses and destroyed ten million dollars' worth of weapons!" Maksim snarled.

O'Rourke shrugged, "The cost of doing business, surely. However, while we all *respect* the close connections between your bratva and the Doyle Clan, surely you see that Patrick must develop his own connections outside of your circle? Zhèng's organization is looking for a stable, consistent trade partner here in Ireland. He came to personally negotiate with the *Ceann Fine* of the Doyle Clan."

If I had a choice, I'd have shot that well-dressed bastard right in the face, but O'Rourke had a point. The Zhèng Triad was far more civilized than some of their rivals, not that this was much of an accomplishment. However, killing the woman tasked with murdering the wedding reception's guest list pointed the finger right at him.

"I'm happy to act as an intermediary," O'Rourke volunteered, "why don't we arrange a meeting at my new distillery?"

My jaw tightened before I nodded. "Send me the details."

"Perfect!" O'Rourke clapped his hands as he left the room, looking at everyone cheerfully. "I'll be in touch."

"What do you think the chances are of Zhèng being the one to attempt poisoning the wedding party?" Yuri asked, pulling Tania down on his lap and rubbing her back soothingly.

"Knowing our past with him? Around seventy-five percent." I estimated, rubbing the back of my neck. "Wiping out the Six Families in one fell swoop would be a masterstroke, sure. However, the mayor was here, along with two members from the *Seanad Éireann* and some very wealthy and connected men and women. It doesn't make sense. Killing powerful members of government would create a firestorm no organized crime outfit could survive."

"What about O'Rourke?" Tania asked, "Could this be another one of his sick little games?"

"How would he know that I'd catch the poisoned wine?" I frowned.

Maksim shook his head, "I'm in your territory, but I'd like to offer you Andrei and Igor to do some digging around."

He was being generous. As his former *Obshchak,* I knew how talented those two were in getting answers. "Thank you, but I have men of my own - and Lydia - who are excellent in this particular field."

"Ah, your female Arbiter," Yuri nodded. "Progressive of you, Patrick."

I laughed, "She's more dangerous than the rest of my men put together."

We all said our goodbyes, as both couples were heading back to St. Petersburg in the morning.

"Give Aisling a hug goodbye for me, okay?" Tania asked, "Tell her she's welcome to call me anytime."

I raised my brow, "How did you manage to bond within a single afternoon?"

Ella leaned in, sharing a glance with Tania. "Girl magic, do not question it. Besides, Aisling's going to need us, sooner than later."

"I appreciate your faith in my skills as a husband," I said dryly.

"You know it's not that," Tania defended, "this is just... a lot for anyone, much less a twenty-two-year-old."

"Aisling was raised in this world," I said coldly, "she's better prepared, far more than you two were."

Yuri glanced at Maksim. "I can't help but feel that was directed at us, brother."

Maksim shook my hand. "Good luck. This is your birthright. Enjoy it."

My smile faded as I watched them drive away, their entourage of bodyguards trailing them. I might give them shite about their marriages, but at least no one had attempted to murder their entire wedding parties.

The weight of this new life suddenly pressed down on my chest like a load of bricks, and I breathed slowly, trying to push the emotions away. This was my choice, and there were hundreds of people who counted on me now, including...

Shite. Aisling.

Aisling...

I might have clung to Bridget a little longer than was necessary before she left.

"It's just the kids, they've been alone for a while and they're still really clingy after their Da was…" she trailed off awkwardly, smiling at me.

"I know," I hugged her one last time before forcing myself to let go. "I'm glad they got to come to the reception for a bit before heading home, though that turned out to be a great idea, all things considered. You know. With the poisoning."

She hesitated, "Maybe I should stay until Patrick comes out of his meeting, then? I'll just keep you company."

Rolling my eyes, I said, "Don't fret. He's holed up in there with his Bratva buddies, doing… who knows, critical billionaire mobster things. I'm just going to bed."

"Really?"

"No pity, Bridge. I don't need your pity. I didn't want that man touching me anyway."

Sure, yeah. Tough talk but I was still fighting a toxic mix of rage and humiliation.

He'd left my side to say goodnight to our guests, who could not leave fast enough after the almost poisoning and the dead body of our wedding coordinator was dumped in the middle of the dance floor. His guards had locked down the estate, so I didn't feel unsafe. Just alone. It was bad enough that I didn't want this wedding, but to be abandoned in the middle of it?

Bridget kissed my cheek. "In the grand scheme of things, it's not the worst mob wedding in Dublin history. Remember the King's wedding, where the groom shot his father-in-law in the face and the bride stabbed the best man?"

"Well then, this night was a success after all." My tone might have been a bit sarcastic, and her smile was sad as she hugged me again. "If you can't hope for happiness in situations like ours," she whispered, "the next best thing is a husband who ignores you."

After she left, I raced up the stairs and slammed my bedroom door shut before the tears came. This was my life now, hoping that my mobster spouse will just... leave me alone.

Weeping, I stood in the middle of the room because the bed and the chairs were all covered in dog hair. Fortunately, Doris was out, no doubt gobbling down all the untouched food from the wedding buffet.

There was a knock on the door that made me nearly jump out of my skin.

"Aisling, open up." Patrick, being his usual charming self.

"Just a minute!" I called, scrubbing away the tears with the back of my hands and managing to smear the mascara down my face instead. "If this outrageous gobshite thinks he's getting me into bed after this day..." I mumbled angrily.

Whipping open the door, I stand there, hands on my hips and trying to look cold and untouchable. "Yes?"

Patrick, damn him, still looked amazing. Other than his loosened tie and a couple of buttons open on his shirt, he was still as put-together as he was at the cathedral before this whole mess started. He frowned, looking me over.

"Are you all right?"

"What?" I frowned back. Ferociously. It was a ferocious, 'You're not getting anything from me' frown. "I'm fine. In fact, I'm just going to bed. I'm exhausted."

"Hmmm..." he mused, still looking me over, no doubt focusing on my raccoon eyes. "I know you haven't had anything to eat since before the ceremony, come down to the kitchen with me, you need to have something before you go to bed."

The automatic answer came before I could even consider it. "Oh, that's fine. I'm not hungry."

Patrick cocked his head. "I have never seen you eat. Not a bite."

I thought of all the times my father screamed at me for my "fat arse" and told me it was unladylike to eat so much. "I'm fine."

"Nonetheless," he said, his tone cooling, "come down with me. The wedding cake is almost untouched. I believe the catering staff caught Doris gnawing on one side."

"Of course, she did," I sighed. "You get that corner, then."

The caterers had done a good job, the giant kitchen was spotless, even the flagstone floor and stainless-steel appliances gleamed. Like most Irish country kitchens, this was the warmest room in the house, even with the exposed stone wall and giant skylights.

Patrick opened the fridge and pulled out a platter holding the top tier of our wedding cake. It started out as such a beautiful thing at the reception. Now, the meringue peaks were flopping over a bit and some of the spun sugar flowers were crushed. What a metaphor for the start of our marriage.

"Half of the second tier is missing," he chuckled, "because Ella wanted to take it back to the hotel."

I shook my head. What every bride dreams of for her once-in-a-lifetime wedding cake. Gnawed on by the dog and carried off by one of the guests. Though Ella was very kind to me so I certainly didn't begrudge her. "Is she a fiend for sweets?" I opened a cabinet, pulling out the plates.

"Specifically, cake," he said, "I'm the one with a sweet tooth so intense that it's problematic."

We both take a fork and dig in. "Sweet baby Jesus and all the saints that's good." I blurted.

"What's in this?" Patrick took another huge bite.

"Layers of almond cake, almond meringue, praline, chocolate mousse, and hazelnut ganache," I answered, reverently licking the rest of the chocolate off my fork. "It was Maureen's suggestion-" I stopped short in horror, "Do you think she poisoned it?"

He shook his head. "I've already had the surveillance tapes examined and the food tested, the only thing she touched during the day was the wine."

"Good," I said, going for another bite. "Because it would be a true sin to throw away this cake."

We ate in silence for a moment. From his expression, I suspect he was also thinking about how the day nearly ended in a mass poisoning. "What did you all decide in your secret meeting?" I asked, "Who do you think is responsible?"

"Ella had the wine sample tested, it was laced - no, loaded with Strychnine." He watched me shudder and put a hand on my arm. "I know the wedding planner was vetted thoroughly, and still, someone got to her. We'll be relying on our inner circle from now on."

I should be horrified, nauseated. I took another bite. "Who do you think is after you?"

Patrick laughed mirthlessly. "The list is long, but I have my suspicions."

Waiting for more information, I realized he was not going to tell me. *Of course,* I thought bitterly, *I'm just the bride. An O'Connell.*

He put down his plate and removed his tux jacket, stretching his long arms with a sigh. He pulled the cufflinks off and started rolling his sleeves up, revealing his thick, corded forearms and a multitude of tattoos. My chewing slowed as I watched him. It was like porn. You should look away, but you just can't. Patrick continued this little strip tease by opening a few more buttons on his shirt and his sculpted pecs came into view.

With his need for sweets, the man must work out like an animal, I thought, *because he has a body like nothing I've ever seen in real life.* Lowering my gaze, I stuffed another bite of cake in my mouth.

"What were you and that Kelly daddy's boy discussing tonight?" Patrick asked abruptly. His eyes had that chilly sheen again.

I should have told him that Cillian kept pushing me for information about the Doyle Clan's plans. How the eejit kept telling me that he would "save me" from Patrick once I got his information. How he kept pawing at me like I was still his fiancée.

Staring at his frozen, impassive expression, my jaw tightened. He left me at our own wedding reception to hole up with his Russian Bratva buddies. Even Tania and Ella were in on the discussion, though apparently, I couldn't have anything to offer. This cold-hearted bastard could not make it more clear how meaningless I was in the Doyle's grand scheme of things.

Putting my plate in the sink, I walked out of the kitchen.

"Aisling! I asked you a question." Patrick was already in front of me, blocking the staircase.

"Nothing, oh, mighty *Ceann Fine*. He didn't say a thing."

He let me go then, and I angrily locked the door of the guest room, struggling futilely with the zipper to my wedding dress until I gave up and fell asleep, buried under a pile of white silk.

Chapter Eleven

In which Aisling discovers some men will not take, "Hey, I'm married you idiot!" as a rejection.

Patrick...

I stopped on my way to my bedroom at Aisling's door, feeling like a bit of a bastard. I'd left her alone for hours on our wedding day, trying to plot our next move with Maksim and Yuri after the attempt at poisoning us during the reception. I wanted the moment in the kitchen to give her a chance to relax and tell me more about Cillian Kelly.

One of the Six Families or no, the next time he attempted to touch my wife I'd shoot him.

After talking to Marty, I knew Kelly had pressured Aisling to find information about our shipping routes and the details of our partnership with the Morozov Bratva. When she lied to me and said they'd talked about nothing, I was surprised at how disappointed I was in her.

I was a fool. Why would the granddaughter the O'Connell fucks be loyal to me? We may be married, but that meant nothing but a clan alliance and eventually, an heir. She was a cunning little thing. I'd have to keep a close eye on her.

Stripping down in my bedroom, I stood at the doors to the terrace, feeling the chilly salt breeze sweep in off the ocean. A lifetime with the offspring of Padriac O'Connell stretched before me. My father was a strong *Ceann Fine* for the Doyle clan, brutal when necessary, but he loved my mother, and she, him.

Yuri and Tania gave me endless grief about being a hopeless romantic after I'd gotten them back together, however, there was truth in it. The vision of a life with all the power of the clan but nothing else was bleak. Nonetheless, this was what I'd fought for and by god, I would stay the course.

Early the next morning, I was heading downstairs to find the coffee before yet another day of meetings when I heard a loud 'thud!' from Aisling's room. I paused, listening as it sounded like something got knocked off a table, shattering on the floor, an exclamation of pain and a muttered series of curses from my new bride.

"Aisling? You all right?" I called, trying the door handle, but it was locked.

"Good, yes!" Aisling snapped, before going into another round of profanity.

"Open the door and show me you're well or I'm breaking it down," I warned her.

"It's your house," she snarled, "demolish away with my blessing."

"You have until three to open up. One... Two... Thr-"

The door was unlocked and I whipped it open to find her writhing like a demented eel, still in her wedding dress and trying to get at the zipper in the back.

Leaning against the doorway, I folded my arms and watched her for a moment. "You slept in your wedding dress, then?"

"Aye, your powers of deduction are masterful, Sherlock," she said, glaring at me resentfully.

I bit my lip, knowing this was the wrong time for a hearty laugh. "Did it occur to you to have someone help you last night?"

"The only people around were the guards and you, so there was no one to help me unless Doris managed to develop opposable thumbs," Aisling said defensively. "Unless you wanted me to ask one of your boyos?"

Shaking my head irritably, I took her arm and spun her around. "Put your hands down."

She gathered her long mass of curls, pulling them over her shoulder and I unbuttoned the little cluster of pearl buttons before finding the hidden zipper and slowly pulling it down. Her skin was silky and pale. I could see the bumps of her spine. Was she one of those women who'd rather starve than have a normal, healthy female body?

The backs of my fingers brushed against her skin as I moved the zipper and she shivered, making me grin. The sides of the dress fell away and Aisling gave a sigh of relief as the tight bodice loosened against her ribs. The zipper stopped at the base of her spine, and I appreciated the top of her lacy little white undies and the two dimples just above her pert ass until she stiffened, moving away from me like my hands were on fire.

Clutching the dress to her chest, she raised her chin. "Thank you," she said, "I've got it from here." Her cheeks were flushed, and she kept her narrowed gaze on me as if waiting for me to leap on her like some Neanderthal. I was hit with a vision of doing just that; seizing her waist and throwing her on the bed, flipping the skirt of her dress up and burying myself between her legs. She'd be so hot inside, her silky lips wet and thighs open to me…

Shaking my head with a silent groan, I turned on my heel, leaving the room.

Aisling…

Slipping the dress down over my hips, I looked at it as it puddled around my feet. Part of me just wanted to throw the cursed thing in the fireplace, but... it really was pretty. Maybe someone else would like to wear it one day. I refused to allow myself to think about the possibility of that being a daughter of mine.

Children with *this* man?

Patrick was beautiful, tall, and had an insanely perfect body. He was clearly intelligent and cunning. And he didn't give a shite about me. The closest interaction we've had here in my elaborate prison was when he unzipped my dress.

I'd expected that he'd want to bed me last night, but other than our cake fest turned interrogation, my new husband didn't seem to want to have anything to do with me.

So why did that make me feel worse, instead of better?

"Mrs. Doyle, there's a flower delivery for you."

I looked up from my book to see Maeve lingering in the doorway, holding an enormous bouquet of roses, lilies, and snapdragons.

"Put that down before you throw your back out. And Maeve, please! Call me Aisling. No fancy titles, surely we're past that."

She shrugged, carefully putting the arrangement down on one of the old wooden tables. "Fitting to have it in the conservatory, eh? Are you thinkin' of bringing it back to life?"

I discovered this glorious place during my explorations a few days ago, and I spent most of my time here. It was built onto the back of the house, overlooking the gardens and the beach below. Circular, with thick glass panes in white iron frames with a gothic arch and a flagstone floor. The peaked roof soared up another story with a wonderful view of the sky.

There wasn't much in here now, aside from some comfortable white wicker furniture I'd dragged in - well, I'd made Jack drag in - from the garden. The sturdy old wooden tables were bare, aside from a few broken pots and a stubborn bit of ivy.

"I want to," I admitted, "it's so beautiful, can't you picture it with dozens of blooming plants? We could eat out here at times..."

She laughed, "You're not so fond of the dining room, are you now?"

"It's dark and formal and... I don't know, it doesn't feel very welcoming," I said. "Look at the light! I could paint some beautiful- anyway, it doesn't matter. It's a good project."

"Paint?" Maeve smiled, "You're an artist?"

"Oh, no!" I laughed, "I haven't painted in years. I used to love it but..." I shrugged awkwardly, "My Da thought it was a waste of time."

Her shrewd brown eyes studied me, and she smiled suddenly. "Well, I hesitate to speak ill of the dead-"

"Oh, go ahead," I urged her, "I certainly do."

"Your Da's not here," she said, "and it seems like if you wanna start painting again, there's nothing the old man can do about it, then?"

Just the thought of it - that all the things my Da forbid me to do - I could do them now. Maybe I wasn't as trapped in this life as I'd thought.

"Do you think Patrick would mind?"

"Heavens no!" Maeve scoffed, "He'd be thrilled you were taking an interest in the old place. You know where your credit cards are? I noticed you haven't touched them yet."

I frowned, "I have credit cards?"

"Aye," she nodded. "I thought the mister had shown them to you, but he's got a line of credit for you and two credit cards for your own use."

"Really?" My voice cracked a little in shock. Patrick thought about me long enough to set up something like this? "That would be grand."

"I'll put them out for you when you come in for lunch," she promised, sidestepping Doris, who came galloping through the conservatory and nearly knocking over the massive arrangement of flowers.

"Curse ye, Doris!" I shouted, just barely catching the vase before the whole thing splattered on the floor. Something dropped out of the arrangement, landing on the table. "Off with you!" The dog gave me a deeply reproachful look and sulked her way out of the conservatory.

I picked up the item; a white box about the size and shape of a mobile, which was exactly what it contained. It was a fancy new iMobile, shiny silver and I checked for a note. A card was at the bottom of the box, and I unfolded the paper.

Dear Aisling,

I'm sorry that I came off as too strong last night.

I was angry with how Doyle was treating you - ignoring you at your own wedding reception! Forgive me for pushing you for information, but even though you're married now, if he's gone against the Council with his ties to the Bratva, you can be set free. I just want you to have a choice.

This mobile can't be linked back to you or me, and there's no tracking app on it so Doyle can't invade your privacy. I'm here for you if you need help, or just want to talk.

If you were mine, I would treat you like a queen.

Love, Cillian

I turned the mobile over in my hands, thinking about it. Cillian had really irritated me last night, pawing at me and asking me so many questions. His note sounded suitably apologetic, though I couldn't understand how he was so sure he could get me out of this marriage. He said I should "have a choice," though to choose what, I wasn't certain, though I suspected he meant becoming "his queen."

Fanning myself with the note, I rolled my eyes. Flying free from one cage just to land in another? Still… I would hold onto this mobile. I hid it between the lining and leather in my purse. You never knew when it might come in handy.

Chapter Twelve

In which Aisling and Patrick encounter mysterious billionaires, idiot dinner guests and sinister business proposals.

Patrick...

After a meeting with my inner circle at Lydia's pub, we were no closer to determining who had poisoned the wine at the wedding reception.

"I got into the wedding coordinator's texts," Lydia said irritably, "there was nothing suspicious. I traced back all the calls she'd made in the last month, they were all what you'd expect, florists and the like."

"What about money?" I asked, "Any unusual bank transfers?"

"That was the odd thing," Lydia said, "a sudden influx of money would make sense. There were no large sums of money in any of her accounts. I also checked back for larger, monthly payments that might indicate she's working some angle with a rival family. Again, nothing."

"So that leaves blackmail as the most likely option," I said. "Lydia, get into any surveillance cameras around Maureen's shop and house. See if you recognize anyone coming and going in the past week or two. Liam, take a look at her family and circle of friends. See if there's been any odd activity, people suddenly missing, maybe held captive."

"Aye," he nodded. "Anything else?"

Running my finger over my lower lip, I wondered what my new bride was doing. Maeve had contacted me for permission to give Aisling the credit cards I'd opened for her. Was she running up a tab at Brown Thomas? Blazing through Armani, Dolce & Gabbana, and Chanel? It was expected of an Irish Mob wife to dress to the nines, though she seemed to have had a relatively small amount of luggage to bring from the O'Connell house.

"Anything else, *Seann Fine?*"

I looked up, realizing that Liam had repeated the question. "Nothing for now, you've all done good work. Liam and Lydia, stay behind."

Waiting until everyone else filed out, I pulled up the accounting from our warehouses in the Dublin Docklands. "Two of our facilities in the Docklands area have consistently shown low or no activity. This is a prime shipping hub. Tell me why we're not at capacity."

Liam frowned, "Well, this is under Niall's command. The warehouses are far enough away from the major hub to be used for arms shipments. Most of our legitimate trade runs through the warehouses closer to the Grand Canal Dock."

"It doesn't make sense that we have empty space," I growled, "pulling together the O'Connell trade and ours? We should be filled to bursting."

"Especially since you ended the Red Trade," Lydia pointed out, quick fingers skimming over her keyboard. "All the books look legitimate; your Purser went through all the O'Connell assets with a fine-toothed comb when you appointed him."

"Who do we have overseeing those warehouses under Niall?" I asked.

"Some of the Old Guard, your Da's men," Liam answered, "and some young guys that Niall brought in."

"He was the only one who vetted them," I said, "no one else?"

They exchanged glances. "You're doubting Niall?" Liam asked, "He was your Da's Clan Chief."

"That's why I gave him his position as Counselor with us," I said. "But he pushed mighty hard on the trafficking."

"Fecking tool," Lydia muttered.

I tapped the table for a moment, thinking. Niall was my father's second in the clan for ten years, I was certain he would be one of the most trustworthy men in my crew. "Divert some of the shipments from the Northern area to those two warehouses. Let's see if Niall puts up a fuss. Lydia, get some new surveillance cameras installed without his knowledge."

"Sure, yeah," she nodded. "Anything else?"

"That's enough to keep you both busy," I said dryly.

Heading back home, I ran into our gardener, Colin, who was grinning ear to ear.

"Thank you, sir! We're so excited for the new plants!"

I smiled blankly. "New plants?"

"Well- Mrs. Doyle and I just ordered all the new plants and trees for the conservatory, I assumed that you requested it?"

Colin was a stocky, ruddy-faced man who was rapidly losing his enthusiasm in the face of my confusion. "Ah, not to worry, Colin. Redecorating is part of Mrs. Doyle's role as the lady of the house. She's enthusiastic, eh?"

"Yes, sir," he said, clearly relieved.

I found Aisling in the conservatory, watching as a sour-faced Jack balanced on a ladder, hanging a huge old iron chandelier.

"Right there," she said, waving both hands in opposite directions, "do you see the hook? It's perfect!"

Leaning against the doorway, I folded my arms and watched her. She was more animated than I'd ever seen her, smiling and laughing eagerly as Jack irritably fastened the light fixture on the crossbeam. She was wearing old shorts and a shirt that rode up on her smooth stomach when she reached for another light bulb. I couldn't stop staring at that sexy little gap of skin and I was suddenly irritated that Jack might see it, too,

"Where did you find that old thing, then?" I asked, strolling into the room. The glass had been cleaned, and there was a window washer balancing over the roof, carefully soaping down each panel, cleaning away ten years' worth of neglect.

"You're back," Aisling said, not looking nearly as happy as she had before.

"Well, I live here," I reminded her.

Rolling her eyes, she turned back to Jack, who'd anchored the chandelier and was climbing back down the ladder.

"I can't believe that ladder held you," I chuckled, grinning at his disgruntled expression.

"I could feel the thing bulge every time I climbed a step higher," he groused. Looking up at the light fixture regally hovering over the conservatory, he said, "It looks grand though, doesn't it, then?"

"Agreed," I said. He left with a polite nod to us both and Aisling watched me uncertainly.

"Maeve said-" She cleared her throat and started again. "Maeve said you'd set up house accounts for me? I thought this would be a good place to start?"

"You jumped right in, eh? It's going look like it did when…" I shook my head. I wasn't going to tell her about my mother. How the conservatory was her favorite room in the mansion. She'd stay in here for hours, pruning the little trees and the flowering vines, humming happily.

Aisling's head tilted curiously. "Like it did when?"

I felt the polar bite of my hate for the O'Connells move up my spine. Because an O'Connell murdered my mother in this room. They took my little sisters.

Aisling was standing in front of me, her big green eyes looking so innocent. She didn't know what had happened in this room, it wasn't her fault. However, she was remaking my mother's old domain into hers, and I wasn't sure how I felt about it.

"It doesn't matter," I said coldly. "We have a dinner with Nolan O'Rourke and some potential Chinese investors tomorrow night. Be ready at eight."

I turned and left her before the disappointment in her gaze weakened me.

Aisling...

"Rat bastard," I mumbled. "Thick-headed gobshite, bossing me about."

I was getting ready for the business dinner Patrick had ordered me to attend with him. I never saw him again after our 'tender' little moment in the conservatory, though I knew he had to be the one who unlocked my bedroom door last night, because Doris was sleeping next to me when I woke up this morning. That infuriating bag of fur even had her head on the pillow next to me, blinking up at me with a limpid gaze.

Oh, dear Lord, I hope she didn't have fleas...

Putting on my pale green dress, I adjusted the back so it didn't plunge quite so much. I'd watched Bridget dress up for nights out as an Irish Mob wife before, so I hoped I'd struck the right note between not too sexy, but expensive-looking. Well, Bridget dressed like that for my horrible brother Mickey, at any rate.

Maybe I should be more buttoned up? Hair up? Hair down? What did Patrick expect? Again, the helplessness of knowing nothing about my new husband was swamping me. The vision of a life where there were no birthday parties - because I didn't know the man's age, much less his birthdate - no evenings sitting by the fire, or watching a movie together made my heart hurt.

Just his chilly indifference for company.

A knock on the door thundered from Jack's meaty fist. "Mrs. Doyle? The *Ceann Fine* is waiting for you in the car."

He knocked one more time and I watched the sturdy wooden frame bulge ominously. "Jack, please don't break down my door, I'm coming!" I snapped, whipping it open before he could assault it with another knock.

It was silent in the car until we were nearly at the distillery. The one my lunatic grandfather bought and then lost in one night when the Doyles and their Bratva buddies mowed them all down in a hail of bullets. Not that I held this against Patrick, exactly. But since he took over the O'Connell assets and all my Da and Grandfather's dirty dealings, I'm not sure if it was any better.

"The distillery was taken over by Nolan O'Rourke," he said, "do you know who he is?" Patrick didn't look at me, his gaze still focused on some document he was reading.

"Sure, yeah," I shrugged. "He's an eccentric billionaire who dabbles on both sides of the law, I'm guessing. He had dinner over at our - the O'Connell house - a couple of times. Wasn't he at our wedding?"

"He was," Patrick said sourly. "He is facilitating tonight's meeting between us and the Zhèng Triad, who are very anxious to do business."

I was trying not to stare at him, but... was this my husband? A man who was actually talking to me and *explaining things?*

"What can I do?" I asked without thinking. The standard Mob clan wife just stood there and smiled. No doubt that was what he expected of me.

Patrick tapped the screen of his mobile. "O'Rourke loves his games. So, I don't know who will be there tonight. Watch and listen. If you hear anything that seems... off, talk to me, yeah?"

The rush of gratitude I felt was almost embarrassing. He thought I could be of use? "The clan wives are used to being seen and not heard," I said with a twist of my lips. "It gives us a bit of room to listen without being noticed, really."

The car stopped and Patrick helped me out, looking me up and down. "I fear they'll be noticing you in that dress." He leaned a little closer, murmuring, "But I'm thinking that makes you prime distraction material."

I shook my head as he ushered me through the doors of my family's old distillery. What entity had invaded Patrick's body? Whatever it was, I hoped it stuck around.

We weren't the only family of the Six invited to this little get-together, it seemed, and they were as displeased to see us as Patrick was to see them.

"Rian Dwyer's boys," I whispered to Patrick, "but not their Da. You think this is an unauthorized excursion, then?"

"I know he still holds the reins," he spoke quietly into my ear, pretending to fix one of the curls that already fought loose from my updo. "Do you know them?"

"They're both complete arseholes," I said flatly, "Their Da went through three wives before he got his sons. I went to school with the youngest, Brendan. He's the worst, mean as a snake, and twice as dumb."

Patrick smothered his chuckle, "Let's go ruin their night." I felt a stupid little tingle run down my spine as he leaned closer, his warm breath on my bare shoulder. He smelled so good; like sea salt and his cologne and the memory of him, bare-chested and carrying his surfboard rose with technicolor accuracy in my mind.

Focus! I lectured myself, *this is an important night to prove myself.*

I'd seen the distillery once when our family had owned it and they were in the final process of renovations. It was one of the oldest distilleries in Ireland, with beautiful copper pot stills and tubing and gorgeous, battered oak floors with giant, gothic-style windows.

I tried to imagine where the bullet holes would have been... if they could get all the bloodstains out of the exposed brick walls. Just being in this place where the O'Connell Mob was wiped off the face of the earth was so much more gruesome than I was prepared for. Did my grandfather know what was about to happen that night? Did my Da? Did they care that the men who followed them would die, too? Closing my eyes, I tried to take deep breaths. I could *not* melt down here.

"Aisling?"

I jolted, opening my eyes and seeing Patrick looming over me, looking concerned. "I didn't think about this," he said, "I shouldn't have brought you here. I can have Jack take you home."

"It's all right." I shook my head, trying to smile, "It just... hit me all at once. But I'm fine. I am. Let's focus on this evening, then?"

"If you're sure," he said, running his hands up and down my arms. It was the kindest touch he'd ever offered me and it felt so much more comforting than it should.

Nolan O'Rourke stood at the head of the table, his arms out in a flamboyant welcome. "A pleasure to have you all here at the new O'Rourke Distillery," he said benignly, "My chef here has created an excellent pairing menu tonight with our line of whiskeys, accompanying French and Irish dishes, created with all locally-sourced ingredients. Business can wait until after dinner- unless you want my chef to have a panic attack." There was polite laughter from around the table. "Enjoy, my friends!"

O'Rourke was almost unnaturally handsome with his blond hair and his outrageously expensive suits, though he looked *weirdly* perfect; like he'd been photoshopped to erase any flaws.

Admittedly, he was the consummate host; the meal was quite grand, with outrageously rare and expensive whiskey and a superb menu of Salmon Brochettes with Harissa, Lamb Tagine, and a Bouillabaisse made with freshly caught lobsters and crab. Keeping quiet for the most part, I sipped my whiskey, though I would have rather had wine.

Watching Patrick slip into the role of "in charge" Clan Chief was a surprise. The cold, withdrawn man I knew was gone, this Patrick Doyle spoke with authority and the other men listened. He was charming and charismatic. He knew everyone at the table and what their organization's dirty dealings were and wasn't afraid to allude to them.

He was deep in conversation with the man from the Zhèng Triad on his right, which meant I had the misfortune to endure the eejit to my left, which turned out to be Brendan.

"You've cleaned up nicely, haven't you?" Brendan had always thought he was a real stunner, which was incorrect. His skin and hair and eyes were all a sort of beige shade... like, if clammy was a color.

He was leaning in, sweat dotting his upper lip and sparse goatee. He squeezed my shoulder, "So how's married life? True love match, this one?"

"Just as true as your incurable chlamydia infection," I sneered, batting his hand away. I'd always hated that guy. He was the one who tried to corner girls in empty classrooms back in school and called them "slags" and "hoors" when they fought him off. And he never got into trouble, thanks to his Da's big donations.

He squeezed my shoulder harder, his beady eyes darting around to see if anyone was watching. "You should shut your mouth.

You know what I could do to you when *I'm* Clan Chief?"

I burst into laughter. "Uh, blame me for your erectile dysfunction?" His face flushed red and his mouth opened to spit something back, and Patrick's frigid tone interrupted his big comeback.

"Touch my wife again and I'll break your arm into three pieces."

Brendan's hand disappeared and I looked at Patrick gratefully. His eyes were a frozen blue, like a glacier, and they glowed with fury.

I wasn't doing anythin'!" Brendan protested, "We were just talking." Patrick's gaze dropped to the red mark on my shoulder and a muscle ticked in his jaw.

"Brendan!" His older brother Flynn spoke from across the table. "Don't you have some calls to make?"

The oaf got up immediately, sending me another nasty glance before smoothing down his tie. "Aye, I'll just go... take care of that."

"Are you all right?" Patrick's lips were against my ear and I shivered.

"I'm fine," I assured him, "though he hasn't gotten any more charming since school."

He helped me out of my chair, putting his hand on my lower back and walking me over to the deck area, looking out over the street. He was wearing a strange expression.

"What about you?" I asked, "*Your* memories from this place can't be... grand."

"What happened here is something I never want to do again," he said, lips compressed.

"Ah, there you are."

It was the man from the Zhèng Triad, that I'd seen briefly at our wedding. When he was standing over the body of our wedding planner. He wore a perfectly tailored suit that possibly rivaled the cost of O'Rourke's and a practiced smile that was meant to be interpreted as friendly, though I was pretty sure he didn't understand what that emotion meant.

Patrick said, "May I introduce my new bride? Aisling, this is Fu Shan Chu Zhèng."

"Call me Bobby," the man interrupted, "most businessmen from China take a Western name to use in Europe and North America."

"A pleasure, Bobby," I said, nodding politely. He didn't look like a man who would want to shake hands. He also did not look like a Bobby. Maybe more like a Draco. Or a Damien.

"If I may, Mrs. Doyle, I'd like to borrow your husband for a moment?"

With a quick glance at Patrick, I said, "Of course." Turning, I headed over to the glowing bar and gratefully ordered a glass of Chenin Blanc, nursing it while I watched the two speak.

I'd gotten good at reading body language over the years, it had saved me from a beating more than once when I knew my Da or Grandfather were about to blow up over something. I'd make myself scarce before the inevitable explosion. Patrick was leaning away from Zhèng like he was diseased, his head-shaking became more frequent the longer the other man kept pushing his argument.

Wandering casually along the wall, reading the quotes about the distillery's history, I got close enough to listen in.

"If I'd known that you'd be pushing the Red Trade, I wouldn't have come tonight," Patrick said coldly. "I'm not a slaver. And we do not traffic humans."

"Ah, but the O'Connells did," Zhèng replied placidly. "Your refusal to open your docks to our shipments is impacting our bottom line in an unacceptable way."

"That's not my problem," Patrick retorted, "go to one of the other families in the Six that are willing to sink low enough."

"None of the others who want our accounts have the right docks and warehouse space," Zhèng said, keeping his composure. "The docks here in Dublin are crucial, now that the Brexit policies closed all available docks in England. I assure you, *Ceann Fine*, it is merely business. We would ship tree bark if it was as profitable a product. This is not personal."

"I've seen the results of your 'business,'" Patrick snarled, "and this conversation is over. The answer is no. And it will always be no."

"We'll talk another time," Zhèng said, still completely unperturbed. "I will give you a chance to think about it. I think you will find the profit margin for you would be double the numbers of any other product you could use your facilities for."

"They're not *product*," Patrick was leaning dangerously close to the other man, "they're humans. We will never work with you." For a moment, it almost looked like he was going to punch Zhèng, and I was certain that would be a disastrous thing.

"Sweetheart?" My voice was as high and innocent-sounding as I could make it, "I'm so sorry to interrupt, but I'm not feeling well." I squeezed Patrick's hand as he looked down at me, clearly surprised at my coyness.

"Ah, well." He finally nodded, "Of course." Turning to Zhèng, he curtly bid him goodnight and hustled me out the door.

We were silent in the car, driving home but once we were inside the house I followed Patrick, after we settled in the kitchen, I couldn't keep quiet.

"You're not in the Red Trade?" I blurted out.

He was pouring a drink and looked up at me. "No," he frowned, "absolutely not."

"But…" Inside, I was bubbling with something that felt a lot like happiness mixed with relief. "The O'Connell Mob was, and you took over all the assets, I just thought…"

"You thought I'd be a goddamn slaver?" Patrick said incredulously. "I know you believed I was the devil, but even Lucifer would be disgusted to be called that. I cut off all their access to our docks, warehouses, the overland transport - everything the Zhèng Triad used to move the women."

"That's so…" I beamed; I couldn't help it. Not having to keep living with the horror of what the O'Connell men had done to so many women and children? Not having to live with the shame that I could do nothing to stop it? I wanted to hug him. I wanted to kiss him for taking that stain away from us.

"So, you knew old man O'Connell was in the Trade? Your *father?* You knew where all the blood money was coming from that put you in the lap of luxury?" Patrick was looking at me, cold again and his eyes bright with contempt.

"How *dare* you." My hand shot up and slapped him hard across the face before I even recognized what I was doing. "Yes, I knew what those evil bastards did. When some of the women got too old to work in the-" My voice hitched with a sob and it took me a minute, "when they couldn't survive the brothels anymore, a lot of them were sold off as servants. My father-" I spat his name like it was poison, "brought some of them into our household to work. That's how my Ma discovered what they were doing, the… the things they were doing to these poor girls. She confronted my father, told him she was leavin' him and taking us away…"

I turned my back on Patrick and swallowed hard, trying not to vomit. I gagged a little as tears poured down my face. I could still see the expression on Ma's face. The smell of her perfume and her blood mixed together. How I screamed while one of my grandfather's men held me back.

"What happened, darlin'," he said, carefully putting his hand on my back, "what did he do?"

"He killed her. What do ya think? He killed my Ma and he told me that if I ever talked about it again, he'd kill Bridget," I hissed. "Ya think I don't know that my family's a fecking curse? That's why I came here with almost nothing. I never wanted to use their dirty fecking money. But I thought you were just…" I threw up my hands in despair. "I didn't know you were any different."

"Shite." Patrick's hands came up to cup my cheeks. Big, warm, capable fingers stroked my cheekbones. "Shite, I'm sorry. How old were you?"

"I was twelve," I said, heaving for breath. "He pulled Bridget and me out of bed and made us watch. Ma kept telling me to close my eyes…"

"Sweet Jesus," he sighed, wrapping me in his arms, holding me tightly. "You were a baby. No wonder you thought I was the same kind of monster, you didn't know that anything had changed. We both just… assumed the worst of each other, didn't we?"

"I hated it!" I sobbed, "Every time someone new would come into the house? And after my Ma died, some of them were…" my stomach nearly turned inside out, "they were young. Really young and I know the old man and my father kept 'em to use…" I put the back of my hand against my mouth. "Those evil bastards."

"Hey darlin,' hey." Patrick kissed my forehead, my wet cheeks, my mouth. "I'm sorry you had to live with that. I'm so sorry about your Ma." His thumbs passed over my cheekbones again, his eyes were so sad. He put his mouth on mine and he kissed me. A proper kiss, not that I'd had many of those, one with lots of firm pressure and a bit of tongue and it was good.

"I don't wanna think about it anymore," I said, my voice small, "I just… I wanna forget."

My new husband kissed me, longer this time, his hands moving me a bit to fit against his lips.

"I can make you forget," Patrick said. "Will you let me?"

I sniffed, trying to talk. "Yeah. Please."

With shocking speed, he lifted me up in his arms and started loping up the staircase.

Chapter Thirteen

In which Patrick proves just how romantic he can be.

Aisling...

It was a miracle Patrick didn't trip over Doris and send us both back down the stairs, because she came galloping out of my room to greet us, her long, pink tongue flapping out of her mouth. He gently nudged her away with his knee and got the master bedroom door closed before she could squeeze through.

Maybe some men after heartbreaking confessions might gently put their bride on the bed, and undress her slowly with kisses. Patrick didn't do any of that. The minute the door closed he pressed me against it, his big hands cupping my face again and kissing me. I could feel something hard and hot against my stomach and the idea that he was already wanting me was so erotic. His tongue thrust into my mouth, tangling with mine and tracing my teeth. Pushing his chest harder against me, he groaned into the kiss.

"You're gorgeous, *mo stór.*" Patrick pulled my leg up, hooking it over his elbow and opening me up to him. My dress slid up my thigh and his hand followed it, gently squeezing my ass. He pushed his hips against my center and this time, both of us groaned. His cock felt thick and it was so long. I wasn't sure it was supposed to fit inside a human body, much less my sad, virginal one. But I wanted it, more than anything right now because my brain was blessedly fuzzy and I couldn't think of anything else besides this tall, beautiful man.

He circled his hips, pressing his cock against me and it was possible I could come just from that. Patrick's lips moved down my throat, to my chest and his hand was yanking my dress down to my waist, sucking a nipple through the lace of my bra and I groaned, pushing my hips against him. The rasp of the lace and the warmth of his mouth was almost too much.

His lips pressed back against my throat and I let out a squeal when he lifted me up, carrying me over to the bed. Breathless, I stared up at him standing over me, his hands yanking away his jacket and shirt, his eyes glowing with something animalistic, almost greedy.

Sweet baby Jesus, this man... Patrick was a kaleidoscope of tattoos; Celtic knots and daggers blending into stars spread over his shoulders and arms, and a menacing dragon spanned his chest with vivid yellow eyes, seemingly staring right at me. His chest was thick and broad, sculpted beautifully down to his toned stomach and a thin line of hair disappeared into his pants.

He chuckled when I yelped again as he pulled my dress down from my hips and off, throwing it on the floor.

"Put your hands over your head," he rasped, and I did, fingers nervously gripping the comforter. He knelt in front of me, planting my feet on his shoulders. Wrapping his long fingers around my thighs, he tugged me against him, so close that I could feel his hot breath on my center. Suddenly self-conscious, I tried to close my knees, but his hands pulled me apart.

"You're too beautiful to hide anything from me, *mo stór*," my husband groaned, his eyes focused intently on me. His knuckle ran up between my wet lips, rubbing against my clitoris and I moaned, loudly, then cringed, trying to cover my face. "Put your hands back where they were," he ordered me, his knuckle still stroking my seam and his thumb moving to circle my clitoris. "There you are..." he murmured raptly, "Those pretty moans-fuck!" He groaned, leaning closer and moving his thumb to nudge me with his nose.

"Oh, god…" I moaned. "Please let me touch you!"

He took my shaking hand, sliding it into his hair. It was softer than I thought and thick, my fingers gripped a silky lock of it and pulled when his tongue started circling my clit and a thick finger slid inside me. My thighs tightened against his shoulders and he placed a kiss on my inner thigh. "I've been thinking about tasting you since I laid eyes on you," he murmured, his lips moving against my painfully sensitive center. "How your lips would spread for me, showing off this pretty pussy." He suckled my clitoris into his mouth and I cried out, gripping his hair harder.

Patrick's finger was leisurely sliding in and out of me, the first thing that had ever been inside me aside from my own inexperienced fingers. "So tight, gripping me," he groaned. "Are you going to clench down on my cock when I put it inside you?" I must have garbled some kind of response because he laughed, biting the spot on my thigh that he'd just kissed. The calloused tip of his finger stroked against the front of my channel and when I gasped, my back arching and moaning, he grinned against me, making me feel his teeth against my clit as he circled the spot again.

"There it is," he purred, "there it is, *mo stór,* I'm gonna make you come like this first, and then again on my cock. You want that? It feels like it." He groaned again, "So silky and wet. So hot. I'm going bury my cock inside you and make you so slick…"

He very carefully suckled my clitoris between his lips and batted it back and forth with his tongue, adding another finger inside me and making me already feel the burn and stretch of it and when he pressed hard against that place inside me, I was shocked into coming. It blazed up my spine, arching my back and making my thighs shake. None of my own feeble efforts ever felt like this, like the lower half of me was blazing hot and when he ran the flat of his tongue up and down between my slick center, spreading me wider I came again, so fast that I wasn't sure if the first one ended before the second began.

Giving my painfully swollen clitoris a gentle kiss, Patrick stood up to pull off his pants and boxer briefs. I had to look, though the sight of him; thick, throbbing and the broad head already slick and shiny, made me rise to my elbows and start inching back up the bed.

"I don't- maybe we should wait- it's..."

He gave me an evil grin as he put one knee on the bed and then the other, crawling over me and caging me between his arms. His cock slid between my lips, spreading them and nudging against my clitoris, back and forth, over and over, and making my legs wrap around his lean hips, tightening mindlessly against him.

"I'll fit, *mo stór*, I promise I'm gonna make you feel so good," he purred, kissing me and pushing his tongue in my mouth, making me taste myself. It felt dirty, maybe a little shocking but he was earthy and greedy and he had no shame about what he wanted and god, I wanted it too.

Spreading my legs wider, I let him slot more comfortably between my thighs and he pushed the head of his cock against me. I stared into his eyes, the pale, glacier-blue glow of them. Patrick kept his cock pressed against me, not moving, just rocking his hips slightly until I moaned. "Please," I gasped, desperate enough not to care that I was begging him, "please..."

"I'll give you what you want," he soothed, "when I'm ready. The way you come so pretty, the way you feel... that belongs to me. Just like you do."

Then his thick cock was sliding into me and I threw my head back, moaning and the time for conscious thought was over.

Patrick...

"Oh, *fucking hell...*"

The *feel* of her.

Aisling's heart was pounding so hard that I could feel it against my chest. She gripped my arms as I slid into her, and the heat and the way she squeezed me was almost too much to take. Gritting my teeth, I watched her pale skin flush a beautiful pink as she gasped.

"You're taking my cock so well," I praised her, barely getting the words out. Nothing had ever felt as good as this, her walls gripping me tightly, her breasts pushing against my chest. "I'm at the top of you," I whispered, kissing her, "nowhere else to go. But there's still more of me. Let's see if I can make it fit inside your perfect pussy."

Moving my hips slowly, circling to loosen her up a little, I sucked on her nipples and my thumb stroked her clit softly. She was too sensitive I knew, but I didn't want to stop, moving my finger around her strained entrance, feeling my cock stretching her wide.

"Draw your knees up, darlin,' let me make you feel good," I groaned, sliding in and out of her slowly. Every second outside of her cunt was torture, knowing the heat and tightness of her inside. "You okay?" I asked, brushing her hair away from her face.

Aisling's eyes opened and she gasped as I pushed back in, harder than before. "Mm-hmm," she managed.

"Good girl," I praised her hoarsely, "my good, sweet girl." It had been a long time since I'd been inside a woman. Getting shot and nearly dying had killed my libido, too. I tried to slow down, but the feel of Aisling strangling my cock, her hands gripping my back, her wide eyes staring into mine… I groaned. I wouldn't survive her.

Thrusting harder, I felt her back arch and the slick warmth of her rippling against my cock. Nothing could ever be as good as this, this beautiful woman and her tight heat squeezing my shaft. My knees slid under her hips, pushing them up, angling her while I stroked harder to find her G-spot, putting my hand on her stomach and groaning, feeling myself move.

I watched her closely, how her breath came faster and her fingers dug into my arms, her nails nearly piercing my skin and I was fine with it because my beautiful girl was about to come and this was good, because I had the patience of a teenager at this point.

"Do you want to come again, *mo stór?*" I whispered against her ear, biting her soft skin. "I can feel you tightening against me. And here I thought I loosened this snug little cunt of yours. You fit me perfectly." I slid my hand under the small of her back, lifting and angling her just so and Aisling's eyes opened wide, the pale green of them like tidepools.

"Patrick- I feel... oh, god this all feels..." Her breath hitched and she came against me, so hard that my cock was wedged inside her, unable to move, it was too much and I came too. Her perfect pussy squeezed me dry and I pressed mindlessly, wanting to stay buried in her forever.

The only sounds in the room were the soft roll of the waves against the beach outside and our labored breaths. I knew that I was sunk, completely. Because nothing would ever feel this good again. No one will ever feel right under me. No one but Aisling.

Chapter Fourteen

In which Patrick and Aisling discover that unfairly, consummating a marriage and a mass shooting can happen at the same time.

Aisling...

We were in the shower, and Patrick was holding me up because I was too limp and weak to stand on my own. Not that I was complaining. Also, the master bathroom was grand, with a huge shower and multiple showerheads. We were currently enjoying the rainfall one, pouring down over us as I laid my head on his lovely, broad chest.

"I'm so glad you don't have a brand," I blurted.

He looked down at me, appalled. "That will never happen in my clan. I would never brand a man like an animal."

"Thank god," I sighed.

Being so close to him allowed me to see the scars under his tapestry of ink. A beautifully shaded Celtic knot in black and gold, located on his ribcage covered three puckered knots of tissue. Running a finger over them, I asked, "Are these from... the O'Connells?"

He nodded. "The three points of life, death and rebirth on the knot seemed right to cover the three bullet holes."

"I can't believe you survived it," I shook my head. "I'm so sorry."

"Those aren't the only ones from that day," he said, guiding my hand to one on his hip, covered by a woven knot designed to look like a snake swallowing its tail. There was another on his thigh covered by a dragonfly in vivid blues and greens.

"Five bullets," I whispered, "it's all so wrong." My hand moved over to his other side, tracing one on his shoulder and another two over his left pectoral, all hidden under his serpent. "What are these from?"

"Ah," he said, "*those* are the ones that nearly killed me."

"When?" I asked, feeling some echo of his suffering, just by touching his scars.

"In New York City, as the Morozov *Obshchak.* I was guarding Yuri and we were ambushed..." he hesitated.

My hand dropped. I didn't deserve to touch him. "It was my family, wasn't it?"

"Aye," Patrick admitted. "They thought they'd killed me, and they kidnapped Yuri. Your father nearly tortured him to death before we rescued him."

I turned away, my shoulders hunched. "How can you stand to even look at me? How-" I choked on a sob, "you should hate me."

There was a sigh as he wrapped his arms around me from behind, putting his chin on my shoulder. "You are not your family," he said quietly, "and you could say the same thing about me. I killed all the O'Connell men."

"They deserved it," I whispered, laying my head on his thick bicep. "For what they did to you, and your people. For those poor girls. I'm glad they're gone."

"No more tears then," he said, turning me around. "Give me a smile. We're alive, you and I. That's what matters."

This time, I kissed him, putting my arms around his neck, rising on tiptoe and trying to push everything I was feeling into it. The heat of his body and the steam swirling around us in the shower made the frozen, brittle shell around my heart thaw just a bit.

Maybe a corner.

But it was a start.

I don't think we saw the outside of the master bedroom for the next three days, not that I was complaining. There was no way I could get out of bed, not while Patrick was intent on pleasuring me like we were mankind's last hope for survival.

On the third night, I was beginning to wonder if this man would ever get tired. He was taking advantage of the dark in the early morning hour to pound into me on one of the big, comfortable lounge chairs out on the terrace, the wind was tearing around the stone house and the waves crashing madly against the beach, but none of that seemed to distract him. My legs were up over his shoulders and his arms were looped under my back, his hands holding my shoulders to keep from thrusting me off the chair.

There was no way I would ever get used to the size of him, how he slammed into me. Of course, neither one of us was willing to hold off long enough to let my poor, sore lady parts heal, but every time I didn't think I could take anymore, he... *did* something. Something as simple as the evil gleam in his glowing blue eyes when he looked at me. Or how he'd pull my hair, yanking my head back to kiss me. Last night I begged him to get that thing away from me, so Patrick held me down and licked and fingered me instead. For hours. Until we were both covered in sweat and I was crying from coming too much, which was not a thing I had known was possible.

The wind whipped around the corner again and I shivered.

"Are you cold, *mo stór?*" Patrick asked, his hips slowing.

I tightened my legs around his shoulders, enjoying his corresponding groan. "We're so sweaty that my hands can't even get a grip on you, so no. Are you sure you should be..." My eyes drooped, he was thrusting inside me again like a madman. "Are you sure you should be calling me *mo stór?*"

"You *are* my treasure, *mo stór.*" he crooned, kissing me and lifting my leg to press it against my chest, going deeper than I thought was humanly possible.

"Really?" I said, trying to concentrate. The size of Patrick inside me always made me feel like my lungs were being compressed, like there was no room for anything but him. "I reckon if I'd asked you a week ago, you would have thought *mo dhliteanas* would be a better name for me."

Now, he stopped, still wedged inside me. "*Mo dhliteanas* - my liability?" He started laughing, "Never would I call you that." His laughter was making his cock vibrate inside of me, and my thighs tensed, my nails digging into his shoulders and I came. Again.

"Darlin,' you have to relax," he groaned, "when you go over like that you wedge my cock in you. I can't move."

"Maybe I don't want you to," I wheezed, "maybe I'll just keep you inside me forever."

Now *he* came, groaning as the heat of him filled me up inside, and he pulled out long enough to see his come spill out of me before circling my clitoris with it and then pushing the rest back inside with his cock. He stroked up into me a few more times before collapsing, keeping his chest from crushing me by balancing on his forearms.

Patrick smoothed my hair away from my face, smiling down at me. "I need to take you inside, darlin'."

Sleepily, I tightened my arms and legs around him. "Stay in me. Just a little longer, then?"

I felt his kisses along my jawline, on my shoulder, and on the tip of my nose. "Of course," he murmured, and we both fell asleep, the howling, chilly wind be damned.

Patrick...

The first rays of the weak sun penetrating the clouds woke me and I groaned. We'd never made it to the bed last night, though apparently, I'd found a blanket on one of the chairs and thrown it over us.

Cracking my neck and groaning, I looked down at my bride. Aisling was still asleep, mouth slightly open, and even with her snarled, tangled mass of hair, she was beautiful. Fierce. Brave.

She had been a virgin the night I took her to bed. I'd cursed myself when I discovered her blood on my cock, on the sheets and she had flushed a bright red. I hadn't even thought to ask, it had been so long and she was so sweet with her wet eyes and her mouth... I should have known.

Of course, she would be a virgin. These ancient fuckers still placed so much importance on something that mattered so little. Certainly, not something important enough to keep their daughters locked up like sheep in a pen. I should have been gentle, I should have been more careful.

All the same, I was shocked that night to feel a huge surge of lust and an odd kind of pride, that I would be Aisling's first. And her last. And all between.

As long as I lived, at any rate. Given my line of work, that might not be very long. But with the time I had, I was determined to worship her body and treat her with all the care and kindness I could muster. They weren't qualities valued as the head of a criminal organization, though I could still feel some stirring of my romantic soul.

"*Mo stór,*" I murmured, running the back of my hand against her cheek, "I'm carrying you to bed now."

"But you're warm," she whined, half awake, "let's just stay..." And she was snoozing again.

Chuckling, I wrapped her up in the blanket and carried her back into the bedroom, tucking her under the covers and heading in to shower. Despite having less than three hours of sleep on a creaky chaise lounge, I felt good. Strong.

My Ma always told me, "It's when you get to thinking nothing can stop you, that bad luck comes barreling around the corner and you're the one tied to the tracks."

As always, Ma was right.

"What the hell happened?"

I clutched my mobile hard enough to crack it, and Liam's image rippled on our Facetime call.

"You were lucky, boss," he said. "While you were finally consummating your-"

"Don't say it or I'll punch your teeth down your throat."

"While you were, uh, busy, ya missed the Six Families' meeting at the Kelly restaurant. I don't know how the gunmen got past the combined security of all those Warlords but they opened fire, turned the entire room into rubble."

I rubbed the bridge of my nose with my thumb and forefinger. "How many dead?"

Liam heaved a sigh, "Rian Dwyer."

The memory of his idiot sons at the O'Rourke Distillery was not a good one. "The eldest is the new *Ceann Fine* for their clan?"

"Sure, yeah," he said gloomily, "Flynn. A right bastard."

"Who else?" I asked.

"Michael Kelly. His boy Cillian's in charge. I saw his tender moment with your bride at the wedding. Not a bright one."

Growling at the memory, I said, "Go on, let's have it then."

"Flanagan survived, he's in the hospital with three bullet holes, the tough old bastard," Liam continued. "Campbell and Burke both escaped, though they lost a lot of men."

"Shite, what a mess," I groaned.

"Boss... there's more." he hesitated. "Because you were the only one of the Six not at the meeting, there's talk that you were behind it. Cillian and Flynn are blathering about bringing you up in front of the Council."

"You'd think those two bastards would be thanking me, if they really believed I shot up the Council," I got up, too angry to do anything but pace. "This stinks of a coup. Whoever's behind it wants a scapegoat."

"Which would be you," Liam added helpfully.

"Thank you, brother," I snarled, "I appreciate the clarification. Get Lydia and your uncles over here. Oh, and Finian. As my Enforcer, he must be able to gather some intelligence. It doesn't make sense that a direct attack on the Council could happen without some chatter somewhere."

"Do you want your Counselor?"

Hesitating, I shook my head. "Not Niall. We don't know if we can trust him yet. Keep this meeting quiet."

"Sure, yeah," Liam agreed. "Be there soon."

"Patrick?"

I turned to see Aisling standing in the doorway of the study, hesitating as if she was not sure of her welcome. She was just wearing jeans and an oatmeal-colored sweater and she could not have been more beautiful.

"C'mere," I said, reaching out my hand. When she took it, I pulled her in for a long kiss, resting my forehead against hers, smelling her light perfume and the peppermint of her soap.

"You have that look…" she ventured.

"Oh? What kind of look?" I said, kissing her again.

"The look that says there's been bad news and I'm not gonna be seeing you for a while?"

"You would be correct, *mo stór.* I'm sorry," I admitted, "someone got gunmen past all the captains at a meeting of the Six. Rian Dwyer and Michael Kelly are dead."

"How can that be possible?" Aisling gasped, "They're… shite, they're the Six! What about Declan?"

"He's alive. Barely," I said.

Absently smoothing my tie, she asked, "Well… who stands to gain?"

"That would be the question, wouldn't it?" I asked. "The two sons who just stepped up and took over their clans certainly benefited."

She frowned. "You think they're working together, then?"

"Possibly," I agreed, "they're looking for a scapegoat, and since I was the only one of the Six not at the meeting…"

"Oh, no," she groaned, "our timing is the worst!"

Biting her shoulder, I murmured, "I'm not sorry. I'll never be sorry for that."

Her fair skin flushed a pretty pink shade. "Nor I, to be honest." The realization turned her pale again. "Oh, my god! You could have been there! You could have been killed!"

"But I wasn't," I countered, pulling her into my arms. "I wasn't. You don't worry about me. I've survived two assassination attempts."

"Third time's the charm," Lydia said brightly, entering with Liam and the rest behind her.

"Not helpful, Lydia!" Aisling scolded her.

"Sorry," Lydia gingerly patted her arm, never one for physical displays of affection, though rumor held she'd conquered the hearts of several of my men in private. "Hey, do you have any of those biscuits left?"

"The gingersnaps?" Aisling asked.

"Aye," Lydia beamed.

"I'm assuming this isn't a subtle way to get me out of this office," Aisling said sourly, "I *will* be back with the biscuits."

"I'll save you a seat," Lydia promised.

We watched my bride head out the door with a sense of purpose, and I looked sternly at my Arbiter. "Inviting my wife into a clan meeting?"

"Oh please," she scoffed. "I've been waiting for you to notice she's a smart one who survived twenty-two years with her arsehole Da and that psychotic prick Padraic. You don't think she's got a handle on who's who?"

Rubbing the back of my neck, I scowled at her. "I don't want my wife in the middle of this."

"Too late," she said bluntly, "she already is."

Chapter Fifteen

In which there are ginger biscuits, plots and machinations, and spectacular oral sex.

Aisling...

Despite my bold words, I wasn't sure that I would be welcomed back in to Patrick's meeting with his inner circle, but I straightened my shoulders, knocked, and sailed back in with my tray of biscuits. I knew better than to bother with tea, and I was right about that since everyone had a full whiskey glass in front of them.

"Darlin,' I think you know everyone?" Patrick graciously re-introduced me around the table. I was touched by his thoughtfulness and by making a statement that I had something to offer.

I hoped I *did* have something to offer.

"Back to the main issue," Patrick said. "The two newcomers are already gunning for us."

"Nice to see that they spent a full fifteen, maybe sixteen seconds being distraught over their fathers' untimely demise," snarked Lydia.

"Sentiment is not popular in the Irish Mob life," said Finian. He was a genial-looking guy with red hair and eyeglasses. I knew from the rumors that he was brutal in a gunfight and even better with quick, quiet ends to troublesome people.

"I've known Declan since I was a little girl," I offered, "he was friends with my grandfather well before I was born, but he's not as evil."

"Strong words," approved Liam.

"I'm not saying anything about my grandfather that you aren't all thinking. But Declan is… saner, for lack of a better word? He's not going to jump into the idea you were behind it so easily. He might also be the man to ask about any recent threats or rumors," I said.

"A good idea," Patrick smiled at me. "You and I should have a visit with him at the hospital."

"Aside from Cillian and Flynn, who else benefits from this?" Lydia asked.

"About twenty other crime outfits," Patrick admitted. "New, less experienced Skippers are easier to manipulate, or take out."

"What about Bobby?" The others looked confused and I explained, "The Second in the Zhèng Triad, I met him the other night when he was pushing for the…" I stopped short and looked at Patrick, not sure what he'd told his inner circle.

He smiled at me proudly. "Aye, Aisling's right. Zhèng was pressuring me to continue the O'Connell Red Trade. I made it clear that would never happen."

"I can see why Niall wasn't invited," mumbled Finian.

"We can't trust him," Patrick said sharply.

"Seems like keepin' him in the loop isn't the wisest thing, then," Finian agreed.

"He was my father's Second," said Patrick, rubbing his eyes, "I owe him the benefit of the doubt until we can prove he's dirty. But control the flow of information around him."

"Back to Zhèng," I pursued, "if he had some new blood on his side, could he keep trafficking…" Self-disgust and shame for my family clogged my throat, I forced myself to continue. "Could his Triad keep bringing women and children through here with their combined assets?"

"It's a good question," said Patrick. "Is it possible? Zhèng would get his trade route and we'd be weakened by having to protect ourselves against the other families in the Six."

One of his Bosuns - Dylan, I remembered from the introductions - spoke up. "It's a possibility and it makes sense, but neither clan has access to the kinds of docks remote enough to bring in human cargo. The J2 is paying a lot of attention to human trafficking, President Higgins made it clear he wanted the intelligence agency coming down hard on it. I'm not sure the Kelly and Ryan Clans have enough dock space and warehouses between them."

The second Bosun, Cormac, another of Liam and Lydia's uncles, jumped in. "Sure, yeah. But they do have the overland transport resources. If those feckers can handle the dock situation, they can definitely get the poor souls out of Ireland."

I felt so profoundly grateful for these people. Not one looked at me with disgust or contempt as the granddaughter of Padraic Lucifer O'Connell. It was obvious they despised the Red Trade as much as I did.

Patrick rubbed his eyes again. I knew he had to be exhausted, he'd had half the rest I'd had last night, which wasn't much. "Here's where we are," he said. "Finian, get your guys and start digging up some intel for us. This was too big to not leave a trace. Dylan and Cormac, button down all our sites that are too tempting not to hit. Put everyone on guard. No starting something you hear me?" He was looking pointedly at Cormac, who glanced elsewhere, whistling innocently. "Lydia, do you have our surveillance equipment up on those docks yet?"

"Not completely," she said regretfully, "Niall's got more security on them than I'd thought. Can you arrange to pull some of his men for other areas right now? Tell him you're running short?"

"I can," Patrick agreed, "and Liam, go get into something that resembles a good suit. We're going to be paying some calls to the rest of the Six today."

Holding my breath, I wondered if I was involved, still valuable. He smiled at me, "Aisling, you're my 'in' with Flanagan, then we'll sort out Campbell and Burke."

I grinned back, looking a little stupid, I'm sure. But this man? I could see why the others loved and respected him. I could see myself possibly feeling the same, one day.

Once everyone had left the study, saying goodbye to their *Ceann Fine* and respectfully nodding to me, Patrick leaned against his desk.

"You look tired," I ventured, "something keeping you up at night?"

Laughing, he retorted, "Yeah. My cock. And you, who will not let it go down."

"Hmm…" I sat down on the big leather sofa by the fireplace. Patting the seat next to me, I said, "Why don't you come over here?" I put both arms over the top of the sofa, trying to look sultry. What was I *doing?* I was not the sort of woman who- Oh. Patrick was already in front of me, brushing my hair off my face.

C'mon, I coached myself, *you can do this.* I felt at a huge disadvantage here, since it was obvious from Patrick's skill in bed that he had fucked his way through three continents.

Reaching out, I unbuckled his belt and spread his trousers open as I pulled down his zipper. Tentatively placing my hand on his cock, which was all ready to go in the amount of time it had taken to unzip his fly, I stroked it, running my thumb over the tip. He groaned and looking up, I found his gaze fixed on me, not moving his hips, just smoothing my hair into a ponytail.

Not that I ever thought I'd be finding a dick attractive, but Patrick's… Smooth, silky skin, lightly roped with veins and rock hard. He had something to brag about, that's certain. Putting my mouth on the tip, I kissed it, running my tongue in the slit before circling the head.

"Shite, *mo stór,* what are ya doing to me?" He groaned, gripping a handful of my hair tighter.

"You do it to me," I said between licks, "I owe you."

"You never owe me for that," he said sternly, pulling my head back by my hair.

Tightening my grip on his thick cock, I gently rolled his balls with my other hand. "Am I doing this right?"

"Everything you do is magic," he promised, "never worry about that."

I drew him into my mouth, all the way to the back of my throat and hesitated.

"Breathe through your nose," he coached me, and I did, gagging a bit, but taking a breath and sucking him harder. I wanted to be as good as the women in his past, I wanted to make him feel as good, as overwhelmed as he made me.

Sliding him in and out, I fluttered my tongue along the bottom against the thick vein there and he groaned again, louder. Tears were rolling down my cheeks but I ignored them, feeling powerful, loving the feel of his thick thighs tensing and how he'd twitch when I gently squeezed his scrotum.

Patrick moved his hips, going deeper into my throat and I choked before shaking my head when he tried to pull back. "Don't," I gasped, wiping my mouth, "I want you to."

Wrapping my hair around his fist, he moved his hips faster, still giving me room to lean away, but I didn't. I would *own* this man's cock and this was step one. The taste of him was slightly salty, and his shaft, slick with my undignified drooling was so much hotter than I could have expected. I rubbed my thighs together, trying to create some friction.

Abruptly, he pulled his cock from my mouth and I gasped for breath. "Hey! I wasn't done."

Shaking his head, my husband pulled my jeans and undies down. "I can't wait, I need to be inside you."

I let out a yelp instead as he spread my legs, wedging his broad shoulders between them and pushed me back against the couch. He attacked my center with that talented tongue of his and my arms flailed, trying to find something to hang on to. How could this man make me flare up like this? I could already feel the sparks circling through my clitoris and radiating out to heat up the rest of me.

Throwing my head back, I was right on the precipice of one of the hardest orgasms he'd given me yet when he stopped. My eyes popped open and I scowled, "Hey! I was- Oh! Oh, holy-"

Rising, he'd notched his cock into me and speared upward, grinning at my shriek. His hips were pistoning so fast that I could only wrap my legs around his hips and hang on for the ride.

"Do you like this?" Patrick grunted, "I think you want it, being fucked hard, just hanging on, knowing you're about to come, feeling it barreling up and you can't stop it…"

He changed his angle and my back snapped into an arch, squeezing him inside me, helpless to do anything but feel it. Every cell was alive inside of me, feeling the heat, and his thick, beautiful cock splitting me open.

Patrick ran his knuckles through the slick coating us both and captured my clitoris between them, tugging it and making a whirlwind of need and energy and desire and an almost painful need to come control me. I was a vessel for him and nothing else right now and my vision narrowed down to a pinpoint, only the sight of him slamming into me and how unreasonably large he was and how could he even fit?

"Show me, you perfect, filthy, dirty girl. Show me how pretty you are when you come on my cock. Make a mess, darlin', soak me." He raised his hand and slapped me - hard - on the ass, once on each cheek.

I always thought women screaming when they orgasmed was some silly, fake porn thing. But as his last, almost vicious thrust made him bottom out inside of me, I did scream. Like a banshee. Like a lunatic. Like a woman well-pleasured.

Just like dominos toppling over, my orgasm triggered his and my husband bit into my shoulder, almost hard enough to break the skin and I clenched up on his cock again, holding him tightly inside me.

We ran our hands over each other, stroking, soothing scratches with our tongues and kisses for the bite he'd left on my shoulder, just waiting for our breathing to even out again.

"Oh, dear Lord I screamed," I moaned, utterly mortified.

"Yes, and it was *so* hot," Patrick growled in my ear. "I couldna' stop coming if you'd held a gun to my head."

Leaning back, I eyed him. "I didn't know you were into that kinda thing, husband." I burst into mortified laughter and he chuckled with me, our chests rubbing together in a very distracting way... it was another hour before we could finally get out of his study and go get cleaned up.

Chapter Sixteen

In which there are discoveries of allies, enemies, and deep-seated phobias of innocent house pets.

Patrick....

Liam was lounging against the hood of my Range Rover when we were finally presentable enough to visit the surviving members of the Six. He'd put on one of the expensive Armani suits I'd bought for him and looked all manner of surly about it.

"At last!" He swept a deep bow. "Your Lord and Ladyship, 'tis an honor."

Aisling leaned closer to me with a hint of a smile. "I thought Seconds were supposed to be respectful and maybe a little in awe of their *Ceann Fine's* authority?"

I laughed, "Yeah, but none of them are Liam."

He held our doors for us with exaggerated deference and we pulled out, bracketed between the two SUVs carrying Patrick's Bratva security detail.

"Ya know," Liam said, "I was talking to Dima from the other crew," he nodded to the car in front of us, "and he was telling me that the *Pakhan* has a Maserati SUV. It's bulletproofed. Tell me why we're riding around in this boring Range Rover?"

I was secretly pleased that he was finally warming up to my Russian crew, but I kept my tone even. I knew the little bastard was trying to rile me up. He was worse than Yuri in that regard. The two of them put together would no doubt create some sort of global catastrophe.

"This car cost nearly 200,000 Euros," I said, refusing to look up from a report from our legitimate trucking. "I hardly think it's boring."

"Does it have a rocket launcher?" Aisling asked.

"What?" I said, frowning at her.

"Does it have a rocket launcher," she repeated, giving Liam the slightest of winks.

"No, darlin.' I am not James Bond," I sighed, "though it does have all the top-of-the-line security features Range Rover can offer, in addition to bulletproof glass, and non-flattening tires. That will have to be enough."

We drove in silence for a moment.

"Still needs a rocket launcher," Liam suggested. I put up the security partition between us.

"How well do you know Declan?" I asked Aisling as we pulled up outside Beacon Hospital.

"He was over at the house quite a lot as I was growing up," she said. "Declan was always kind to me and he'd sometimes distract the old man when he was screaming at me or threatening to hit me." She shook her head, looking out at the hospital, a huge glass and brick monolith surrounded by park-like grounds. "I never understood why he tolerated my grandfather, they must have had something in common. Besides crime, I mean," she amended.

This struck me as hilarious, but I choked back my laughter, it was time for me to slip into my *Ceann Fine* mode. Stern. Authoritative. Deadly. "I will leave you alone with him at some point," I said, "he might tell you something he won't discuss with me."

Aisling looked doubtful, but she nodded as I helped her out of the SUV. "I'll do my best."

"I know you will," I leaned down to whisper in her ear, "and I'll reward you for it tonight." I sucked her earlobe for a moment, feeling her pleasurable little shudder.

How did I last so long before making her mine? My new bride was a goddess.

"I'm not in favor of this," the doctor said sourly as he led us through the ICU, "but Mr. Flanagan was insistent. Please try to avoid upsetting him. The man is sixty, I'm still stunned he's survived three bullet wounds."

Glancing over to see me glaring at the man, Aisling smiled at him warmly. "Mr. Flanagan is like family to me. We'll take care."

He hovered in the door of the private unit until my stare made him find something else to do. Flanagan's personal bodyguard stood by his bed, giant arms folded and staring at us.

The unit was darkened, only the lights from the medical equipment keeping us from tripping over various obstacles in the room. If I were to guess, that had been his bodyguard's decor contribution. The man in the bed seemed shrunken from the *Ceann Fine* of the Flanagan Mob who escorted Aisling down the aisle at our wedding. His hospital gown was clean, but there was still some blood spotting multiple white gauze bandages.

"You got a cigar?" Declan wheezed, "I'd kill for a good Cuban right now."

"Hey, Uncle." Aisling leaned over to kiss his cheek. "No cigar, I'm afraid. Just flowers this time." She arranged the huge spray of tulips in their crystal vase after putting them on his bedside table.

"Hmph," he growled.

"Some of your medical team are thinking you might be

immortal," I said, seating myself by his bed and angling so he wouldn't have to twist his head to see me. "They're doubting a mere mortal could escape Death this many times."

"I'm not certain I've got more holes in me than you do," he said. "This is a fecking mess."

"Oh, yeah," I agreed, "what the hell happened?"

"Just what you've heard, I'm sure," he shrugged painfully and winced as he regretted it. "We were having the Council and somehow, twelve gunmen got through all our security details. Which means at least half of them had to have stepped aside for it to happen. But no one can seem to pin it on any of the clans. No brands, no tattoos." His mouth tightened furiously, "They killed three of my best men to get to me, including Piran's brother." He nodded at his bodyguard, whose expression seemed sculpted in stone.

"Just so we're clear," Aisling said, "you can't think Patrick had anything to do with it."

"He'd have to be an idiot," Declan scoffed, "brand new in his role after a brutal takeover and immediately going after the other clans in the Six? That's a walking death wish right there."

"Kelly and Dwyer's lot are claiming I'm behind it," I said.

He chuckled derisively and a slight foam of blood came to his lips. Aisling moved faster than the bodyguard, gently wiping his mouth and offering him some water.

"If I were a betting man," he said, his voice weaker now, "I'd be putting the odds on those two. But they're too stupid and greedy to have come up with this on their own. The trick is to look for who's wanting to ally with them. I declined the request to bring you before the Council. Work on Burke next, he's less likely to believe you had a hand in it."

"Thank you," Aisling said warmly, "what can I bring you?" She put a hand up, "Don't even start with the cigars or the whiskey."

"Socks," he said. "Cashmere. I hate these cursed things the nurse put on me."

I stood up, "Excuse me for a moment, I have to take a call." Watching from outside the room, I saw Aisling lean over his bed, taking his hand in hers, nodding as she listened to him. He tapped his cheek and she kissed him again before leaving.

"He says he wants to see you alone."

"Stay here with Liam, in sight," I said, squeezing her hand.

"If you're asking me for cigars behind my bride's back, you know she'll kill me," I grinned, sitting down again.

Declan didn't smile at my feeble joke. "I need something from you," he said hoarsely.

"Yes?"

"My son- my youngest, Jamie. He's flying home from the Ares Academy."

"I'm an alumnus," I nodded.

"He's my last son," he said, the effort to talk was beginning to show in his expression. "My two oldest are gone."

"I remember," I said.

"You need to help him. He's going to need plenty of guidance. My Second is gone, shot in front of me. Jamie needs someone who's not there for the power or to manipulate him for their gain."

"You're thinking too highly of me," I warned.

His brown eyes were still shrewd. "No, I'm confident about you. Jamie will be a strong leader. He's just... so young. If I don't make it out of this fecking bed, I want you to promise me that you'll help him."

"My Aisling told me you used to stand between her and her grandfather when he wanted to use his fists," I said, hate for Padraic O'Connell swelling in my chest. "I'll be there when he needs me."

The relief on his exhausted face was palpable. "I'll put out my position on the attack, that you had nothing to do with it. I'll refuse any disciplinary hearing. But you better work fast. This isn't the last of it."

A chill spread over my back as I stared at him. I knew he was right.

Aisling...

Back in the car, Patrick took my hand, resting it under his on his muscled thigh. "What did he say to you when I was out of the room?"

I sighed, "He was being all..." I waved my other hand, "ambiguous, enigmatic. He said something about how young hotheads and idiots can be dangerous if there's enough of them. He told me to be careful and watch after Bridget and the kids." Frowning up at him, I asked, "Do you think she's in danger, then?"

Kissing my hand, he thought about it. "She should be out of the line of fire, since you're officially the heir that cemented the alliance between our clans, but... your nephew Finn. He's still a direct descendant from the male O'Connell line."

Briefly, the thought that my grandfather had murdered everyone in his family, even the children made my stomach lurch. "But- he's a little boy! He should be safe."

"Not if someone has a use for him," he said grimly. "I'll put an extra security detail on Bridget and the kids, all right?"

Kissing him fervently, I whispered, "Thank you. So much. Can we go see them right now?"

I knew we had other calls to make. Important people to sway to our position. So did Patrick. But he sighed, and nodded. "Sure, yeah. We can do that."

"So tell me what's happening, then," Bridget said, eyeing me sternly.

God bless my sister-in-law; she saw right through my "social visit." She had been in this game longer than I had and she knew when things were going sideways.

Glancing over to make sure Zoe and Finn were busy, I quickly explained everything we'd learned that day. By the time I finished, she looked pale enough to pass out.

"They think someone could go after my boy?"

"Patrick's just covering every potential threat, all right? He's doubling your security here, just in case." I looked over to see him speaking with Yevgeniy, whose jaw looked tight enough to crack a walnut.

"Besides, that walking segment of the Ural mountains over there isn't going to let anything or anyone near you. He looks like he could stop bullets with his teeth," I teased her, relieved to see her smile again.

Bridget's smile turned evil and she nudged me, nodding at Patrick. Zoe was chatting with him, holding up one of her rats like some kind of offering to the gods. He was leaning as far away as he could without falling through the door. She carefully placed the rat - I think that one was Tofu - on his jacket and the little rodent quickly made her way inside his Brioni suit.

"Hey, hey, lassie, get your rat-"

"Her name's Tofu, Uncle Patrick. She likes you." Zoe said, smiling happily as he held out his arms like a terrified scarecrow and the rat's little furry face peered out from one sleeve.

"This is the perfect revenge for him, after making me share a bedroom with Doris." I said, "I don't know when I've ever felt this happy." Bridget smothered her laugh.

We watched Patrick try not to tear off his suit jacket and shirt to get away from the rat until Zoe took pity on him and got Tofu back.

He was mopping his face as he walked over to us. "Holy Mother of God, that thing is not a pet. It's a demon."

"Are we off to meet with Campbell and Burke?" I asked, trying not to laugh at his pale, sweaty face.

"No," he said with a shudder, "we're going home and I'm taking a shower."

"My big, strong husband, a walking cack attack about a little, sweet rat?" I said, lightly tickling the back of his neck.

He batted my hand away.

Chapter Seventeen

In which Patrick's Range Rover really should have a rocket launcher.

Patrick...

Aisling was watching me with amusement, arms folded and twisted a bit in her seat. "Are you going to be okay? You're still sweating like a sinner in church."

"You have no idea what that thing felt like running around inside my jacket," I snapped. "That long, scaly tail... it wrapped it around my neck for balance at one point. Or to choke me."

She laughed, far too happy about this. "I wouldn't put it past Zoe to train them into attack rats. She has a very vivid creative streak."

"Teach her how to use her powers for good, then." I scowled at her.

She was about to give me some sassy retort when an ear-splitting crash knocked us sideways in a spray of glass. The Range Rover spun, tilting dangerously until finally crashing over on its side. I shook my head, trying to focus and wiped the blood out of my eyes.

"Aisling!"

She was limply hanging in her seatbelt above me. She was unconscious and bleeding from several little cuts. Pulling myself free from the broken back of the seat, I rapidly crawled to her.

"Liam, you okay? Talk to me! We have to get Aisling out of here-"

I was cut off by the staccato beat of automatic gunfire. The front of the car was crumpled, the hood torn half off and a thousand tiny cracks in the windshield, but it held. "Liam!"

There was a groan, and his voice was slurred as he said, "I'm here. You two okay?"

"I must get Aisling loose, she's unconscious. Can you see our guys?"

His head rose over the seat, but his attempt to answer me was cut off by more gunfire, I tried to determine if was from my security detail or the suicidal bastards who ran us off the road. Liam pulled his gun and tried to open his door, but the metal was too bent.

"Shite, I can't see a damn thing," he groaned. "Is Aisling hurt?"

I held her face carefully, trying to determine if anything was broken. "Darlin' you must wake up, c'mon now. Open your eyes." I yanked uselessly on her seatbelt and finally pulled my knife, cutting her free. Landing with a thump in my arms, her eyes shot open and she sucked in a huge breath.

"Patrick? What's- you all... you all right?" Bloody and hurt, and her first thought was for me.

"We got hit," I had to shout in her ear over the roar of the gunfire. "I need you to stay down and low. Does anything feel broken? Can you breathe okay?"

"Don't worry about me," she managed, "I'll stay put."

She huddled in the little pocket made by the broken seat and made herself as small as possible as Liam and I searched for our men through the cracked window. The SUV that led the caravan was also on its side, spun around and facing us. I groaned, seeing the limp body of one of the men thrown from the car. Two others were sheltered behind the wreck, shooting at the bastards with the Heckler & Koch MPS rifles who were creeping closer.

I kicked at the door with all my strength, "Open up, you fecker!" I shouted. Liam managed to wedge his gun in a crack in the metal and was taking potshots at the two men with the machine guns, nailing one in the thigh, dropping him. He sprayed our car in return, but it pinged off the glass, though one bullet punched through the metal.

There was return fire from behind us, giving me hope that the men in the third car survived.

"Don't you kick that door open!" Liam shouted, "You're protected in here."

"Not if they light the car on fire," I said grimly, slamming my heel over and over into the twisted metal. I glanced down at Aisling, she was still crouched where I'd put her, hands over her head. She looked up and tried to smile at me, and I roared, finally kicking the door with all my strength and it finally flew open.

Liam rolled out first, firing at the men surrounding two big trucks with reinforced bumpers. There were at least fifteen of them, but five were down, likely dead and two others firing randomly in all directions. One hit one of his own men and I shook my head, taking down a giant bastard who was firing his weapon like he knew how to use it.

Heat shimmered in, warping my gaze and I realized the SUV in front of us was on fire. "Move!" I shouted to the two men crouched behind it. "I'll cover you!"

"Make 'em count," Liam said grimly, "if that SUV goes up, the flames could hit us, too."

I scanned the area, looking for shelter and spotted a stone shed behind us. It wasn't far, if I could get Aisling secured behind it…

Dima shouted directions in Russian from behind us, laying down cover fire with me as the two surviving men in his car fanned out, trying to flank our attackers.

I leaned back into the backseat, holding out my hand. "Come to me now, sweetheart. I have to get you out of here." I could feel the heat from the SUV in front of us and groaned. It was going up like an atom bomb any second.

Aisling shakily pushed herself up, trying to reach my hand. "C'mon love, grab my hand. You can do it." Gritting my teeth against a torn piece of metal digging into my side, I managed a smile. She slipped and I could feel my terror for her choking me. "C'mon. Almost there."

Another splatter of automatic fire hit the car, making it rock and Aisling fell backward, crying out in pain. I wedged myself in as deep as I could. "Look at me. Aisling, look at me now. Give me your hand. C'mon darlin' you can do this!"

Gritting her teeth, she straightened her legs and strained, reaching with both hands for me. This time our fingers touched, I gripped her wrist and pulled, hard enough that I thought I might have dislocated her shoulder. Holding her with one arm and firing with the other, I backed toward a stone shed behind us.

The front SUV blew up, spectacularly, whiting out my vision for a moment until I blinked furiously. Shards of flaming metal struck one of their trucks, torching it instantly, along with six of the men around it. The two that remained raced for the last truck, backing down the road at speeds that told me they were no amateurs.

"Keep one of them alive!" I shouted, covering Aisling from the flaming debris still raining down around us.

"Your sleeve's on fire," she said faintly, trying to put it out.

We were lucky, five wounded - two seriously - but my entire team survived. Liam dragged the only survivor left away from the corpses of the rest of his men over to me, dumping him like a sack of rocks.

"I hear the sirens," he said, "you might wanna decide what to do with him in a hurry."

I looked down at him. The man's hair was smoking, big chunks singed off and he was groaning from a bullet in his shoulder. Putting my foot on the wound, I leaned in, enjoying hearing his scream.

"Who sent you?"

"Fuck you," he spat.

"Wrong answer," I said, pushing my foot down harder. "Who sent you?"

"Sirens…" Liam murmured, looking over his shoulder.

"Put him in the back SUV. Is it drivable?" I craned my neck, it looked like it, no flat tires.

"Da," muttered Dima, holstering his gun.

"Good. Gag him and throw him in the back. Get the wounded to the safe house, I'll call Doc Meyer to meet you there."

He nodded, dragging the wounded man by the back of his jacket and ignoring his howls of pain as he threw him in the car. They disappeared just before the *gardai's* cars came into view, lights flashing and sirens blazing.

Crouching next to Aisling, I cupped her cheek. "I'm sorry, *mo stór*. I'll get you out of here as quickly as I can."

"It's all right," she smiled tiredly. "It's not my first gunfight."

Cupping her face gently, I whispered, "I hope to Christ it's your last."

After an insistent round of questioning from the *gardai'*, I cut it off, curtly pointing out that my wife was hurt and they were welcome to call me tomorrow. Two of the more sympathetic officers - and on our payroll, I knew - helped push the Range

Rover back on all four tires, which were all full. The SUV was battered, but drivable still after being sprayed repeatedly with automatic fire.

"I take it back," said Liam, holding a wad of gauze to a cut on his forehead, "this *is* a James Bond car."

"Still needs a rocket launcher," Aisling groaned painfully, letting me help her into the back seat.

Chapter Eighteen

In which Aisling rides a unicorn to Gumdrop Island and Patrick visits The Sliver.

Patrick...

"They attacked my wife."

"*Ceann Fine,* we know, we are-" Finian began,

I swept everything off the long table we were gathered around, shattering whiskey glasses and sending my laptop flying.

"They. Fucking. Attacked. MY WIFE!" I roared. Everyone sat silently, frozen in their seats as I paced around the table.

"These fecking sods used a specialty-reinforced tractor-trailer truck to roll my car and you're saying none of you have fuck-all to tell me?" My fists clenched and unclenched as I took a deep breath, trying to clear the red haze before it took me over.

"The captive is still waiting for you to question," Liam said carefully. "The doc stabilized him, though he wasn't happy about it."

"One of our contacts in the Forensics department ran the images of the dead shooters through their files," Finian spoke up. "Only two matches in the criminal database. Both mercenaries. However, one of the bodies matched up from a speeding ticket, if you can believe it. Brogan Kennedy. He was a dockworker over in the Campbell shipping yards."

Lydia frowned. "Bard Campbell is the most conservative of the Six Families. It doesn't sound right that he'd come gunning for you - with fifteen shooters, no less - without any backing from the rest of the Six. Plus, he's dealing with a labor dispute in his legitimate trucking company in Belfast." She paused, eyeing me cautiously over her glass. "How *is* Aisling?"

I ran my hands through my hair. "She's got a broken arm, the one I hauled her out of the car with." There was a collective sympathetic wince from around the table. "She didn't scream. Didn't make a sound. She said she didn't want to distract me."

"Shite, I would have screamed," mused Finian.

"Several small cuts, nothing that needed stitching," I added.

Liam shifted irritably, "How did they find us today? In a fairly deserted area, quite convenient for attacking us?"

"Your convoy is not inconspicuous," Lydia pointed out, "but it is interesting that you visited Flanagan in the hospital today. He certainly knew where you were going."

I frowned, running my finger over my upper lip. "That seems the least likely, based on our conversation at the hospital. However, no one can be ruled out right now." I stood up, heading for the door. "I'm going to check on my wife, then I'll meet you at the Sliver."

Aisling was curled up on her side in bed - what was now *our* bed, something that made me grin - with her broken arm resting on a pillow. There were a couple of small cuts on her face, a few more on her arms and shoulders. I felt self-disgust like a punch in the stomach. She should never have been hurt.

I should have had better intelligence.

I should have protected her.

"How are you feeling, *mo stór?*" I sat down on the bed, careful not to jostle her.

"I'm fine," she smiled a little dreamily. "Your doctor gave me some pain meds that might be a bit too good. I'm sittin' on a candy floss cloud with a unicorn. He's takin' me to Gumdrop Island."

Bursting into laughter, I gently kissed her cheek. "I think Doc Meyer is more used to gunshot wounds and stabbings, but still." I frowned, all the humor gone. "I can't believe I yanked you out of the car by your broken arm. I'm sorry, sweet girl that I didn't know. After that? You deserved the good stuff."

Yawning, Aisling squeezed my thigh with her good hand. "You saved me, husband. I think that's the important thing here. Besides, he only gave me a brace. He said the break's not bad enough for a cast."

I kissed her with more enthusiasm than was proper for an injured woman. "You were brave and kept your head. I'm proud of you."

"As I said," she hummed lightly, "it wasn't my first gunfight. When I was ten, a rival of the O'Connells attacked us on the way to church on Easter Sunday. They may have been bastards, but they were better than my Da. He used me as a shield when they started shooting at him and they went after our security men instead."

Just when I thought my disgust for the O'Connell men couldn't be greater…

"What happened, *mo stór?*"

Clumsily trying to brush her hair out of her eyes, she said, "They killed a bunch of ours. Da and his men killed a bunch of theirs. Everyone drove away and he made us go to church anyway because we couldn't look like they'd scared us off. I had wet myself when he pulled me in front of him when they were shooting, so Ma did her best to clean me up. I got a whipping when we went home. For bein' weak."

I put my head on her chest. "My sweet girl. Shite. I'm sorry."

I wish I'd taken my time with Colm, made him suffer for days before letting him die.

I felt her hand in my hair, the warmth of her fingers stroking my head, soothing my ever-present headache, and making my tight muscles loosen. I hadn't allowed anyone to do something like that in a long time, something so intimate. This sweet woman shouldn't be caring for me, I should be giving this to her.

"Not your fault." She twined a lock of my hair through her fingers. "An' you took me away from that. Ya' saved Finn and Zoe from growin' up with another bastard like I did..." Aisling's words were slurring, she was apparently not joking about the strength of those pain meds.

Gently kissing her, I leaned closer, cupping her cheek. "I will give my life, to keep you safe. To protect Bridget and her kids." I shuddered slightly. "But not the rats."

Giggling, a high, sweet sound that made me laugh, too, Aisling said, "Fair enough. I think I'm gonna nap now."

"Good idea, ya stoner," I tucked her in and watched her as her giggles died off into soft snores. I kissed her one more time on her forehead, looking at her broken arm, curled protectively against her chest.

My smile faded as I headed down the hall. I was getting answers from that bastard who tried to kill my wife, and I would do every ugly thing in my arsenal to get them.

"Explain to me," Dima asked, "why you call this Sliver?"

He was driving with me to the location because Liam was busy moving men around to bolster our defenses.

"The Sliver's a strange bit of land that technically doesn't belong to anyone," I said, looking at the passing countryside. "The British government has been scooping up property, taking it away from Ireland and then returning it since the 1550s. All these old records got mixed up, burned, lost… At any rate, there's bits of land like this all over Ireland, small plots that don't show up on maps, no taxes paid to any government, under no one's jurisdiction. And in this particular case, remote enough that legal scrutiny passes over it."

Dima grinned darkly, "I begin to see the advantage."

"Exactly," I agreed, "the Doyles built a facility here on this bit - shaped like a sliver, hence the name - about forty years ago. It's very useful."

The Sliver was built into a small hill; with two steel doors that could be made inconspicuous when not in use. We'd stored sensitive cargo there many times, used it as a safe house… and a torture site. When we pulled up, the doors opened and we drove through them, parking in a large storage area.

"Much bigger than I expect," Dima said, looking around.

"We have work to do," I said, tightening my hands into fists, "you want to soften him up?"

"Da," he said cheerfully, cracking his knuckles.

The air grew colder as we descended the steps, our shoes clanking on the steel grid treads, echoing off the cement walls. The hallway at the bottom of the stairs stretched ahead of us, with four steel doors on either side. I led Dima to the last one on the left.

"Hey, boss!" Finian greeted us, looking far too happy. The prisoner was unconscious, hanging from a hook in the middle of the room, blood dripping into the drain beneath him.

Finian had a cigarette hanging out of the corner of his mouth, and he was shirtless.

"You working up a sweat, then?" I asked, taking off my suit jacket and rolling up my sleeves.

My Warlord shrugged. "Just having a bit of fun. Hey there," he greeted Dima with a nod. "You wanna take over? I'm gonna get a jar."

Dima smiled with anticipation and nodded back, rolling up his sleeves as well.

Following Finian out of the room, I heard the first meaty "thunk!" of Dima's fist into some portion of the unlucky sod's body.

"What did you get out of him?" I asked.

He took a lager out of the fridge in the next room. I never understood why my men wanted a break room next to the place we conducted interrogations... but whatever made 'em happy.

"He's one tough fucker," he said, opening the can. "No affiliation tattoos, brands... but, it looks like he had some tattoos on his fingers to cover whatever was there before. Could be a naked tattoo of his Ma, I don't know. But I took some pictures and sent them up to Lydia. She's running them through her scanner."

A slight flush went up his neck when he mentioned her name.

"Christ almighty, are you another one of my men whose heart Lydia's crushed under her size six combat boots?" I groaned.

"No!" Finian said defensively, "She's just real smart with those things. Now don't you want to know about our prisoner?"

Smooth shift in the subject matter, I thought, shaking my head. "Yes, of course."

"Only thing I got out of him so far is that it doesn't look like any of the Six Families," he said. "He refused to give me anything good, but he's got his tells, like any man. There's a bigger group involved here, some kind of collective."

I frowned, watching him chug down the bottle and get out a fresh one. "A collective? Of who? What nationality? What criminal organization?"

"Whoever they are, they got him scared," he said, "I was very persuasive."

"It's a start," I said, slapping his shoulder. "I'll go in and see what Dima's prised out of him. When'd ya last sleep?"

"Eh," he shrugged.

"At least use one of the cots down the hall, you eejit," I said, "take a few hours."

Dima must have moved on to some new techniques because our prisoner was screaming. I cracked my neck and thought of Aisling's pale face, her splinted arm, and joined him in the interrogation room.

Aisling...

When I woke up the next morning, Patrick was asleep in the big armchair by the fireplace, shirtless but still wearing his dress pants. Creeping over, I tried to cover him with a quilt, and he woke up instantly, standing and grabbing my shirt.

"Sorry?" I offered, "I just wanted to cover you up."

The coldness left his expression. "I didn't mean to startle you, darlin,' how do you feel?"

"Much better," I said, flexing my shoulder experimentally. "What about you?"

"Fine."

Liar. He looked exhausted, dark circles under his eyes and a cut on his forehead that could have at least used a bandage, if not some stitches.

"Why didn't you come to bed last night?" I asked, "That chair doesn't look that comfortable."

"I didn't want to disturb your sleep," he said, hesitating, "but I didn't want you to be alone, either."

The thought of this man keeping watch over me when he was

so beat up and exhausted from that car crash and the attempt to shoot us into pieces was so... *sweet?* It was sweet, though. "Well, can you just lie down for a minute a take a quick snooze?" I asked, "You know you'll be better for it."

Patrick hesitated, looking from me to the bed like it was a succulent chocolate dessert. I knew the look; he'd eaten three of them yesterday.

"Just for an hour," he said, rubbing his eyes.

"When did you get in last night?" I didn't ask where he'd been. I didn't want to know.

"About five this morning," he admitted. I shoved him onto the bed, using my good arm and pulled up the silk comforter. "*Mo stór* if you wanted me, you could have just said," he grinned up at me shamelessly, and damn him if my lower half didn't warm up.

"Later," I whispered, biting his ear.

He was asleep before I left the room.

"Where are we going again?" We were in another heavily reinforced SUV, this one was a Mercedes G-Class, and Liam had happily filled me in on every, excruciatingly boring detail about its safety features.

Patrick was going over some documents on his iPad. "Into the office." He was dressed in a dark blue Armani suit and looked delicious enough to nibble on.

"The office?" I asked teasingly, "The one where all the proper work is done?"

Patrick raised his brow. "Are you thinking you can get away with sass just because of one little broken arm?"

I put a hand to my chest, pretending to be deeply shocked. "Oh, heavens no!" Liam laughed from the front and Patrick went back to his paperwork, muttering something about "cheeky sods."

Stepping out in front of the tall, glass, and granite office building in North Wall Quay brought up no happy memories. I almost never came to the O'Connell offices for their legitimate enterprises, just once or twice so Da could show off his "perfect" family to clients and investors.

Patrick walked differently here, tall, commanding, though without the inherent sense of menace he seemed to wear as his mantle as *Ceann Fine*. Gliding up the glass lift to the fifteenth floor, I watched our reflections in the mirror. With his hair slicked back and that suit; he perfectly looked the part of a rich, high-powered businessman. A hot as hell businessman.

He caught me staring at the mirrored door. "What are you looking at, pretty girl?" Stepping behind me, his hands slid to my waist, pulling me against him. "Are you admiring how sexy you are in this dress?" His long fingers drifted down to my hips, squeezing me. "Looking like such a proper businesswoman, when I know just how pretty you'd look if I pulled this up a bit and shoved into you from behind?"

I made a high-pitched noise that resembled something like a seagull and he laughed softly, edging up the hem of my dress. I put my hand on his, trying to stop him. "Patrick, we can't..."

"Tell me, *mo stór,* if I were to put my fingers inside your lacy little panties, would I find you wet?" He placed slow, sucking kisses down the side of my neck and I squeaked again, watching the numbers climb on the lift display. "Would you be all hot, and slick for me?"

With a cheerful "ding!" the lift reached the top floor. "Oh, thank god," I wheezed, yanking my hem back down and not-quite racing out into the lobby.

It was a large, airy space, decorated in Office Chic with low, black leather couches on the granite floor with bright, abstract paintings on the walls.

"Mr. Doyle, welcome back!" A cheerful-looking woman in her forties was seated at the huge reception desk, and her smile slipped a bit when she spotted me. "And... Mrs. Doyle. Hello, ma'am."

"Oh, just call me-" I squinted. "Cara, is that you?"

Her light complexion went even paler, "Y- yes, Mrs. Doyle."

I realized then that she was terrified, and the shame of my family's legacy choked me again. "No, it's just- really, Cara, it's so nice to see you! And you're clearly in charge of this place so I'm having higher hopes for Patrick already."

Her hunched shoulders went down and some color came back into her face. "Thank you," she said with a small smile, "I enjoy the work."

"It's really good to see you," I said, trying to pour all the relief and warmth I felt at seeing her alive and well into my smile.

"Cara, we'll be in my office. When is my first appointment?" Patrick asked.

"Four o'clock, Mr. Doyle."

"Excellent. Thank you," he smiled at her before walking me into his office and closing the door just as I hugged him fiercely, knocking him back against it. "What is this for?" He kissed my neck. "Not that I'm complaining, mind."

"That's Cara. She was one of the women- the women my grandfather brought into the house when they couldn't work in the... How did she end up with you?" I smoothed my hands down his jacket lapels, patting his chest nervously.

His hands came up to stop my movements, holding my hands to his chest. "About six months ago, your father was selling some older women in an auction for domestics. It was a bad one," he said, looking disgusted. "Yuri and I bought them all and got them jobs or some training. I kept Cara out of Dublin and put her in some business courses until I took over."

"Thank you," I whispered, kissing him over and over. "Thank you so much. She just disappeared one day and I never knew... I hate those bastards for what they did! I hate that I'm part of that family!"

"Shh... my sweet girl. You're a Doyle now, and you'll help me make it right. We'll wipe any fecking trace of the Red Trade from Ireland, one way or another. This isn't on you."

I kissed him, gripping his lapel with my good arm and going up on my toes to lean into his tall, solid body. "Thank you, thank you, thank you." I punctuated each word with a kiss until, with a growl, he took over, sliding his hands down to my arse and gripping me tight, yanking me up until I wrapped my legs around his narrow waist.

Placing me on his desk, he pulled down the neckline of my dress enough to reach my breasts, sucking hard on my nipples until they were almost painfully tight. "I love these, so sweet and pink," he gloated, pulling on one and making me yelp. Those big, warm hands of his moved back to my arse, squeezing them again and making my back arch, pushing my breast against his mouth.

Sliding one hand inside my undies, he groaned. "I knew you'd be so slick for me, ready." Twisting his fingers, he pushed two of them inside me. "Still as snug as the day I first took you to bed, aren't you?"

I vaguely heard the 'clink' of his belt buckle and the rustle of his pants sliding down as Patrick pulled my thighs wide. "I can't wait, *mo stór,* I need to take you," he said, eyes glowing, this time with lust.

"Then have me," I gasped.

Anything else I could have meant to say was gone, forgotten as he shoved into me, greedily, without finesse and with the savagery of a man starving for me. Every time with him stung like the first time, and I suspected it would always be like that. But I had learned to love how it burned, how he spread me wide and hammered into me like he wanted to split me in two. My heels tightened against his flexing, perfect ass as he held onto my breasts, looking down at where we were joined.

"You are beautiful," he growled, "so beautiful with this tight, sweet cunt and your slick on me, dripping down my balls? God!" He braced his feet, thrusting into me, harder and harder as his thumb began circling my clitoris. "Can you come like this, *mo stór*? I'm too hungry for you, I can't-"

His head threw back and his neck tensed, his jaw tight. My husband was beautiful in his savagery, even more after letting loose from the authoritative, composed businessman that I'd come into this office with.

Pressing his thumb hard against my painfully sensitive clit, he thrust faster, with harder, shorter strokes and I was half out of my mind with need. I couldn't think about anything but his cock inside me and how good he felt, too big somehow but still so...

"Come, my beautiful, filthy, perfect girl," he growled, "come with me now."

My back arched, tightening down on him inside me and I felt like I burst open, and everything poured out of me in a white blaze of light and his hand came down over my mouth as I screamed, telling him how beautiful he was and how good he felt and a bunch of nonsense that I just couldn't stop saying.

It felt like hours later when I finally came back to my senses, and Patrick carried me over to the leather couch in the seating area. I relaxed on his lap, so content and feeling loose and boneless.

"You know," he chuckled, "I'd had a thought that I would bring in some champagne so we could christen the new office together. I like this way much better."

I slapped his shoulder, too weak to do anything else. Looking around his office, I sighed. "It's funny, I always dreamed of working someplace like here, making my own money, having a life…"

He tilted his head to look down at me. "Did you go to business school? I can't picture the O'Connell men letting that happen."

"I did," I said proudly, "Trinity Business School, Marketing and Advertising."

Patrick whistled, "That's huge, darlin'."

"I took the courses online, in secret so my Da wouldn't catch me and force me to stop. I always had this dream that maybe I could get free, you know? Go somewhere else and make my own way."

"Go where?" Gently, he pulled the strap of my dress back up.

"Oh… well, I had a secret file on my laptop where I'd put pictures from different places that inspired me, Seattle, Vancouver. Barcelona looked amazing, and Paris… Anyway. I knew they were just dreams. I knew my Da would never let me go."

His hand went to my hair, gently untangling the worst of the knots. "There's always room for a motivated, up-and-comer in this company."

I sat up, wide-eyed. "You'd really let me work here?"

"Of course," he said. "We have a good marketing department and you could learn a lot. You'd be valuable here."

Straddling him and wincing just slightly at the ache between my legs, I cupped his cheeks, kissing him tenderly. "If you're trying to make me think you're the greatest thing to ever return to Ireland, you're going the right way about it."

Chuckling, he kissed me back. "You've caught on to my evil plan, darlin'."

Chapter Nineteen

In which Patrick introduces Aisling to a punishment that is not really a punishment.

Aisling...

"We're going to St. Petersburg this weekend."

Patrick was looping his tie into a tidy Windsor Knot, looking back at me in the mirror as we dressed for the day. I was heading into the office to meet the Marketing Director and he was off cracking skulls or extorting funds or whatever a *Ceann Fine* did during his day.

"Oh?" I asked, trying to get the zipper up on my black pencil skirt, "Any particular reason?"

"It's our first tribute for the Morozov Bratva," he said, "but a bit more ceremonial. Maksim is throwing a party, we'll be seen as the heads of our Mob organization, meeting with a few allies. Bring a couple of fancy dresses."

I couldn't help noticing that he said "we" when talking about establishing our position as head of the Doyle Clan and I grinned a little.

"Why don't you call Ella and Tania?" Patrick suggested. "Get some suggestions on what to wear? I want you to feel comfortable."

"Thank you, that's a good idea." I was so warmed by his kindness.

He smiled at me, shrugging on his suit jacket. He pushed his hand through one of the sleeves and paused. "What the-" A stuffed rat came shooting out the end of it as he yelped. "What the hell is that!" Patrick shook the jacket violently, as if another dozen would fly out.

Kicking the innocent rodent stuffie with the top of his dress shoe, my husband glared at me. "Really, Aisling? *Really?*"

I shrugged innocently. "I have no idea how that got there."

"That's low, woman," he grumbled, stalking out and muttering down the hallway.

I knew the O'Connell clan had a private jet, but I'd never been on it. When the Mercedes pulled up to a Gulfstream at a private airstrip by the Dublin International Airport, I wondered if it was my grandfather's. Patrick must have read my mind because he put his arm around me, leading me to the steps.

"I just purchased this jet," he said, "I sold off your family's and it was a good thing. There was enough cocaine residue in there to supply every club in Belfast for a month."

"Of course there was," I sighed, climbing the stairs to be greeted by a startlingly good-looking male flight attendant, who shook my hand with a big smile until he noticed Patrick's chilly gaze behind me. There were three banks of wide, comfortable grey leather seats in an L shape, a separate dining area and I caught sight of a bedroom behind the opened door at the back of the jet.

"Fancy, look at you," I teased Patrick, who rolled his eyes.

"That would have been a waste of space in my life as an *Obshchak*," he said wryly, "but now that I have a beautiful wife..." He nuzzled my neck and I laughed.

"The flight's only what? Three and a half hours?" I teased. "I don't think there's going to be time for any sleeping."

"I wasn't thinking about sleep," he retorted, still kissing my neck until Jack and two of his Russian guards stepped into the main cabin area. "Back to work," he sighed, letting go of me.

We sat in the same bank of seats; I pulled out my laptop to look over some press releases I was assigned to proofread and Patrick and Dima pored over a series of complicated-looking inventory lists as the jet took off. Whatever they were searching for, they weren't finding it and when Dima left to speak to his other man, I slid over.

"What are you looking for?" I murmured.

"There are some discrepancies in the cargo logistics loaded into a few of our warehouses," he said, running his hands through his hair. "So, someone's stealing from us, or the inventory is getting manipulated before delivery, then." Patrick flashed a smile at me. "I'm still nailing down all the discrepancies left behind by the..." he hesitated, "the old crew."

I looked over the floor plans for the warehouses he was examining, I recognized them based on their proximity to the docks. "These are the ones near the far West side of the Docklands, right?"

"Sure, yeah," he said, looking at me with a new appreciation. "How did you see that?"

"Da intercepted my Ma's security detail one day," I said, tracing the lines of the floor plans, "we had to come there and drop off all of our bodyguards before he'd let Ma take me to school, so I recognized it."

When the flight attendant asked if we were ready to eat, I insisted on moving some of the paperwork to put down a plate of steak and risotto for my husband. "You have to have more in your stomach than vodka by the time you meet with the Morozov men," I scolded. When he sighed and picked up his silverware, I felt a warmth blooming in my chest. It was nice to take care of someone. To have Patrick trust me enough to take care of him.

Flying into St. Petersburg was surreal; the massive stretch of forest, the shimmering water of the Baltic Sea... it was beautiful in a wild, untamed way that I didn't expect for such a major cultural city. Patrick laughed at me for eagerly leaning over him to drink in the beauty of the Hermitage Museum as we passed by.

"There should be a few hours of free time if you want to take Jack and explore a little," he said. "However, you'll need a larger security detail here. The Morozovs may be one of the Russian Six Families, but we made enough enemies in my time with the Bratva that extra men are a good idea."

Jack looked deeply offended at the insinuation that he couldn't protect me on his own, and I patted his arm soothingly. I'd come to be very fond of the mountain-like ginger who followed me like a massive shadow.

A representative was waiting for us outside the magnificent entryway of the Hotel Astoria to take us to our rooms, and I tried not to gawk like Culchie on her first trip into the big city but the hotel was legendary.

"Did you know that Rasputin used to hide out here for assignations with some of his married lovers?" I asked excitedly, wandering from room to room in our suite. "Prince Charles has stayed here, and Elton John, and HG Wells."

"And now you," he said, smiling at me fondly, watching me touch the elaborate gilt scrollwork on the walls. There was a huge main room with beautiful old furniture covered in green and gold silk, three bedrooms and bathrooms, a private kitchen, and a balcony that stretched around the corner and ran the length of the entire suite. "I thought you'd like the balcony," he said, "you can see St. Isaac's Cathedral across the way."

I melted for a moment, admiring how kind this man could be. He was giving instructions to some of our security men and finally looked up to see me, smiling at him like a simpleton.

"What?" Patrick asked, gesturing for the men to leave.

"You're just..." I shrugged awkwardly, "you're so good to me."

"You deserve it," he assured me, walking over to capture a kiss, sliding his hands down over my arse and squeezing it, making me yelp against his lips.

"Hey, now! No groping, Mr. Doyle!"

"Why do you think I got you such a nice suite, Mrs. Doyle?" He smiled devilishly, "I'm softening you up so I can debauch you."

I was moments away from letting him when there was a knock on the door. "So close..." he groaned before pulling away.

"There she is! Hey girl!" Tania and Ella came into the room, giving Patrick a hug before not-quite pushing him away to get to me.

"So, Yuri and Maksim will have this guy locked up in boring-ass meetings for the next two days," Tania said, "so we're here to kidnap you."

Patrick was beginning to look concerned, and Ella noticed. "Surely you trust us with your wife," she said, looking wide-eyed and innocent.

"Maybe," he said skeptically. Turning to Jack, he murmured, "Take three more men with you."

Tania and Ella rapidly ascertained that I wasn't that eager to shop for clothes, to their relief, and we strolled through the Grand Peterhof Palace before stopping for lunch. On the way back to the hotel, I spotted a little collection of stuffed animals in a shop window.

"Can we stop here?" I asked.

"Of course," Ella said, watching with amusement as I headed for the pile of stuffies. "Are you looking for something for your niece and nephew?"

"Not exactly," I grinned, pulling six toy rats from the pile. There was one with a long pink tail that looked especially threatening for a sweet little stuffie.

Patrick still wasn't talking to me after opening his shaving kit to find one of my new rats lurking by his razor. Despite that, dinner with the other two couples was so much fun. Tania eagerly introduced me to *Pelmeni*, glorious little dumplings stuffed with lamb or pork. The *Shashlik* - marinated meat and veggies on a kabob - were so delicious as the spices exploded on my tongue, that I stole several juicy pieces off Patrick's plate while he was busy talking to Yuri.

I thought he hadn't noticed until he leaned over, whispering in my ear. "I'm glad you like them, should I order you more?"

"Oh, it's plenty..." I started mentally reciting my script from childhood, don't eat too much... don't be a pig... "Actually, I would love more."

Patrick kissed my cheek, gesturing to the server and ordering another round of *Shashlik.*

"Why does every story from you involve crime, violence, and booze, though mostly a combination of all three?" Tania asked, shaking her head at the fifth story - and the fifth round of vodka - as we all lingered at the table.

"It's a magical combination," Yuri said, raising his glass.

I was still giggling at the story of the three of them escaping naked from a Moscow sauna after an encounter with some enraged members of the Yakuza. Looking around the table, I could see the love Patrick had for these two Russians. They'd saved his life from the O'Connell Mob's attempt to destroy his family, gave him purpose. They backed his bid to take back the Doyle Clan's rightful place. None of those things were necessary to build their Bratva, but they did it anyway.

Since my family had also now shrunk to a narrow group of people, I hoped that maybe there would be room for me in this little circle, too.

The following afternoon...

"*Aisling!* Bloody hell, woman!"

"What was that?" Tania asked. She'd called me to tell me what to wear tonight; there was a big gathering of the Morozov Bratva's inner circle and their allies at one of the clubs Yuri owned.

"I think Patrick found another rat," I whispered, trying to smother my laughter.

"Girl, you are pure evil," she said, trying not to laugh, too. I'd told her and Ella about the poor man's violent aversion to Zoe's rats.

"You're thinking it's too much, then?" I asked.

"Oh, hell no. You have to get every advantage you can over these men," she said, "keep digging. You can never have enough dirt on a Crime Lord. It's our job to keep them humble."

Patrick stalked through the door into the sitting room, shaking the stuffed rat at me.

"Oh, shite, I have to go," I said, trying to smother my laughter at my enraged husband.

"Good luck," Tania snickered.

"Do you know how much trouble you're in? Do you?"

Patrick stood over me, hands on hips and outraged. One little chuckle slipped out of me and I knew it was a mistake. His eyes turned that spooky, frigid shade of blue and he scooped me up off the couch. Carrying me over to the desk, he stood next to me, arms folded. "Take your clothes off."

"What?" I looked around. There were several floor-to-ceiling windows lining the wall of the big room.

"You heard me," he said.

"It was just a stuffed toy," I said weakly, already slipping my dress over my shoulders. He nodded at my bra and I took it off, uncomfortably crossing my arms across my chest.

Patrick snapped the waistband of my undies. "These, too."

I had never felt so exposed before, standing in front of my husband - dressed in his suit - while I was naked. He took off his jacket, rolling the sleeves of his dress shirt up. While I definitely appreciated the show, I got increasingly nervous about his silence.

"Bend over the desk," he said.

"It wasn't a real rat!" I protested, but when he put his hand between my shoulder blades and pushed gently, I bent over. The glass edge was uncomfortable against my hips, and my nipples stiffened from the chill.

"Say another word," he warned, "and I'll double your punishment." I turned my face to look up at him. He didn't really look angry. The corners of his mouth were turned up slightly. I wasn't sure what was happening here. This was a punishment that wasn't a punishment?

"But I-"

"Now, it's double," he said calmly, his big, rough hand stroking the bare skin of my arse. "Such silky skin... so pale. I think it will be even prettier turned a bright red."

The first slap made me screech, shooting up from the desk, just to have him push me down again. "That's one, you bad girl," he said, just before landing the second blow on my other cheek. The first few blows simply outraged me, making me grit my teeth. But as he precisely, quickly alternated slaps on my reddening cheeks, I was shocked to feel more than just my arse heat up.

This cannot be turning me on, I thought, deeply shocked. But it was. This diabolical sod was absolutely making me wet and I cringed when he slid his fingers through my wet lips, circling my entrance.

Leaning close enough that his lips touched my ear, he whispered, "It's not much of a punishment if you're enjoying it, darlin'."

I pressed my forehead to the glass, refusing to answer him. After another five slaps, I felt his calloused fingertips rub my arse, soothing the heated skin.

"You can stand up now," he said.

Glaring at him, I did, putting my hands over my burning rear. Patrick looked... different. His eyes were narrow, but he had a little smile playing over his lips as he looked me over thoroughly, shamelessly. He walked around the desk and seated himself, opening his laptop.

"C'mere, bad girl," he said, beckoning with two fingers.

My feet moved without thought to guide them, walking over to stand between his knees. When he unzipped his pants and pulled out his cock, my eyes widened. Apparently, I wasn't the only one who enjoyed that spanking a little too much. He lounged in the office chair, stroking his thick cock as I stared. Holding it upright, he tilted his head.

"Turn around." Brow furrowed, I did, gasping when his hand on my hip guided me - I thought to sit on his lap - but instead, he angled me to slide down on his cock.

"Oh! Oh, my god, what are you *doing?*" I gasped.

Patrick leaned into me, his broad, hard chest pressed against my back. I could smell his cologne, the starched cotton of his shirt, and some unidentifiable spicy element that was just him. "You're getting your punishment now."

I angled my shoulders, trying to look back at him. "What was that spanking, then?"

Oh, he had the most evil smile. "That was just the warm-up. Now, you're going to be my good little cock-warmer while I get some work done."

My mouth kept trying to form words without knowing what I could possibly say. He kissed the back of my neck and pushed me down a bit more, making sure he was completely buried inside me, scooting in to get a bit closer to the desk and started tapping out a reply to an email.

What was I supposed to do? The *feel* of him inside me was overwhelming. He wasn't moving at all, just his long arms tapping away casually on his damned keyboard. Was he really going to make me sit here, perched on his dick and not allowed to move?

I was so turned on right now. This can't be the plan. How was this punishment?

"Patrick, I-"

"Shh..." he bit my neck sharply. "Not a word. *This* is your punishment. You will sit quietly while I work. You will not move." Then, unfairly, his hand went to my hip, adjusting me slowly for a moment and pushing his cock against the front of me. "Did you know there's another spot inside you that feels just as good as the G-spot?" His hips moved again, subtly, and I felt a jolt of electricity clear down to my toes.

I sucked in a breath so quickly that I coughed it back out.

"This right here?" He pressed the heel of his hand just under my belly button. "This is the A-spot. It's a very sensitive little spot at the very top of you, next to your cervix." My head drooped as more electrical impulses zinged around my lower half, making my legs try to close against his cock.

Patrick slapped my clitoris with the tips of his wet fingers and the sting and corresponding bloom of heat made me shriek. "Ah-

ah! Keep your legs open."

It felt like an hour of this torture. Maybe two hours. Possibly a week but I didn't know anymore because I was nearly crying with my desperation to come. The heartless git would occasionally move slowly to keep himself hard, then go back to work before I could get any stimulation.

"Please..." I cut my pathetic little plea off abruptly, biting my lip, but I was dying. I could feel the rasp from the wool of his trousers against my thighs, and I was pretty sure I was making a mess of his dress pants. Slumping against his chest, I wanted to cry. I wanted to punch him in the face. I wanted... ah, god I wanted to come.

"Oh, sweet girl, you're so wet," he soothed me diabolically, his hands coming down to smooth along my inner thighs. "You must be so uncomfortable right now. Wanting to come." He sucked a red mark onto my shoulder, "Needing it so bad, don't you?"

I wanted to tell him to go straight to hell. I also wanted to bounce up and down on his nice, thick cock and it was all killing me.

"Do you want to come?" Patrick whispered in my ear. "How much do you need it, sweet girl?"

I nodded mindlessly, "Please? A lot, I need it..."

"Good girl." He slapped my wet lips and I yelped.

Oh, my god I'm going to die right here at this desk. He helped my shaky legs by putting his hand on my hip, thrusting up sharply with his hips and almost knocking me off. Each time he thrust back up into me, he slapped my clitoris and counted softly in my ear. "Five... good girl, taking every inch inside..."

I came at "six," gasping and whispering his name over and over like a secret too precious to share, writhing as he cupped my pussy and slammed up inside me, one, two, three more times before groaning and flooding me with heat, so much that his come leaked out on to his fingers and my thighs.

Lifting me up, he carried me over to the bed, putting me down gently and getting a cool, wet cloth to wipe over my shaky, sweaty body. "Do you need some aspirin, sweet girl?"

"No," I said drowsily, "I'm really good."

Patrick wrapped his arms around me, holding me tightly in the afternoon sun, whispering how beautiful I was, how sweet, what a good cock-warmer I had been. I felt filthy, and exhausted, and so perfect.

Chapter Twenty

In which there is vodka, dancing, and heartbreak.

Patrick...

"Aisling seems to have settled into married life," Yuri observed, watching her laugh and clink glasses with Tania and Ella. She looked delectable in a short gold dress that shimmered over her perfect hips - which were finally filling out a bit now that she felt comfortable eating a full meal - and showing off her sleek legs. She was so distracting in that dress, in fact, that I almost wished I'd put her in a turtleneck before we came here. Or a nun's habit.

"It was a rough start," I admitted.

"Something we all understand," chimed in Maksim. He was watching Ella with a look of devotion that I'd never seen on his face. Ever.

"And here we thought you having to drag your bride kicking and swearing to the altar would be an inauspicious beginning," Yuri smiled pleasantly, making me want to dump my drink over his head.

"How did you keep from killing him as a child?" I asked Maksim.

"Believe me, it was a constant struggle," he sighed before changing the subject. "What did you learn from the shooter? Dima told me he was very unwilling to offer information."

"I have to tell you," I said, "if Bogdan ever decides to retire as your torturer, Dima should really step up and take his place. The man had some techniques I'd never seen before. And he's not as creepy as Bogdan."

"No one is as troubling as he is," Yuri agreed, gulping down the last of his vodka. Bogdan was a valued member of the Morozov Bratva who enjoyed his work to the extent that no one wanted to be around him. And these were hardened Bratva men.

"What we finally got out of the bastard was that his team was hired by someone new; the Collective? Does that sound familiar?" I asked, watching my bride uncross her legs and cross them again, the light gleaming along those smooth thighs…

"Patrick? Are you listening?" Yuri flicked me on the forehead.

"Arsehole!" I snapped, "Sorry, you said?"

"I said," Maksim repeated with exaggerated patience, "that there have been some rumblings in the various Chinese Triads about a new European partnership for the Red Trade. No one can pin down who the Collective is, but they're already buying up property all over Europe and Asia to build sex resorts. One stupid bastard from the Jiang Triad had the balls to approach us, thinking we were involved."

"That's it?" I ran my hand through my hair, "There has to be something crucial about the ports in Ireland. Something that they need badly enough to take us out. I assumed it was Zhèng's bloody bunch, he's been pressing us hard for our docks and overland transport for his captives. I told him it would never happen, and he laughed it off like I was just trying to drive a hard bargain."

"So, we hit them hard," Maksim said, "blow up a couple of their empty ships and cripple their operation."

"This is larger than just the Zhèng Triad," Yuri said, frowning, "the plans for these sex resorts, the hundreds of millions this Collective is pouring into the plan… We are missing a few puzzle pieces."

"There's another development," I said, "you got my messages

about the attack on the Six. The sons stepping up to take over for their fathers are loathsome little shites. Cillian Kelly in particular is all over courting the Triad for their trafficking partnership. The head of the Flanagan Clan is in our corner, but we visited him in the hospital, and he's not looking good. His surviving son isn't ready to lead."

"Hey! Get your fine butts up and dance with us!" Tania seated herself on Yuri's lap, giving him a kiss.

"We will be there in a moment, darling. Just finishing some business," he purred, giving her a long kiss.

"This is a club night!" Tania protested, "You know, we're here to have fun? We'll be the super-hot ones down there on the Reggaetron floor when you decide to stop being boring."

Aisling gave me a small wave and I smiled and nodded, mentally wishing everyone within five meters of her elbows the best of luck.

Aisling...

Oh, I adored those girls! Ella, Tania, and I spun and swayed around the floor, making our poor security guards chase after us to keep anyone from approaching us. As if anyone could actually see around Jack's massive bulk. Finally taking pity on them, Ella led us to the rooftop.

"This is beautiful," I sighed. The top of the club was covered with all kinds of blooming plants and little islands of couches and tables, with lights strung overhead for a softer glow.

"Isn't it?" Ella lifted her hair to let the cool breeze flow over her sweaty neck. "You know, Maksim actually re-proposed to me during dinner, right over there." She nodded to a secluded little area surrounded by low walls covered with ivy.

"Re-proposed?" I asked.

"Oh, hell yes!" Tania chimed in. "We all had terrible weddings. In fact, it's a Morozov Bratva tradition that all weddings suck. You must demand a do-over! Trust me, you didn't look any happier at your wedding than we did at ours."

"Tania had to get married in the entryway of the Kazan Cathedral because the priest thought it would be an offense against God to marry her and Yuri in the iconostasis, you know, the altar?" Ella offered helpfully.

"Yeah, and I had to lock Ella in the restroom at her reception to talk her down before she ran screaming out of the Four Seasons," Tania retorted. "See? You're in good company."

"Sure, yeah. But my wedding has the distinction of nearly poisoning everyone in attendance. I can't help but think I win this round," I said, refilling my glass from the bottle we'd grabbed on the way up here.

"True…" Ella allowed.

"Did Patrick ever tell you what he did for Yuri and me?" Tania asked.

I shook my head.

"Yuri had left me and moved back to St. Petersburg because he was so fucked up from the kidnapping…"

I shrank back in my chair. "From my piece of shite Da, I know."

"Not your fault," Tania said, patting my knee. "Anyway, so Yuri's set to marry this Bratva princess from Moscow as per the usual arranged marriage alliance bullshit, and Patrick comes charging back into our lives and tells me I have to go stop this wedding."

My eyes were cartoonishly wide, I knew, but I could not comprehend the outrageousness of this act.

"I'm telling him no way," she continued, waving her drink around and splashing a little vodka on my knee. "But Patrick told me this. He said: 'That's something that does not go away, a love that gives the strength to endure all things.' Your man is a romantic, honey. A romantic through and through."

I had tears in my eyes and I was embarrassed about it. Patrick risked his position in their Bratva to bring them back together.

That was the most beautiful thing I had ever heard.

When we got back to the hotel early in the morning, Patrick checked his mobile and groaned. "Excuse me, *mo stór,* it's Liam, I have to get this."

"No problem," I said, giving him a kiss, "I'm going to take a shower."

Walking unsteadily into the bedroom and cursing that last bottle of wine, I heard something buzzing insistently. It wasn't my mobile, sitting on the bed. After looking around for a moment, I located the noise in my other purse.

Oh shite, the mobile from Cillian, I thought, digging between the lining of the purse to get it out, shocked that I'd completely forgotten I still had it. He was persistent, I'd give him that. The vibration stopped for a minute and began again, like one of those persistent bees that always insisted on buzzing around your head when you were just trying to have a nice, quiet picnic.

Answering it before Patrick could hear it, I hissed, "Hello? Why are you calling?"

"I've been worried something fierce about you," Cillian protested. "I heard about the attack and then you disappeared and no one's heard from you. I didn't know if you'd really been hurt and they were covering it up, or…"

Rolling my eyes, I wondered how polite I had to be. "Look, really, I'm fine, thank you for your concern." I looked over my shoulder, hoping Patrick was still on his call, wondering why I'd been foolish enough to keep Cillian's mobile. Then, I remembered his father had been murdered and instantly felt guilty. "Oh, my god!

I'm so sorry about your father. You must be heartbroken." To be honest, I didn't know if he was upset about it at all. If his father was anything like mine, this could be a blessing.

"Thank you," he said sadly, with an appropriate tinge of anger underneath it.

"Uh, are your people doing all right? Your mother?" I was definitely a little drunk and trying to find the right words to say.

"She will be," he said, "I have a lot to learn, though."

So humble, I thought, *that's new in this world.*

I can barely hear Patrick in the other room, but his voice was rising, he was angry at whoever he was talking to.

Cillian was saying something and I forced myself to pay attention. "I'm just glad you're well, Aisling. But I have something I need to tell you."

"What... would that be?" I asked, confused.

"How much do you know about what Patrick's been doing with your grandfather's business?"

Lips compressed, it took me a minute to answer. "He could burn it all down for what I care."

He sighed. "I heard he was making a big noise at that dinner at O'Rourke's distillery, claiming there would be no more, uh, trafficking. Human trafficking."

"I know what it is," I said steadily, "I know the filth my grandfather was involved in. Patrick ended any involvement from our clan."

"*Cailín álainn...*" Cillian sounded a little sad, maybe embarrassed. "That's what he told you?"

"Look- I know what I know, and don't call me that! I'm a married woman," I spluttered. I didn't want to know what's going to come out of his mouth next. Damnit! Why did I drink so much tonight? He was talking so fast and my addled brain was trying to keep up.

"Doyle's got your lot mixed up in some serious shite," he said regretfully. "He didn't end the trade. He's doubled it. There's a cargo container full of those poor souls at the O'Connell docks right now."

My hand went over my mouth. I was going to vomit all over this antique bed with its fancy silk cover if my mouth opened again. "I don't believe you," I whispered.

"I'm at the location with some of my men," he was trying to sound soothing, like he knew he just tore my heart out of my chest. "We've been trying to stop the Red Trade on these shores, but... Doyle's making it hard by stepping up. I was hoping I could get enough proof to stop him by documenting-"

"I don't believe you!" I was too loud, I was almost yelling and I had to shut up, but my heart was hammering so hard that I could barely hear myself speak.

Cillian sighed. "You know the O'Connell docks and warehouses, the ones on the far western side?"

"I do," I managed, unsteadily making my way into the bathroom.

"Hang on, then." There was a series of 'pings' as pictures were sent to my mobile, maybe six of them. The light was not good, but it was crystal clear what was happening. A ship docked. Another picture showing a crane lifting a steel shipping container off the deck. And then...

I dropped the mobile, kneeling by the toilet, throwing up everything I've eaten for the past week. Resting my forehead on my arm, I can dimly hear him calling for me.

"Aisling? *Cailín álainn?* Please answer me."

"I'm okay," I said, wiping my mouth with the back of my hand, "are you sure it's him? He was just showing me plans from the warehouses, saying there was something going on?"

"His Counselor is down there," Cillian said, "Niall. He was the Doyle Second under his father. You know him?"

Another cheerful 'ping!' alerted me to another picture and the end of my hopes. It was an image of Niall, directing crying girls, some of them helping younger kids, into the dark opening of one of the warehouses. I had only met him once when he was at the house for a meeting, but I recognized his face, warped with anger, looking like he was screaming at the girls. His hand was raised, he had a… Sweet Mother of God was that a *whip?* He was *whipping* them?

The next image was too clear. I could see the red marks across the girl's back that he was hitting. I could see her expression of anguish.

I stared at these girls. Every one of them bone thin, dirty. How long had they been in that horrible container? Where did they get taken? Walking home from work? Going to school?

"Aisling? Hey…"

I blinked and tried to come back online. "Sorry?"

"This is bad," he said sadly, "I'm so sorry. But I'm going to fix this, all right? We're going to take out the men on the ground and get the girls out of there. I have trucks standing by. We'll nail Doyle for this, I promise."

"Tell me what you need," I answered numbly, "just tell me what to look for. I'll get you everything I can."

"Good, *cailín álainn.*" His voice softened, "That's good. We'll get this bastard, and when we do, the only thing I'm asking… it's not contingent, mind, but…"

"I'll marry you," I said blankly. "Of course. Just please take care of those women, okay?"

"I will," he sounded so kind, like he really understood that my faith in anything good left in this world was gone. "Keep the mobile close, but don't let him find it! I'll contact you tomorrow. Stay safe, *cailín álainn*."

"Sure, yeah," I cleared my throat, "you too, all right?"

"Always," Cillian said with a touch of the swagger I saw the first time I met him.

I dropped the mobile on the counter and buried my face in my hands.

"You picked the wrong side, Aisling."

Yelping, I accidentally knocked the mobile to the floor, where it spun around and around as I stared in the mirror at the expression on Patrick's face. It was a frostbite level of cold, his mouth was in a thin slash but his eyes glowed with disgust.

Chapter Twenty-One

In which the scales are lifted from Aisling's eyes.

Aisling...

I didn't remember getting back on the jet or anything, really, that happened after Patrick leaned down, swiftly retrieved Cillian's mobile, and locked me in the bedroom without another word.

On the jet, he nodded to Jack to take me to the bank of seats in the back, as far away from Patrick as he could put me. My mountainous bodyguard sat across from me, hands on his knees with a blank expression.

It was hard to care. I was so stupid. The eejit virgin granddaughter of Padraic O'Connell. My job would always be to act as the pawn in someone else's game. A living, breathing piece of collateral.

I *believed* him. I believed everything he said to me. Jesus, Mary, and Joseph, he must think I'm such a fool.

Why did he bother to be sweet to me? He could have just raped me. No one would have done anything about it. Was it sweeter for him because I was so stupid and gullible when I gave it all up to him? He must have been laughing at me every time I told him something painful, all those ugly truths from my past. Was I really that desperate for someone to care about me?

Of all the times the men in my family mocked me, beat me, told me I was nothing but a tool to use for furthering their filthy business, none of them ever hurt me as much as this.

The terrified, exhausted faces of those women. The disgust and contempt in Patrick's eyes.

I bought his whole load of bullshit.

"Take her home. Keep her in her bedroom. Make sure she has no electronic devices."

Patrick was talking to Jack as I stood there, staring down the runway for the private airport. There was a jet taking off, I wondered what it would be like to be on board, going somewhere else. A place no one knew who I was. I was put in one SUV, Patrick got into the other. I caught a glimpse of Liam's concerned face before the door shut and they drove off without looking back.

Back at the Doyle House, I passed the master suite and went straight to the guest room. Doris sat up on the bed, her tail wagging madly, thumping on the pillow.

"Mr. Doyle told me to put you in your room." Jack's gravelly voice was not unkind, which was a little surprising.

"This is my bedroom," I said. "Go ahead and lock me in."

Jack sighed and made a gesture at Doris. "C'mere doggo." She didn't move a muscle, staring at him with her usual simple-minded, pleasant expression.

"Doris! Come! Come here!"

She stayed stubbornly on the bed.

While he continued his efforts to lure her from the room, I walked in and sat down, staring out the window.

Jack sighed again and fell silent. When I heard the key turn in the lock, tears came flooding down my face, Doris whining anxiously and trying to lick them off my cheeks.

Patrick...

"How did we find out in time?" I said, striding down the rotting wooden walkway to the dilapidated-looking warehouse.

"It was Cian Murphy," Liam said. "He's your smuggling expert, after all. He was running a sweep of the waterfront and the radar caught the cargo ship hovering off Howth."

"And I thought we'd have to keep an eye on that one," I shook my head. "I'm giving him a raise."

"Whatever that weaselly little feck Kelly was sending to Ais-" he caught a look at my expression and said, "to your wife, it must have been from an hour before. Niall and the others had the women and some kids packed onto the trucks before we could get there, but Lydia accessed all the street cameras within a three-mile radius, and we caught 'em."

"Where's the ship's captain now, and the arseholes driving the trucks?" I asked, my gut tightening at having to face what was in that building.

"At the Sliver," Liam said, "they're getting worked over while Finian and a couple of his guys go through all the records on board."

"There has to be some connection to the Triad," I said. "As soon as you find it, take the ship out far enough to avoid detection and sink it. Use a helicopter to get our guys off before you detonate the charges."

"You got it," he said, nodding to one of the guards to roll open the door.

I'd seen this before, more than once and every time it gave me nightmares for ages. Dozens of girls, some huddled together, some sitting silently against the wall, staring at nothing. All my men were on the outside of the building, Lydia and a group of other women from the clan - and a couple I recognized from her pub - were helping serve food and bandaging cuts.

"About goddamn time, Liam," she said without looking up, "you got my goddamn interpreter?"

"She's on her way," I said.

Lydia's head shot up, and I almost took a step back. My ever-unflappable Arbiter was on *fire*. Rage radiated from every pore in her body and if her glare could start a blaze, the entire west end of the coast would be in flames right now.

"Tell me you got that fecking Cillian Kelly and his nuts are sewn in his mouth right now."

"Not yet," I said, "but I'll let you be the one to cut 'em off. How bad is it?"

She moved us back out the door, and I didn't take offense. Not one of those poor souls wanted to see a man anytime soon. "I haven't had a chance to get the rundown from the doc yet- she's a close friend of Dr. Meyer, he says she's trustworthy. But some of these women-" Her pale eyes narrowed behind her glasses. "Broken arms and legs, nothing set or splinted, all kinds of bad shite." She turned her face away.

Liam tried to offer her a handful of napkins, to use as a tissue, I guess, and she slapped his hand away. "I'm not crying, you arse!"

"Sorry, yeah of course," he tried to appease her.

She ignored him, using the napkins to wipe her glasses before facing us again. "A couple of the women knew a little English, and there's a kid in there, Miras - he can't be more than fourteen – who's pretty fluent. They're been in that fecking shipping container for almost six weeks- he made scratches on the side to count because they only fed them once a day." Her eyes lit up like the fires of Hell again. "Except for when they took some of the women out."

"What did they know about the bastards who collected them?" I asked. My skin felt like it was on fire. I wanted to tear Cillian apart. He and his shitty lot would pay for this if it was the last thing I did on this earth. They had to be a key part of whatever this Collective was. I would hunt down every one of them.

"Some got drugged by some pretty bastard out at a club, others snatched off the street." Her lips tightened again. "Some were sold by their own parents."

"Best guess on where they're from?" I asked.

"The boy said he and a bunch were from Kazakhstan," she said. "I think I heard some Polish, I'm not sure of the rest." Swiping some hair out of her face, she asked, "Where's Aisling?"

My jaw tightened hard enough to crack a molar. "She's locked in her bedroom at home, of course. Where the hell else would she be?"

"Here!" Lydia retorted. "I don't care what that bleeding sod sent her on the burner mobile. Bring her arse down here and make her see what he's done."

I focused on some scraggly-looking trees in the distance. "I can't… look at her. Ready to give it all up for that pathetic prick."

"Hey!" She slapped my shoulder and I grabbed her wrist, yanking it up and nearly taking her off her feet. "Sorry, boss. But think this through. You must show her who he is. Kelly doesn't know she's compromised yet. You can use her to set him up, and maybe we smoke out the rest of this Collective. You must set your personal feelings aside here, cousin. There'll be time for fixing things between you when we blow those sons of bitches out of the water, yeah?"

Sucking in a deep breath and letting it out again, I pulled my mobile out. "Jack? Bring her."

Turning to Liam, I asked, "Do we have enough guards here?"

He nodded, his usual humor gone. "Yeah, sure. There's also surveillance on the Kelly compound and the ship."

"Good," I looked away from the warehouse filled with suffering souls. "Let's go to the Sliver and show that captain what it's like to really hurt."

"You don't want to stay..." Liam hesitated.

I looked at him blankly, still painstakingly dismantling all my pathetic illusions about the woman I married, piece by piece so that eventually, I'd be able to breathe again without feeling the knife in my heart. I'd looked through the pictures that bastard Kelly sent her, I'd heard the entire conversation, him calling her his sweetheart, his sweet girl. She believed him instantly over me. Without a single doubt.

"She'll be supervised. Let's go."

The Sliver was nearly invisible at night, so much that unless you knew where to look for the doors, you wouldn't find them. Inside was a hub of activity; Finian and one of Lydia's computer protegees were going through the ship's manifest, tracking routes, uncovering money deposits and trying to link them back to the source.

"How's it going, then?" I asked Finian, shaking his hand.

"I think we're going to have some very useful information soon," he gloated. "The manifest has been quite illuminating. This trip is the captain's fifth in six months carrying human cargo. There's several specific stops he's made each time. It ties into the intelligence that this Collective group of limp dicks are planning a whole chain of sex dungeons. Resorts. Whatever the feck they're calling them. But it's going to make them easier to track. I think you'll enjoy hearing what the truck drivers want to tell you. They have a map of drop sites for the women and another..." he hesitated, looking ill. "Another drop site for the kids."

I thought about Aisling's shocked face, how I heard her promise that human trafficking piece of shite that she'd marry him, no hesitation. I clenched my hands into fists, hearing my knuckles creak. "Liam."

"Yeah, boss?"

"Let's go visit our friends downstairs."

He gives me a grin like I'd just offered him half ownership in Lydia's bar. "Right behind you."

Aisling...

Watching the light posts become farther apart as we left the city, I wondered if Patrick was sending me out somewhere isolated to kill me. I thought about my Ma, and how even knowing what was about to happen to her, her only thought had been for me.

No matter what he did, I'd try to be strong. I thought about Bridget and the kids, crossing myself and praying for their safety. They didn't know anything. They thought that evil bastard was a good guy. Surely, he'd leave them alone.

When the car finally pulled up to a battered-looking warehouse, I knew what was going to happen to me. I wouldn't beg these bastards. They weren't going to see me cry.

Still, I jumped a little when Jack swung my door open. Looking at the woods around the building, I wondered if I could make a break for it, maybe lose myself in the forest? That hope was abruptly crushed when he took me by the arm. Not hard, more like he was helping me over the uneven ground, which I found kind of funny. Like it mattered if I had a skinned knee when they killed me.

Jack nodded to a couple of other men patrolling the building before opening the door, holding out his hand as if to invite me in.

"Aren't you..." I floundered, "aren't you coming in?"

He shook his head, his giant face was solemn. "No men."

What was happening? I walked in through the door in a daze and froze. Oh, Mother Mary and all the Saints. So many girls, even some kids, crying quietly. Cillian was right, my husband was a monster, the Doyles were just as evil as the O'Connells.

"There you are." It was Lydia, picking up a pile of sweatpants on her way over to me. "Well, come and help, then."

"You must be fecking joking," I hissed. "*You,* of all people helping Patrick do this?"

"Shut it!" Lydia snapped, taking my arm and spinning me around. "What do you see?"

"Get your hand off me," I said between my clenched teeth. After a second or two, my brow furrowed. None of them looked terrified. Exhausted, heartbroken, yes. They didn't shrink from the other women who were helping them. I recognized a lot of them from the Doyle clan, even some of the wives or daughters of fallen O'Connell men. They were serving food, two were carrying medical supplies, following a woman around in a white coat, who was examining the most injured-looking. A couple of the younger girls were playing games with the kids. And no men inside.

"You seeing it yet, genius?" Lydia said coldly. "Does it look like we are the ones who were shipping these people to the auction house?"

"But..." I pressed my hands to my head, feeling like my brain was leaking out. "I saw the pictures! I saw-"

"You saw what that miserable prick Cillian Kelly wanted you to see," she interrupted me, "Niall may have been the Second to Patrick Senior, but he's been working for Kelly and his lot since the beginning. I can show you videos. Pictures. Even audio if you want. Big, clear, high-quality images of the bastards who have been doing this under our noses."

"So..." I was still squeezing my head, as if that would make this whole thing make sense. The reality that Patrick had heard me offer to spy for the bastards who made this happen, how I promised to marry Cillian... Jesus, Mary, and Joseph, why hadn't I *thought* about it? Why didn't I question the pictures against everything I knew about the man I married?

Though... why didn't he talk to me? Why did he go cold and ugly - turn into the Silent Irishman - without even explaining what had happened?

Lydia's chilly expression softened slightly. "You didn't know. Now stop marinating in your guilt and help me. These people need taking care of, and I'm not maternal so it's beginning to annoy me."

I gave a laugh that turned into a sob, but I pressed the back of my hand against my mouth. I didn't get to cry and feel sorry for myself. Not now. "Where do I start?" I said.

She thrust the pile of clothes at me. "Here. There are showers in the back and we're giving everyone clean clothes when they come out. Keep an eye out for injuries the doc didn't catch."

I nod a little too hard, tears stinging my eyes. "I can do that."

Chapter Twenty-Two

In which Aisling shows just how mad an Irishwoman can get.

Aisling...

I was brushing the hair of a girl who couldn't speak. I'd finally gotten her to eat something a few minutes ago, the first thing she'd been able to do since I got here. Her hair was worse than mine after a long day of playing with Zoe and Finn. Even after her shower, it was a snarled, matted mess and her hand crept up to pat at it every now and then.

"I could brush your hair for you, if you like," I offered, "my hair gets like this all the time." After waiting for her faint nod, I borrowed a brush from Lydia's crew and carefully separated her hair into thirds, starting on the first section.

"My Ma used to brush my hair for me," I volunteered, "I'd be yowling like a stuck cat and she'd put up with it, just combing through the mess." She seemed like she was listening, so I kept talking. Silly things, mostly. About my niece Zoe, and her rats. How I took to hiding stuffed rats everywhere to freak out Patrick. I chuckled, even though there were tears in my eyes. "You should have seen his arms flapping around like a windmill."

Her shoulders shook, I wasn't sure if it was laughter or tears, so I kept brushing. "I'm Aisling, by the way."

"M..."

I moved on to the third section. "I didn't catch your name?"

"Maja," she whispered.

"Maja," I repeated, "that's pretty. Polish?"

"Mm-hmm."

I started to braid her hair, waiting to see if she wanted to say anything more. She was silent, so I talked about Doris, the stupidest dog on the planet who tried to jump off our second-story terrace to chase a squirrel, and how I nearly fell over the railing, grabbing her just in time. After a while, I realized she'd fallen asleep.

Putting a blanket over Maja, I stood up, stretching my back. My broken arm was beginning to throb and I wondered if the doctor would have any aspirin to spare.

Lydia was on her laptop, earbuds in, fingers flying, and listening intently to someone sending her information. She glanced up at me, pulling out one earbud. Nodding toward Maja, she asked, "How's she doing?"

"Better," I said, sitting down when she pointed to the seat next to her. "She gave me her name and I think she understands some English. She wouldn't say anything else. But she let me brush her hair. That seems like progress."

"It was," she said, still watching something on her laptop.

"What are you doing?" I asked.

"I got into the bank deposits for that ship's captain and I'm tracking back to the source. The deposit ran through two banks and three different countries before it landed in his account. Once I get back to the source, though, I can see the activity on the original account and start putting together the pattern." She pushed up her glasses and rubbed her eyes.

"What happens now?" I said, rubbing my throbbing arm.

"With what?" Her fingers were flying over the keyboard again.

"For these people?" I asked, "Where do they go?"

"It depends," she said, "most we'll send back to their families. A few were sold - usually the kids - by their own people, so we'll find something better for them."

"You've done this before?"

"Twice," Lydia answered, "once with Liam and some friends. It was more freelance, you could say. The second time, the Morozov Bratva intercepted the shipment and helped us get everyone somewhere safe."

"You couldn't give the *garda* an anonymous tip? Give them a chance to track the traffickers and arrest them?"

Her smile was vaguely pitying. "Who do you think is looking the other way when these poor souls are getting snatched in the first place?"

"That can't be everyone in law enforcement," I protested, shaking my head.

"No," she allowed, "and here, at least, we have some key officials on *our* payroll. But it's not as if we can open ourselves to scrutiny. Should the wrong people get involved, these women end up somewhere even worse. Or dead, if they think they're too much of a liability."

"Oh, good lord, it's like I've forgotten what family I was raised in," I sighed, "asking why we don't call the *garda*."

"Don't look at it like that," Lydia said, "just view it as... radical self-reliance."

"That sounds so much better, then," I said, feeling a little of the wall built up between us start to dismantle again.

I was dozing in a corner when Lydia shook my shoulder. "Wake up, superspy. It's your time to shine."

"Sorry?" I asked, gingerly rotating my broken arm. Getting up, I followed her outside. Patrick's SUV was parked there and I froze.

"C'mon," she said, linking her arm with mine. Lydia slid in the front, forcing me to get in the back. Patrick wasn't looking at me, speaking on his mobile, issuing some terse instructions.

When he hung up, he looked at me briefly. The old, icy Patrick was back. He handed me the burner mobile Cillian had sent me. "Lydia tells me you two have spoken," he said, looking out the window. "Do you understand what's happened here, then?"

I looked down at the mobile in my lap like it was a snake. "Yes. I was completely wrong."

"Are you capable of contacting Kelly and feeding him a little disinformation?" He didn't look at me, as if I wasn't even in the car.

"What do you want me to say?" I asked, feeling like I was floating somewhere above us, watching the collapse of everything I'd dared to hope could be mine.

"Tell him you overheard us talking about a big shipment of guns. It's coming in tonight late, at our Howth docks." He was checking his mobile now, his tone was completely indifferent. "Can you do that?"

"Of course." My voice was lifeless.

"Do it now," Patrick said, looking at me for the first time, and I almost recoiled against the car door. The contempt I saw in his eyes… like I was nothing.

I huffed out something that was half a sob, half a bitter laugh. He was looking at me just like the O'Connell men used to, those bastards.

Well, fuck him, then.

Tapping on the only mobile number on the mobile, I waited for Cillian to pick up, nauseous with anxiety.

"Aisling! Are you okay?" The despicable sod had the nerve to sound concerned.

"Sure, I'm all right," I said, not bothering to hide the tremor in my voice. He would expect me to be nervous. "Look- I- I- have something, I think? Something Patrick said?"

He barely let me get the words out. "Good work, *cailín álainn!* What did you hear?"

"He was on the mobile with one of his Bosuns. He said something about a big arms shipment coming in late tonight," I said, refusing to look at Patrick. "They were talking about the Doyle docks in Howth, do you know them?"

"Yes sure, of course. This is good, sweetheart, really good," Cillian said warmly. His having the nerve to call me sweetheart made me want to punch him right in the goods.

"Hey, Cillian?"

"I'm still here," he said.

"Did you get all the women out of the warehouse? Did you get them to safety?" I knew Patrick was glaring at me for going off script, but I wanted to see what that rat bastard would say.

"Every one of them, *cailín álainn,*" Cillian promised, "they'll be safe from men like Doyle very soon."

"Thank you," I said, still trying to sound nervous, yet trusting. Like the fool both these men thought I was. "Thanks for easing my mind. Look, I'd better go, but... take care tonight, all right?"

"I will," Cillian said, "we'll have you out of there soon."

Disconnecting the call, I threw the mobile on the seat next to Patrick.

"That will be all," he said, dismissing me.

"Boss-" Lydia began, but he cut her off.

I got out of the SUV, then stopped, spinning around.

"Do keep this in mind, *husband,*" I snarled. "You were thrilled to think the worst of me after hearing my conversation about those pictures. You know, the pictures of *your* men. At *your* docks. You're filled with contempt because I didn't magically trust you, but you instantly jumped to hating and despising me. You think I'm worthless now? Well, fuck you. You're no better than my father and grandfather. They looked at me the way you're doing right now. For my entire life. I'll play your game, just because I want to watch that bastard die for this. Then I never want to see you again."

Slamming the door with all my strength, I speed-walked to the building. I wouldn't let him see me cry. Not for him.

Patrick...

A sarcastic golf clap pulled me out of my shock, still staring at the open door.

"Congratulations, boss," Lydia said. "And before you tell me to get the feck out of the car and remember who's in charge, I'll do that for you." She exited as quickly as Aisling had.

I caught Liam staring at me in the rearview mirror. "You got something to say, arsehole?"

"Nah," he sighed, starting the car, "I think Lydia covered it."

It was, of course, lashing rain when we got into place at the Howth location. I couldn't stop thinking about the fury Aisling sent my way. She had *instantly* given up everything we were building together with that fucking call. She couldn't even wait to question me about what she'd seen?

She'd just believed everything that little prick told her.

Was I any better? Her words stung, and I remembered her heartbroken face with a wince. Aisling wasn't hardened enough yet to hide how she was feeling. She'd been furious, but she looked like her heart had been torn out by the roots.

Just like mine.

"You okay?" Finian asked, checking his SIG Sauer.

"Sure, yeah," I said absently, unable to forget how she walked away from me. Shaking my head, I tried to focus. "Is everyone in position?"

He nodded, "The scouts just reported a caravan of six trucks heading down the R105. Twenty minutes out."

"Good." I covered my Glock 20 with my jacket, trying to keep it dry. "Who do we have with the women?"

Liam's voice crackled in my earpiece. "We took half the guards from the warehouse to disperse around here, but there's still fifteen men on watch."

It was logical, but I felt a sense of unease nudging insistently at the back of my mind, a feeling I'd learned to trust since it had kept me alive this long. The size of the convoy heading into this trap was right, it was what I would expect. Kelly's attention would be on his potential gun score, the greedy prick.

"Liam, check in with Jack and Lydia," I said. "Ask them if they've seen anything unusual."

"On it."

Shifting position, I fought the feeling that this was wrong. That I was missing something important. "Liam? What do ya' hear?"

The connection crackled for a minute. "Gimme a minute."

Finian leaned in, "The trucks are ten minutes out."

I ignored him. "Liam! Answer me!"

This time, he came back instantly. "No one's answering. Not Lydia, not any of the guards who are supposed to be monitoring this channel."

The sense of unease I'd been fighting exploded into full-blown horror. "They're going after the women," I stood up, racing for my SUV. "Finian, you're in charge, light the bastards up the minute they get into range." I threw myself into the driver's seat, turning the key as Liam raced across the little clearing toward me.

"Dylan! Get every one of your men on the fecking road, we've got hostiles heading for the warehouse. They're going after the women."

And Aisling, I thought, *you stupid bastard, you may as well have wrapped her up with a bow for him.*

My Bosun groaned, "On it. Does Lydia have her gun? Is anyone inside the warehouse armed?"

Liam looked at me, paler than any Irishman could be without being dead. "Lydia gave me her gun to use tonight. She said mine was shite."

My fist slammed down on the dashboard. "We're thirty minutes away, who can we pull in? Who's closer?" It hit me. "Liam, get Flanagan on the mobile. Get his bodyguard. Get whoever in his clan that's currently in charge."

He was already scrolling through the contacts on my mobile.

This can't happen.

I'd left Aisling thinking that I despised her. This can't be the last moment I had with her.

Chapter Twenty-Three

In which Cillian Kelly is such a complete bastard.

Aisling...

It seemed like it all happened in seconds.

Pop! Pop! Pop!

Lydia shouted, "Everyone get down!" Her hand went to the empty holster at her hip and she cursed. "Ah, fuck! We're under attack, keep your heads down!"

I crawled toward her. "Can you contact Patrick and Liam?"

There was another rapid spray of gunfire that echoed from one end of the building to the other, drowning out the screams and wails of terror, then the lights went out.

They can't get these women again, I thought, looking around, desperate for a weapon. Dr. Healy was crouching behind one of the overturned chairs, the contents of her medical kit scattered on the floor. Scrabbling through it, I found a folded case of scalpels. Handing one to Lydia, I put the other in my jacket, praying I didn't end up just cutting myself.

I met her eyes and we both realized the same thing. "It's Kelly. That little prick," she hissed, "he has to have one fuck tonne of buddies if he's attacking Patrick *and* us at the same time."

"How did he find us?" I gasped, "I thought no one knew about this location."

The doors burst open, sending shards of wood spraying in all directions. The force was almost percussive; Lydia and I flew backward, landing painfully. A truck wedged into the ruined opening, its reinforced bumper and grill not even dented from caving in the entry. The truck's lights blazed into the interior, blinding me for a moment as a dark figure walked in front of the truck.

"There's my girl," he cooed.

Cillian Kelly. That son of a bitch.

Everything we'd tried to do for these women and the kids was gone in an instant. The screaming and weeping, especially from the children was agony to hear. The ones we'd tried to coax out of their catatonic state before were just... gone again. My heart felt like it was bleeding in my chest as I looked at Maya, rocking back and forth, staring at nothing.

"I have to admit, *cailín álainn,* that I'm a little hurt. I thought we were a team, that we were working together." Cillian was strolling around the main room, examining the terrified, shaking women.

"You evil prick!" I hissed, "You're a fucking trafficker! I would *never-"*

"Ah, ah!" His hand shot out and squeezed my cheeks - hard - with his hand, "This is the time for apologies and sweet words, Aisling. I am on a schedule here."

"How did you find this place?" Lydia snarled. She was bleeding from the corner of her mouth. One of the Kelly thugs pistol-whipped her after she called him a 'little mommy's boy with a baby dick.'

Cillian held up his mobile. "Aren't you supposed to be the brains of this operation? You really think I wouldn't put a tracker on the burner mobile I sent to my sweet, future bride here?"

I closed my eyes. I didn't even think of that. I *am* an eejit.

"Getting a call from my *cailín álainn,* here in the middle of nowhere when she's supposed to be home, planting her flowers and playing with that stupid dog?" He chuckled, shaking his head.

"You've got someone in the Doyle House, too?" I snapped.

"More than one," he smiled down at me fondly. "Doyle's not as careful as he thinks he is. Don't worry about his little ambush down in Howth, I still sent in enough soldiers and guns to punch a hundred holes in every one of his men."

Lydia was shaking her head, refusing to let this make sense. "You don't have enough Kelly men to pull off both locations."

"It's not just the Kellys," he grinned, "it's the Collective." He was walking around, examining the sobbing women.

Outside, I could hear a high-pitched voice shouting contradictory orders. "It's the Dwyers, isn't it?" I said, sickened. "You ordered the hit on your own fathers."

Brendan came swaggering in, still barking orders until a look from Cillian shut him up.

"Two loser sons killing their daddies does not a collective make," scoffed Lydia.

"All the *Ceann Fine* were meant to die that night," Cillian shrugged, "including Doyle. He deserved to die much more painfully for fucking up our plans. Every son in the Six was ready for it, but that bastard killed Mickey first."

"My brother Mickey?" I asked, incredulous and horrified. What was worse, I believed him. After being raised under the menacing influence of my father and grandfather, he would absolutely do something like this.

"While we're mopping up these pieces of shite, Campbell and Burke are being finished off by their sons. Flanagan's boy is young. He'll be easy to control." Cillian was so matter-of-fact about it all, as if I'd asked him what the weekend weather looked like.

"We'll be running the biggest sex trade in Europe by this time next year," Brendan couldn't control his excitement.

"Not that it will do *you* any good, what with your chronic premature ejaculation problem, now will it?" I laughed at his stupid, ugly expression of rage.

Brendan's hand came up to hit me, and Cillian grabbed his wrist. "Don't you lay a fecking finger on my fiancée."

"Are you insane?" I snarled, "I will never marry you, you evil son of a bitch!"

He squatted in front of me, and for the first time, I could see it, the madness finally shining out in his gaze, the monster finally shedding its skin of normalcy.

"You *will* marry me, you dirty slag, or I'll put you on that boat with the rest of these whores," he said softly, almost kindly.

"Flynn Dwyer and his pathetic bunch will never kill Patrick," I said. "You and your special little Collective can go straight to hell."

Cillian shook his head, as if deeply disappointed in me. Rising up, he clapped his hands. "Get the product in the trucks," he shouted, "we're running late!"

I fought and kicked, but when Brendan put his gun to Lydia's head, I stopped instantly, getting into the trucks with the others. I held one of the younger girls - she couldn't be more than eleven - on my lap. "I'm sorry," I murmured, "I'm sorry honey. But don't give up." She put her head against my shoulder and sobbed.

"Hang onto that scalpel," Lydia whispered, "we'll have a chance to use them yet."

We were in the last of the trucks to take off, an older model with a canvas covering the open back, rain still crept in underneath the tarp. I nearly screamed when a man wedged his shoulders and head inside as he crouched on the bumper.

"Hush! Just listen," he whispered urgently.

"Cian Murphy what the hell is going on!" Lydia hissed at him.

"We're getting men in place," he said, keeping his voice low. "They're taking you right back to that ship, it's still at the Doyle docks. You have to try to stall them as long as you can, all right? Doyle is close, he's got reinforcements. We have to keep these bastards from getting underway."

"Did you hear Cillian back there?" I whispered urgently, "All the bragging about the other Clan Chiefs killing their fathers tonight? Can you warn them?"

"I already got word to Campbell and Burke," he said, "but they'll be busy fighting their own battles. We have to count on our own people." Hearing the gears shift as the truck made a turn, he gave us one last look. "Don't let that ship leave the dock, you hear me? Do everything you can to keep out of that shipping container."

"Wait! What about Jack and the others? Is he alive?" I asked desperately.

He was gone in an instant.

"That man is a ninja," Lydia shook her head.

I ran my shaking hand through my hair. Keep our people out of the shipping container? How? Those arseholes have machine guns! We had those scalpels, but they weren't going to hold off thirty armed men.

"Okay, I'll just... I'm going to be sweet to Cillian. I'll tell him yes, I'll marry him but he has to let the women go as a wedding present. He won't, but we'll drag out some time while I'm begging him." I swallowed against the disgust choking me. "Let's see if we can get in front of the line so no one can get shoved in the container while I'm begging, then?"

Lydia was not an outwardly affectionate person, I knew that, but her grimy hand reached out for mine and squeezed. We sat in the dark, jostled back and forth, holding hands as I prayed to the Blessed Virgin Mary that I could be strong enough.

I smelled the docks before we saw them, the scent of rank salt marsh and rotting seaweed. The trucks stopped and Lydia leaned over to Miras, the boy who could speak English, whispering fiercely. He nodded, his huge, brown eyes wide in that determined little face.

"I told him to get everyone to slow down as much as possible without getting hurt," she told me. "Let's drag this out. You ready?"

Squeezing her hand one last time, I nodded. "I have to be."

We were dragged out of the truck and I pushed forward until I spotted Cillian. He was talking to that man from the Triad; Zhèng. Bastard. Of course, he'd be here to supervise. No one in any position of power would trust these men not to fuck it up.

"Cillian, wait!" I edged past two of his men, who grabbed me until he nodded to them. "Look, I'll marry you. I'll do everything I can to make this transition smooth. We'll have the biggest and the most powerful clan. I just- I want a wedding present from you. You'd give me that, wouldn't you?"

Zhèng was fastidiously wiping his hands with a handkerchief as if simply being there was tainting him somehow, which I found outrageous for a man trading in human souls. "This was a quick transition from the defiance you told me about earlier," he said to Cillian, ignoring me.

Cillian chuckled indulgently, "You had time to think during the ride, *cailín álainn?*"

I forced a smile, fine. Let him think I was weak. I edged more in the path where his soldiers were ready to take the girls back down to the ship. The steel container was already on board and open, the black mouth of it yawning open like the gates of hell.

"I- I did. I'm a realist. I just-"

Brendan's lot were trying to nudge past me, pushing the sobbing girls. Lydia was my determined backup, planting her feet and blocking their way.

"Sweetheart, you're in the way," Cillian crooned, "come over here."

"Wait, I'm just asking for one thing, please?" I heard Zhèng chuckle, the evil prick. "Please spare this lot? For me?"

"I think you know how this works," Cillian said with exaggerated patience, "we can't open a sex resort without whores, can we?"

"I know," I said, ignoring Brendan's attempt to push me, digging my elbow into his ribs. "But please, I know you have other- other shipments, right? These girls, they can be servants here?"

"We don't need a hundred new domestics," Cillian said impatiently, "what we need are whores, and this shipment's too pretty to waste on scrubbing floors. I'll buy you a fancy new car, how's that?"

I heard Lydia grunt behind me, that little prick Brendan had punched her in the stomach. I gripped her hand tighter. "Will you please ask this pathetic little fuck to stop grabbing at us? Are you going to let him touch your wife?"

Cillian's head tilted and I watched the foul thing inside him come out to play. "It looks more like you're trying to block him, sweetheart." He strolled closer, an amused grin playing over his lips. "Are you trying to maybe stall for time, then? Maybe you're hoping that Doyle might show up, riding in on a white horse?"

He leaned in, his brown eyes sparkling with a mad sort of glee. "He's dead. Flynn blew his head clean off his body. Your husband's brains are lying in the dirt right now. So why don't you step off the path and do as you're told, then?"

My knees almost buckled and I leaned against Lydia. "I'll be everything you want, Cillian. I'll be your perfect wife. Please, just give me this? I'll never ask for another thing, I swear it."

His red, furious face was suddenly in front of mine, close enough that the spit from his screaming mouth hit my skin. "He's not coming, you stupid slag? Don't you fucking get it? Now get your fucking arse over here or you're going in the shipping container with the rest of them!"

"You need me," I hissed, forcing myself not to back away from his terrifying proximity, "I'm your link to the O'Connell Clan. The heiress, remember?"

Cillian laughed. He laughed uproariously like I was the punchline to the best joke ever. "You're forgetting Finn."

I froze, feeling like he'd just slapped me. "What?"

"Your nephew, Finn? You do remember him," he asked politely. "He's the male heir. Sweet Bridget's all alone with two little O'Connells to raise. I wanted you, Aisling. But you spread your legs for Doyle, that piece of shite. So if I'm getting a used one, I may as well pick your sister-in-law. Don't worry," he grinned, "I'll care for that boy like he's my own," he paused, eyes sparkling with his madness. "Until Bridget's pregnant with *my* son."

Everything was gone but the red-hot need to kill him tear his fucking head from his shoulders dig out his eyes and...

Brendan had me in a headlock, choking me as my feet still kicked madly. Cillian was cursing, a long furrow of scratches across his face bleeding and a cut in the corner of his eye was seeping blood, too. A flash of pain blinded me for a minute and I blinked, just as Cillian backhanded me again. "You crazy bitch! You're dead, you sow!"

"Ah, ah!" Zhèng admonished, looking far too entertained by it all. "Do you know how much money she's going to make us? She's beautiful, cultured, innocent. Don't waste valuable merchandise."

Cillian was dabbing his sleeve against his torn eyelid. "I want to kill her."

"It's just business," Zhèng said crisply, "Don't throw money away. You can do whatever you want to her and still make an excellent profit."

"Yeah, sure," Cillian hissed, his ugly, bloody smile stretching as he looked at me. "We'll put her in one of the black-level clubs."

"Black-level," Brendan giggled in my ear, that greasy prick. "You know what that means? Anything goes. *Anything.*" He licked the side of my face and my arms flailed, trying to hit him. "I'll be a regular visitor, love."

"I'll kill you!" I screamed at Cillian, standing shoulder to shoulder with Zhèng, laughing at me. "I'll fucking tear you apart! Don't you touch them! Don't you-"

Pain exploded in the back of my skull and my vision greyed out as I went limp, making it easy for them to drag me down the path to the ship.

Chapter Twenty-Four

In which minutes and seconds are all Patrick and Aisling have left.

Patrick...

"We have *minutes*, Flanagan," I shouted into the mobile Liam was holding out for me. "Your Jamie may be safe, but my wife - our family - they're about to get dragged onto that ship and once they clear the bay, my chances of getting them back alive drop down to next to nothing."

"You've got my men, they're on the way," he said, voice still weak but bolstered by his rage. "I think you'll get there first, though. Tell me what you want them to do."

"Point at every Kelly and Dwyer man and shoot them. Don't hit the women and kids," I said between numb lips. "Liam, set it up with him."

My fingers tightened on the steering wheel. Every glance at the digital readout on the dash ticked away more minutes and made my chance to save Aisling go that much lower.

"Boss?" Liam interrupted my cycling desperation, "It's Cian. He's on-site. Aisling was fighting with Kelly, trying to slow him down. He thinks they knocked her out, they're dragging her and Lydia down to the ship with the others."

"Tell him to find a spot higher up. Start shooting at the men, drop as many as he can without getting killed himself," I said slowly. I could feel my focus narrowing, the way it did in a gunfight. "The gunfire will reduce the chance of them hearing us as we drive onto the staging area. Tell him we're five minutes away."

Five minutes. It was an eternity.

I could hear Cian's gunshots echoing in the little harbor as I pressed down the gas pedal, fishtailing into the turn.

Three minutes.

The lights of the other trucks behind us drew closer, leaning into the same turns. The gunfire stopped.

"God-*damnit*," Liam groaned, "you think they got him?"

Two minutes.

The layout of the harbor housing my docks was circular, and we'd paved a road around most of it weeks ago to make bringing cargo in and out easier. This time, it made surrounding the area almost seamless.

I was out of the SUV, Glock in hand almost before it stopped, shooting from behind the open door, quickly, precisely targeting and hitting every man I aimed at while I searched for Aisling. The screams and wails were a grisly soundtrack as the women flailed and kicked, trying to pull howling children away from the gunmen dragging them toward the ship, slipping on the blood and rotting seaweed on the dock.

"I'll fucking kill her, Doyle!" I heard Kelly roar across the staging area. "I'll blow your sweet wife's brains out! Drop your gun!"

He was almost to the dock, his arm around Aisling's neck. Both their faces were covered in blood and she was struggling sluggishly against him. His Ruger was pressed so hard into her forehead that if he slipped or even changed position, he'd kill her, just the slightest twitch of his trigger finger.

"Boss," Liam hissed, "don't you do it. He's just going to kill you and then her, too."

"There's no choice," I said, still in my narrow, focused mode that didn't allow me to think about things like dying. Not when my wife was half-conscious in his chokehold. Not when I'd failed her so badly. "Hopefully he's a terrible shot. If you get a chance, blow his head off. Don't worry about me. Just get Aisling away from him."

As I stepped out from behind the car, I could hear multiple clicks of safeties being flipped and bullets chambered.

"Throw your gun out where I can see it!" Kelly shouted.

I held up the Glock, wishing to god I could aim it and put a hole the size of a fist through his useless heart. I tossed it away from me, hands up.

Walking closer, I could see Lydia, vibrating with rage as that asshole Dwyer boy held her at gunpoint. All the women and kids were on the ground, multiple rifles pointed at them.

"I'm a little disappointed Flynn let you get the best of him," Kelly said. Brendan's head shot up, glaring at me until his simple brain connected the dots.

Brendan grinned happily, "Doyle, you killed my brother? Fuck you, that means I'm *Ceann Fine* now, ya cunt!"

Lydia may have a gun pointed at her head, but she still rolled her eyes.

Aisling seemed to be able to focus again. "Patrick? Go… go back, okay? Don't-" Kelly's arm tightened around her throat again and her face turned red, fingers clawing at his arm.

"I dropped my weapon," I said steadily, "take your gun away from her head."

He looked at his men, "Load 'em up." Kelly shouted, "Get them in the shipping container. Move your arses!"

"No!" Lydia shouted, bucking against Dwyer again.

"Lydia, stop fighting!" Aisling pleaded with her, her voice was a frog's croak and I knew she'd been struggling against Kelly's chokehold for too long. Her eyes were wide and she looked like she was desperately trying to communicate something to Lydia. I watched her lips shape soundlessly.

One... two... three...

It helped that both men were looking at me, thinking I was the threat. Both women whipped out something that gleamed in the weak light of the moon and swept them across the bodies of the bastards holding them.

Lydia's angle was awkward because of how she was held, but she dug the blade between Dwyer's shoulder and neck. Aisling was battling her broken arm to get at Kelly, but she managed to jam her scalpel viciously into his throat, drawing the razor-sharp steel across it and turning her face away from the violent spray of blood as he choked, dropping his gun.

She bent to seize the pistol, turning to hold it to Zhèng's head. He lost his constant expression of urbane amusement, dissolving into shock. His hand reached for his waist and Aisling sliced at it with her blade, sending up a spurt of blood. "Don't you fucking move," she hissed, "I will gut you like a fish."

Lights blazed on, lighting the clearing up like noon as Flanagan's troops made their arrival known.

"Drop your weapons if you want to live!" I shouted, pulling my other gun from the ankle holster.

"Do it!" Lydia yelled as the men around her hesitated, "Fuckin' drop them, you cunts!" She slashed the bloody scalpel at the closest man, grinning as he dropped his rifle.

"Now you see why she scares me," Liam muttered, coming to my side and handing me my Glock.

"What are we going to do with them?" Lydia asked.

I was crouched in front of Aisling, gently wiping Kelly's blood off her face. I smiled without taking my gaze from my wife. "I have an idea. Liam, go get Cian for me."

Finishing with Aisling's cheeks, I moved to her neck. "You've stopped shaking, that's good," I said, pulling another wet wipe from the package. "I should have the doc check you out, though."

"Her name's Dr. Healy," she said, her voice still a little faint. "She's checking out the women. I'm just fine." She wouldn't look at me, though she held still and let me clean the blood from her skin.

"You always say you're just fine, darlin.' It's okay to not be fine in a situation like this." I hesitated. "Aisling, I need to-"

"You were looking for me?" Cian interrupted my effort to tell my wife what a stupid bastard I was.

"Yeah," I sighed, standing up to face him. "Lydia found something interesting when she went through the steps of how you managed to track that ship hovering off the coast."

His expression never wavered. "Sorry?"

I leaned in to make sure no one could hear us. "The only way you could have found that ship on radar would have been by using a government system. There isn't anything strong enough to have picked it up on any civilian rig shoreside. It had to be a military cruiser or a government satellite."

Cian remained completely calm. Not a tic. Not a twitch.

"You're Irish Intelligence, aren't you? J2, maybe?" I said. "I checked around, you popped up about six months ago, befriending the Fitzgerald's."

His level gaze finally moved to mine. "I don't know where you got your information, boss. With all due respect, that's fucking barmy."

I put my hands on his shoulders. "You saved my wife. You saved Lydia, and the doctor, and all those women and the kids. I owe you a debt I can't repay. What's your plan, then?"

He blew out a long breath, like he'd been holding it. "I've found that oftentimes, even when there's hard evidence and arrests of the right people, once that *airtight* case is brought up, evidence disappears. Other governments step in and demand we release their citizens for…" he rolled his eyes, "…unlawful detainment." He stepped back a pace to light up a cigarette, examining the glowing tip. "And it all goes up in a puff of smoke."

I nodded, watching him carefully. Cian wasn't acting like a man who felt trapped or threatened.

"What's *your* plan for those men, *Ceann Fine*? Because I can tell you they've popped up like a fungus in past cases and I can't count how many lives they've destroyed. But they always weaseled out of it." He nodded at Zhèng, who wore the studied air of a man who found this all too distasteful. "That bastard? His Triad's responsible for half the human trafficking in Asia. He and your buddies there–" he looked over at a very dead Cillian Kelly, "were gearing up to go after the Golubev Bratva to move in on their trade into Eastern Europe."

"Maybe, we can help each other," I proposed. "Lydia's tracked six of the properties this Collective bought up to build their fuck palaces. I can give you the locations and the money trail."

Cian nodded, "And what would you need from me?"

"You've already done it," I said, "you saved my wife. All these people. I would certainly appreciate the Doyle Clan not being involved in your investigation, and I'm guessing this won't be the last shipment of human souls we'll intercept. Can you keep your eyes turned from my other enterprises?"

"You have my word," he said, holding out his hand.

We shook hands, me finding it bizarre and oddly entertaining that my co-conspirator was a J2 operative. Strange bedfellows...

"So!" I grinned, "You want to see what I've got planned for these pricks?"

"You must be insane, Doyle," Zhèng spoke in a clipped, furious way. "Do you know what will happen to you when my *Shan Chu* finds out you've threatened me?"

He was being pushed across the ship's deck to the open shipping container, where most of the men, including a blubbering Brendan and several other key men in the Kelly and Dwyer clans, were already held at gunpoint.

Liam gave Zhèng another shove that could be characterized as overly enthusiastic.

"That will be the last of your worries," I assured him pleasantly. "Aisling?"

She walked over hesitantly, watching the body of Kelly being dragged across the deck and thrown into the steel container with his men. "Yes?"

My wife still wouldn't look at me, and even though it felt like the knife in my heart gave another twist, I'd have to bide my time. I held out my hand, and she looked at it like it was a snake I was about to throw at her. "Come with us for a moment?"

Slipping her hand in mine, she followed me onto the ship's deck, in front of the shipping container, where several of our men held the ones inside right where they were.

Zhèng planted his polished Dior loafers into the deck. "I am not going in there."

"Yeah?" I swept my hand back to the women and kids he'd planned on selling in slavery and if they were lucky, a quick death. "They seemed to survive it, no matter what you sick fucks did to them. You should make it just fine."

Liam put his gun up against the back of Zhèng's head. "Die here or get in the container like the cunt you are. You were gonna put my sister and Aisling in a black-level hell house? Please, boss. Let me pull the trigger."

That was enough. Zhèng turned and walked reluctantly into the dark maw of the steel box.

I looked down at Aisling. "Anything you'd like to say?"

"Yeah…" She stepped closer, close enough to see the body of Kelly, dead eyes staring blankly at nothing, Brendan and all their men stirring anxiously, and then at Zhèng. "I hope your Triad burns to ash, just like your soul in hell, you evil bastard. You'll never suffer as much as the misery you've caused for so many people." She smiled. "But you will suffer."

Hitting the side of the container, I shouted, "Close it up!"

The shouting inside intensified, and my men tapped the steel sides with their rifles, chuckling.

"Enjoy your cruise!" Lydia called with a grin.

Aisling…

Once off the ship and watching as it left the harbor, I said, "Where are you sending them?" I still couldn't make myself look at Patrick. If I did, I knew I'd start sobbing and beg him to forgive me, to thank him for risking his life and coming to save me, even if there was nothing left of us.

Lydia leaned into me. "You're going to enjoy this. First, we have to get these women sorted. Again." She sighed and headed back to help convince everyone to get back into yet another truck.

"I'll just…" I crossed my arms defensively. "I'll go help her."

"Of course," Patrick said, his tone oddly gentle. "I'll be waiting to take you home."

I froze for a moment. "Wait! The men outside the warehouse, what happened? Are they alive? Did anyone make it? What about Jack?"

He sighed, rubbing the back of his neck. "We lost eleven men. But Jack and three others survived. He stayed conscious after they took you and managed to keep the others from bleeding out."

"I'm sorry. I don't..." I heaved a sigh. "I'm so sorry. But I'm glad Jack made it."

"Aisling? Darlin,' we're home."

I bolted upright. "Huh?" It was much later, after everyone had been put into a vehicle that would take them somewhere safe, and I was sitting in the back seat of the Mercedes, drool running in a line down my cheek and smearing the window.

"Oh," I rubbed my eyes, "I'm sorry."

"Don't be." He was out of the SUV and opening my door before I could even touch the handle. "You've been working with those women - with a broken arm - for nearly twenty-four hours. I would have carried you in and put you to bed, but I think you're going to want to see this first."

"Okay?" I followed him into the house and down the hall to his study. Doris came galloping around the corner and nearly knocked me over as she expressed her joy at our return.

Patrick flipped on the massive TV mounted across from the table where his inner circle would meet. I frowned, tilting my head. "What are we watching?"

He grinned over his shoulder at me, and it was so beautiful that it almost hurt. He smiled like he still cared about me, like he didn't despise me and find me useless. "This is the aerial footage from a drone hovering over what Lydia called the 'LE You Are So Fucked'."

"Wait. What? The ship? Why are we watching this?"

"We had to wait until the ship was far enough out into the North Atlantic to do this," he said. "Keep watching." His mobile rang as I watched the screen, as he listened to the caller.

There were a couple of men on board, I couldn't see what they were doing, but they finished whatever task they were at and climbed into the helicopter resting on the deck.

"Keep watching..." he murmured.

The drone's camera glitched slightly then came back, nice and clear. It had pulled back from the ship, the helicopter as well.

"Ready?" Patrick asked the caller. "On your signal." A blinding flare of light whited out the camera. This time when it came back, there were flames shooting out of a massive hole in the hull. The ship was tilted ominously, the bow already almost vertical to the waves. It took less than ten minutes for the entire ship to go down, the massive cargo container sliding across the deck and then sinking under the surface of the water.

"The men," I said, surprised at how calm my voice was. "They were still..."

Patrick turned off the TV, walking over to me. "Yes, they were." His gaze was hard. "Are you all right?"

I looked over his shoulder, staring at the black screen. Thinking about it. "Good. I'm really good."

"Good," he echoed. "Let's go to bed."

We climbed the stairs, shoulder to shoulder and I didn't know what to think. Did he mean, go to bed together? I wasn't sure I could sleep in the same bed with him.

When Patrick opened the door to the master suite, I stayed frozen in the hallway. He looked back. "Will you come in?"

I wished I knew what to tell him. I wished the last seventy-two hours never happened and that I didn't know how easily we could give up on each other. I wished I could tell my husband that I loved him. I don't know if he would ever believe me.

"Hey," he ran the back of his hand lightly down my cheek. "There's much to be said. Much to apologize for, but..." he hesitated. "I would like it if you'd sleep in here tonight. In our bed. Just sleep."

Doris, the ridiculous bag of fur and no brains, took him at his word, racing happily into the room and leaping on the bed.

"No, Doris!" Patrick said crossly, "I didn't mean you, ya git!"

"Doris stays," I blurted, shocking myself.

"What, are ya serious now?" He looked at me like I'd completely lost my mind. "I thought you couldn't stand that dog!"

Shrugging awkwardly, I stepped inside. "She stays."

He chuckled, shaking his head. "She stays, then. Come to bed." He took my hand and led me into his - maybe our - bedroom.

Chapter Twenty-Five

In which life is too short for anything less than true love.

Aisling...

Waking up in Patrick's arms was not what I'd expected.

We'd started the night on the far ends of the massive bed and ended up in a tangle of arms and legs. The slant of the sun coming through the terrace doors told me it was early afternoon. Doris had apparently taken off for parts unknown, or more likely the kitchen to badger Maeve for treats.

I was lying half on, half off Patrick's chest with my legs twined with his. His right knee was up slightly, which meant his thigh was pressed between my legs and firmly against my center, which was warming up in a hurry. In fact, I was seconds away from humping his leg, something that my subconscious and ovaries were in complete agreement about needing to happen. Fortunately, my brain kicked in at the last minute and saved me from abject humiliation.

He was so beautiful, this man. He was still asleep, breathing deeply. His eyelashes made thick fans on those lovely, high cheekbones. A stray lock of his silvering hair slid over his forehead and I fingered it gingerly. When did the poor man start turning gray? Given the life he's had, any time after, say, ten years old would make sense. It was very unfair that it was actually a beautiful silver color. Add that to his blue eyes, and he would be one of those men who just got more attractive as they aged.

I tried to ignore how this observation made my chest hurt. Because this man would never belong to me. The connection we'd made was too fragile, and the ties broke like spun sugar at the first challenge and showed we were more eager to mistrust and despise each other than to try to hold on to what we were building.

"Such a sad face to see when I'm just waking up."

Patrick's hand covered mine before I could pull it away from where it was resting on his chest. "How are you feeling?"

"I'm fine," I said automatically, trying to avoid his gaze, which felt like it was lasering its way into my mind.

"Fine," he scoffed gently. "Broken arm, worked with traumatized women and children for twenty-four hours straight. Got slapped around. Pistol whipped. And you're fine."

"I am," I said defensively.

Patrick put one arm behind his head to see me better and lifted my chin with his other hand. "*Mo stór,* I don't presume to know what your childhood was like. But I'm thinking you were told not to eat too much. Not to feel too much. Not to be too much. To never complain. To never ask for anything for yourself." His thumb traveled over to my cheekbone, rubbing it softly.

"So now the script is set, then. Before you even get a chance to decide if you're hungry, or in pain, or anything that might inconvenience your family, you recite those words beaten into you, yeah?"

"And you got your degree in Psychology where?" That came out ruder than I meant but I was flustered.

Patrick refused to take offense, chuckling softly. "A little too raw, first thing in the morning?"

"It's afternoon," I stupidly correct because I couldn't think of anything coherent to add to this conversation. He sat up, crossing his legs and effortlessly scooping me into his lap.

"There's things I have to say to you," he angled his head, making me look at him. "Will you listen?"

I huffed out a deep breath, blowing a bit of hair off my face. The moment felt oddly fragile, like the words inside my head. The ones I wanted to tell him but I couldn't because if he didn't take them from me they would crash against the hardness of his heart and shatter into a million pieces.

"Sure, yeah," I managed, swallowing the words back down.

"When you tore into me yesterday, every single thing you said was right."

My head jerked up and I stared at him, shocked.

"What," he said, "no one's ever told you that you were right before?"

I frowned as I thought about it.

"That's answer enough," he said, readjusting me a bit on his lap. "You and I... we were just getting to know each other. And when Kelly decided to fuck with you that night, it was late, you'd been drinking, and you're sent these pictures - the worst possible pictures - that showed our docks and our men. That prick knew exactly what would hurt you the most, the thing that would make sure you weren't thinking clearly and you'd agree to anything to help those women."

"Wait," I interrupted, the grotesque images of Niall and that whip hitting me all over again. "Your... that guy Niall. Please tell me he's dead or something."

Patrick smiled, playing with a bit of my hair, rubbing it between his fingers. "He was in the shipping container."

"Good!" I hissed the word out forcefully, like it was something that tasted nasty.

He stayed silent for a moment, both of us listening to my rapid breathing in the quiet room until I could slow it down again.

"And here I come, expecting you to magically know who was in the wrong, that you wouldn't be affected by such horrible images and hoping..." He hesitated, forcing his shoulders to relax. "Hoping that our beginning, tentative as it was, would hold enough for you to talk to me. That you would never think I could be capable of such dark things."

"Something that does not go away," I whispered, not really hearing myself, "A love that gives the strength to endure all things."

He was shocked, and that flush rising on his pale skin maybe indicating a little embarrassment, too. "I see Tania's been opening her big yap again."

"I thought it was beautiful, what you did for them," I smiled up at him shyly.

"Nice to know I can fix other people's love lives' but not my own," he said wryly.

Does that mean... he *wants* this? I skip over the L-word, it's too much right now.

Until he says it.

"Wife," Patrick said, sitting up and cupping my face, "I'm jumping in with both feet here. I love you." He shaped the words precisely as if to make sure I could read his lips in case my hearing didn't register it. "How I behaved that night didn't show it. I was disappointed, and stunned. I thought we'd made so much progress together, and..." He huffed out another breath. "I didn't stop to think how it had impacted you, just floundered in my own misery."

"I..." I was still back on that second sentence in his little speech. "You do?"

Blessedly, he understood what I was asking for. "The most important thing my parents taught me was that whether we're in the Mob life or any life, that our time is short. We don't know how many years we have and they showed me that when you find the person you love, you don't waste a single day." His grin lit up his eyes with a wild sort of beauty. "They said 'I love you' to each other every day. And I'm going to say it to you, and I'll do my damndest to make you want to say it back."

Tears instantly welled up in my eyes and my ability for rational thought just flew out the window like a startled sparrow. "Saying something that beautiful to me, and us not even dressed yet, you arse!"

His look of concern from when I started weeping like an idiot dissolved into relief and another grin. "Oh, I got you, darlin.' Getting all emotional for me? You love me. Admit it then."

"No, I don't," I lied immediately.

Bringing his lips to mine, my husband gave me a long, glorious kiss, full of passion and tongue and the slightest nip of my lower lip at the end of it. "Yes, you do…" he whispered and kissed me. "Say it, *mo stór* and I'll make you come before you leave this bed."

"That sounded more threatening than perhaps you meant?" I said, eyes drooping as he kissed me again. Thoroughly. The kind of kiss you felt clear down in your toes. Sliding my fingers through his hair, I held on as Patrick kissed down my neck, supporting me on his lap with one arm around my waist and his other hand flat against my ribcage, fingers spread under my breasts.

"There's so many things I want to do to you," he groaned, before he ran the tip of his tongue down my throat.

"Still threatening-sounding," I laughed breathlessly, my knees tightening around his hips, which I noticed were suddenly notched perfectly between my legs.

"Hmm… he rested his chin on two fingers as if he was deep in thought. "I'm thinkin' I need to make you come first, and then you say you love me, is that the right order?"

I was giggling helplessly, which was as high and girlish and awful-sounding as it could be but I couldn't stop. He abruptly flipped me over on my hands and knees, putting a pillow under me to brace my broken arm. Caging my body with his, he rested that hard, broad chest over my back. I felt his stubbled chin nudging into the soft spot between my neck and jawline. He rubbed it back and forth, letting me feel the bristles scraping against my skin. My giggling cut off into a low moan.

"Oh, you like that, do you?" Patrick was annoyingly pleased with himself, growling a little as he rubbed his scratchy chin again against me again. I could feel it scrape along my spine as he placed kisses down my back, and then one long, sucking kiss on each cheek, punctuated with a sharp bite. I yelped each time, and he soothed the sting from the bite with his tongue.

I felt vulnerable, kneeling like this, knowing he was looking at the most private parts of me. He went up on his knees, his big, rough hands sliding up the back of my thighs and then his thumbs spread my lips open and my husband ran the flat of his tongue from the top of my slit to the bottom, and back again. It was outrageous, it was embarrassing and I wanted him to do it again.

This was apparently said out loud, and the depraved bastard could not be more pleased.

"I would *love* to do that again, *mo stór*," he says, his mouth still against my center, and he did. And then licked me again and again, until I was wiggling my hips and I could feel his chest shaking with laughter and then I didn't care because his lips fastened onto my clitoris and he *tugged.* As if his lips were directly connected to my orgasm because it felt like my diabolical, outrageously sexy husband tugged that from me, too.

"Please love, you have to stop," I wheezed, as he continued to gently suckle my clitoris, extending the waves of heat washing over me, making my thighs tremble, and drawing in a full breath was impossible.

Sliding his arm under my hips, he kept me on my knees, even when I collapsed face-first into the pillows. "So beautiful," he praised me, "so perfect, *mo stór*. Do you feel what you do to me?" Patrick pressed the hard length of his shaft against me and I shivered. "Nothing feels as good as being inside you," he whispered in my ear, "the way your sweet, snug cunt grips me, how hot you are inside... I want to live inside you. I want to keep you on my cock all day and feel all those tight, coiled muscles squeeze me."

He put the broad head against my opening, pressing firmly against me but not entering. His long fingers slid down to play with my clitoris, circling it, pressing down in long, slow strokes. Arching my back, I tried to pull him inside me.

"I want it," I moaned, "I want you to..."

"You want me to do what?" He angled to press his lips against mine, and I tasted myself and it was shocking and exhilarating all at once. "What do you want, *mo stór?* Tell me and I'll give it to you."

My hips were insistently pushing against his cock and he wasn't taking the hint and I didn't want to say it. He was *right there,* just one thrust and he'd be inside me and it would be so good... I knew how good it would be because Patrick had always given me exactly what I could handle and then a little more. Every time it was so good I thought my nerve endings would fry because I couldn't handle how intensely pleasurable it all was, everything he did to me.

Now, he said, "I love you." He said it again, "I love you, *mo stór,* tell me what you want. I'll give it to you, gladly. Everything and anything you want."

I wasn't allowed to want things. I wasn't allowed to ask. Not when I would be called a "spoiled bitch," but I know Patrick wouldn't do that. He would be pleased that I asked for what I wanted from him.

"I want you, husband," I managed to say, "I want you inside me. I would really like you to- to, uh fuck me and-"

The first thrust made me nearly scream with relief. His fingers were gripping my hips hard and his forehead rested between my shoulder blades for a moment. "Perfect," my husband said hoarsely, "fuckin' perfect, you are." His second thrust inside me was just as good as the first and by the fifth time his cock slammed inside me I was coming again as he praised me and fucked up into me even harder.

"I want you to come again," he said, his head tucked next to mine, "I want you to come all over my cock. Christ, you're so wet. So sweet and slick..." His praise died off into a groan and his arm went under my breasts and he pulled me upright against him, his long fingers sliding down to circle where his cock was pounding into me and rubbing hard against all those sensitive places inside that he'd shown me with his fingers and his dick.

His big, warm hand pressed down firmly against my stomach and Patrick *growled.* He growled like a man who couldn't believe how good this could be. Arching my back into a bow, he put my hand under his. "Do you feel it, love?"

Oh, my god I *did.* I could feel the pulse and push of him inside me from the outside and it was so intensely, outrageously good that I came again, clamping down so tightly on his cock that he froze mid-thrust, groaning like I've killed him. All I can feel is the weight and heat of him as he filled me. Every bit of me felt in tune with every part of him, like we were always meant to be connected and it took all this time to know it.

"I love you, Patrick! I do, I love you... love, love, love you..."

I shouted it the first time then as he carefully put us on our sides, still connected, I whispered it again, over and over like it was the secret that made everything finally make sense.

Chapter Twenty-Six

In which there are fireworks and a little "feck off!" from Patrick.

Patrick...

Two months later...

"Tell me again why we're doing this?"

Liam was pouting and it was just as annoying as one could expect.

"Show some dignity, Liam," I said, resting my wife's hand on my thigh.

"O'Rourke tried to hook you up with the Zhèng Triad in the first place! Why would you want to go back to that smug bastard's distillery for a *party?*"

I smiled down at Aisling, who was giving me the side-eye. She was some *beor* in that glittery silver and black dress, so wildly beautiful. Her perfect breasts swelled just a bit over the low neckline of the dress, taunting me and guaranteeing I would be a walking, erect cock tonight. Reduced down to nothing but my dick.

So, it was fortunate everything was planned out well in advance.

"Trust me, brother. You're going to enjoy this one," I said, kissing my wife's hand as I tried to placate the pouty little arse who was supposed to be at least acting like an adult if not my Clan Chief.

He grunted, pulling up in front of the O'Rourke Distillery, lit up like a Hollywood premiere tonight. "Just send out a bottle of the expensive stuff for me and the guys."

"Liam's so cranky," Aisling murmured, kissing my cheek.

"Come on, *mo stór,*" I said, already out of the Mercedes, nudging the valet aside and giving her my hand, "I want to show my beautiful bride off."

Nolan O'Rourke stood at the top of the stairs, greeting his guests. They were forced to stay in line on the steps, looking up at him like a king as they waited to enter the party. I spent the time nuzzling a sensitive spot I'd located just under Aisling's ear, whispering to her about all the filthy things I intended to do to her when we got home.

"Bold of you to assume I'll be in the mood," she said with the perfect amount of sass.

"Bold of you to assume I don't know how to put you in the mood with a little finger work," I retorted, biting her ear. "You want a wee demonstration?" I loved the pink flush that spread up her neck and over her cheeks. Still making my wife blush was so satisfying.

"Stop it!" Aisling whispered, looking around us, "We're almost up to O'Rourke. Let's make our gesture of cordiality to the miserable sod, drink his expensive booze, and then we can go home and..."

"Yes?" I whispered, kissing her sweet spot again. "Just ask for it. You know I'll give you anything, *mo stór.*"

"Ah, the happy newlyweds!" O'Rourke was all smiles in a tuxedo that likely cost more than the GDP of Ireland. "My dear Patrick and Aisling, lovely to see you. We must talk after I've dispensed with all..." He waved his hand in a self-effacing way, as if greeting the long line of politicians, minor royalty, celebrities, and mobsters like me was just yet another tiresome requirement in the life of a billionaire.

"That will be delightful," Aisling said, smiling and showing all her teeth in a way that was less congenial and more shark-like and it was turning me back into that mindless Walking Cock again.

His practiced smile faltered for a second before slipping firmly back in place. "Enjoy the drink and entertainment, my friends. I will find you soon."

We walked around for a while, greeting other guests and I took a glass of champagne from a passing waiter for Aisling while I sipped from a glass of O'Rourke's excellent whiskey. Best to enjoy it now, since it won't be around for long.

Aisling leaned against the railing out on the terrace, looking down at the crowds below us. I pressed up behind her, making sure she could feel my cock, hard and already throbbing against her lower back.

"Are you trying to tell me something, husband?" She was blushing, despite her taunting little smirk.

"Darlin' I'm hard around you most of the day and night. It's almost a medical issue at this point," I whispered, kissing her. "Just ignore it. It'll go away." She looked down at my tenting pants and reached out to cup her hand against me. Grabbing her wrist, I hissed, "Did I not just say ignore it, not fondle it? Jesus, Mary and Joseph, show some mercy, woman!"

I could hear O'Rourke's booming laughter behind us and turned around, placing Aisling strategically in front of the painfully obvious tent in my tuxedo pants.

"Lovely to see you, lovely..." he patted a gushing guest on the arm as he navigated past her.

"There you are!" His handsome face was wreathed in smiles but his eyes glittered. Fury? Malice? Amusement? It was never clear how he would react. I'd chosen this spot; a place away from the rest of the party-goers. I knew he wouldn't want the rest of his adoring crowds to hear what I was certain would be a fairly infuriated diatribe.

"You have caused me a myriad of problems, Doyle," he said, still pleasant, as if we were having a chat about the weather.

"Some might think it was the other way around," I replied calmly. Aisling took my arm, and if her glare could have started a fire, he would have been a pile of ash by now.

"I've been fielding calls with *Shan Chu* Zhèng," O'Rourke said, "his *Fu Shan Chu* has seemingly disappeared off the face of the planet. You can imagine the agitation this has caused for his organization." He sighed, sounding deeply sorrowful and straightened his tie. "I merely acted as an intermediary between the Zhèng Triad and the Doyle clan, and yet he seems far more interested in holding me responsible."

"You said his *Fu Shan Chu* disappeared?" Aisling asked, her gaze wide and innocent.

"Yes," O'Rourke eyed her, "the locator chip Zhèng had - all the Triad's men have one implanted - stopped transmitting somewhere in the North Atlantic."

"That does cast a rather large net," she agreed sweetly.

"You know, Nolan," I said thoughtfully, "I've been thinking back to that night at our wedding reception, the poisoned wine in the Loving Cup? It was a massive dose of strychnine, as you know. So the results would have been nearly immediate. Not everyone in attendance would have died, just the first few unlucky enough to drink after us. Maksim and Yuri Morozov, their wives..." I watched him closely, but he never deviated from that look of pleasant inquiry. "The people you'd allied with to obtain your distillery."

O'Rourke merely lifted an eyebrow.

"I'd been working through the gifts," Aisling added, "writing thank you notes for such lovely, generous wedding presents.

After Tania mentioned that you had given a belated wedding gift to her and Yuri - a silver Quaich - it made me sort through our gifts to find that *you'd* given us that beautiful Loving Cup. A shame that it was destroyed after the lab analyzed the poison in it."

"A pity," O'Rourke mused, "it was a rare piece, I selected the design for the engraving myself."

"These things happen," Aisling assured him sweetly, "I still sent you a thank you card for your *generous* gift."

I glanced around us to make sure we were still isolated from the others. "You can imagine the kind of suspicion this would rouse, the gift of the poisoned cup from you, the convenient murder of our wedding planner by Zhèng..." I shrugged, still smiling pleasantly.

I had thought many times about how this sociopath in an expensive tux had put Tania, Yuri's wife, in the line of fire that night at the distillery, just to prove a point to her. O'Rourke was so far removed from the doings of regular men that he no longer thought or reasoned like the rest of us.

Aisling spoke first. "Was that some kind of a- a sick- some kind of a sick little test? Something just to amuse you, then?" She looked ill under the pretty lights strung across the terrace.

O'Rourke gave his little, self-effacing smile. "I... wanted to see how it would turn out, I suppose. Patrick here was so very motivated by revenge, but would he stay sharp and strong enough to lead such a powerful clan?" His glittering gaze turned to me. "Look how well you did that night! And then making Zhèng disappear was *quite* the magic trick." He chuckled heartily.

"I hope the *Shan Chu* doesn't continue to hold it against you, since you were the one who tried to broker the deal," Aisling said with the most insincere show of concern I'd ever witnessed.

I felt the stirrings in my cock again and groaned internally. Was there nothing this woman could do that wouldn't make me hard?

O'Rourke shrugged. "I am too removed from such things to be in the line of fire," he said. "I merely facilitate and observe."

Aisling was staring at O'Rourke as if he was a particularly fascinating species of bacteria; hard to look away from, but you'd never want to touch.

"Speaking of observing…" he said, rubbing his hands together. "The fireworks are about to start, they're quite unusual. I'd seen a similar display in Shanghai last year and had to have a show of my own. It's a company owned by the Zhèng Triad, in fact." He looked us over one last time, thoroughly. "You positively radiate love for each other," he mused, "so rare in this world."

As he turned to leave us, I glanced down at my beautiful wife, who looked pale again. "Why did that sound so threatening, coming from him?"

Kissing her temple, I wrapped my arms around her. "Life is too short for anything but the love we feel," I whispered.

"Uh, Mr. Doyle?"

A younger man walked up to us, he wore a good suit but his hair was sticking up in spikes like he'd been running his fingers through it.

"Tony, good to see you!" I said, shaking his hand. Turning to Aisling, I introduced them. "Aisling, this is Tony Kwan, a very talented pyrotechnics expert. Tony, my beautiful bride Aisling Doyle."

"A pleasure, Mrs. Doyle," he nodded with a smile. "So… the show should begin in about fifteen minutes, just so you know."

"Excellent," I grinned, "we're looking forward to it."

He gave us a short, courtly bow and strolled off into the crowd.

"He seems nice," Aisling said innocently, "how do you know him?"

Taking her arm, I led her through the crowds, heading toward the exit. "We've done business together."

Aisling...

"I know you questioned this bed when I ordered it," I said, dodging Patrick's kisses for the moment, "I'll bet you're seeing its value now."

The bed in question was a big, beautifully carved wooden platform that was suspended from the ceiling of the conservatory with ropes at all four corners. Piled high with feather pillows and a green-patterned comforter, it was a perfect addition to the corner, surrounded by ferns and a few small, potted trees.

The bed swung slightly as we both looked up at the night sky through the glassed-in roof. Nolan O'Rourke, billionaire and lunatic, would naturally put on a fireworks show massive enough that all of Dublin would watch, and the conservatory was the perfect spot to enjoy it.

The fireworks had already begun by the time we'd gotten home, and they were beautiful, giant starbursts of red, fading into green and then yellow. Purple shapes of whales and blue fireworks that looked like waves.

"Oh! That's pretty." I sat up to admire what I thought was the finale, an elaborate and beautifully created display of the O'Rourke Distillery logo in sparkling golds and purples.

Patrick sat up, too. "Keep watching," he said with a grin.

I smiled at him, a little confused and turned back to see a majestic spray of silver rockets soar over the fireworks logo and explode, scattering the shape into a thousand fizzling sparks.

Then another round of rockets, this time in red. Because they were that color, it took me a minute to see the crimson flames flaring from a corner of the distillery. It was slow, relentless progress, fireworks blazing and shooting through the building.

"Oh, no! I hope everyone got out in time!" I gasped, shocked but not able to look away.

"They have," Patrick said absently, watching something on his mobile.

"Love, are you seeing this?" I nudged him but he wouldn't look up at the pyrotechnics debacle. There was a tremendous *'boom!'* Something so massive that the percussive effects of it shattered windows, accompanied by car alarms going off and now in the distance, the sirens of fire trucks.

"That must have been the copper pot stills," he said, "they're huge. With that eighty-proof whiskey, it's going to be quite the blaze."

"Patrick!" I shouted, rolling over to him, "This is terrible, why aren't you watching this?"

"I am," he said, giving me a kiss. Looking at his mobile, I could see someone was filming the conflagration and streaming it to him live.

"What have you done?" I wheezed, watching the fireworks shoot back and forth in the building shattering windows, and as the last copper pot still caught fire, the top of it exploded through the slate roof of the building. "You're sure everyone got out safely?" I persisted.

"Of course," he promised, angling the screen at me. Whoever was streaming the footage had a nice, clear closeup of Nolan O'Rourke. He was wailing like a widower, pulling at his hair and watching his beloved distillery collapse into smoking timbers and soot.

"*You evil-* this was you, wasn't it?" I accused him.

Finally putting his mobile away, Patrick wrapped my hair around his fist, drawing me in. "Trying to get the Doyles into bed with human traffickers? Not good," he shrugged.

A polar chill spread over his expression like frost over a window. "Nearly poisoning my bride? Billionaire or no, the man needs a lesson."

Staring at him, then the flames leaping up from the distillery that we could still see from miles away, I shook my head. "Revenge is not a dish best served cold," I said, "apparently revenge is the best pyrotechnics show Dublin will ever witness. Give Tony Kwan my regards."

It was wrong, it really was, but when Patrick burst into uproarious laughter, I did, too. It was hilarious in a horrible, totally appropriate in this context sort of way.

Ripping down his zipper and pulling his hard cock free, my husband lifted me and set me down on his lap, straddling his narrow hips. Holding his dick up for me, he grinned. "Climb on, sweet wife."

Awkwardly pulling off my undies, I angled above him, hoping the red glare from the flames covered the blush I could feel heating my cheeks.

Sliding his hand up to my breast, he pulled it free from my dress, thumbing my nipple. "Go on, darlin,' ride my cock. It's yours, take it."

Oh... it was somehow bigger this way, he went deeper inside me and I put a hand over my abdomen. "I can *feel* you," I moaned, "up here. It's just..."

I rotated my hips, loving the feeling of my swollen clitoris against the curly hair at the base of his cock. The bed began moving slightly with me and I moved up and down, taking more of him each time until his cock was completely buried in me.

"Hold on," Patrick groaned, his fingers digging into my hips, "don't clench down, *mo stór.* You feel too good. I want to stay inside you longer."

Pressing my hands flat against his glorious chest, I tried, fingers toying with his nipples and trying not to think of how thick he was, pulsing inside me. His hands finally slid around to grip my arse and he squeezed me, enjoying how it pushed me forward and rubbed my clit against him.

Yelping as he thrust his hips up and nearly sent me flying, I glared at his unrepentant grin. "Go on, love," he said, "take what you need from me."

Gasping with relief, I slammed back down on his lovely, thick cock, nails gripping into his sculpted pectorals but he didn't complain, merely helping me bounce with thrusts from his hips until the bed rocked back and forth as wildly as I moved up and down and I screamed with relief and pleasure as the sparks cycling through me lit up like the fireworks outside. Patrick sat up, gripping my hair and kissing me, moaning into my mouth as he spurted inside me and I have never felt so full, so completely... well, complete.

Epilogue

In which we find that some surprises can be wonderful.

Aisling...

Two months later...

"Close your eyes, love."

"Why?" It's not that I didn't trust Patrick but the man was very fond of surprises. Sometimes, sweet surprises like more exotic plants for my conservatory, or a kitten that Doris had immediately appropriated as her own child, more canvases and brushes after Maeve had told him that I used to paint.

But most of the time, his surprises involved sex. Not that I complained. So, when he approached me with a blindfold and a diabolical gleam in his eye, I was suspicious.

He had the nerve to look wounded, holding the black cloth he wanted to put over my eyes. "Don't you trust me, wife?"

I gripped his tie, going up on tiptoe. "The last time you surprised me, I ended up hiding - *naked* - behind your surfboard while you chased those tourists off our beach!"

Patrick's grin was filthy, and he ran his tongue over his lips. "You can't do naked surfing if you're not naked. But I made it up to you, yeah?"

"Hmmm..." I reluctantly let him blindfold me, but instead of stripping me of my clothes, he put a dart in my hand. "What's this, then?"

He gently turned me around, positioning me with his hands on my shoulders. "Before you is a big map with the places you've always wanted to see, circled with big red bulls-eyes. Throw your dart, and wherever that dart lands closest to is where we're going for our honeymoon."

"We... we're having a honeymoon?" I asked, "Isn't it a little late for that?"

"Absolutely not," he scolded, lifting my hand, "I am taking my beautiful bride on a honeymoon. All we need is a destination. Ready?"

I shrugged. "Let's give it a lash." He held my wrist steady, and then I flicked the dart, hoping for the best. I could hear the *'thunk!'* as it hit the board.

"Good hit, good hit," he said. "Let's try it again."

"I thought I hit a target?" I asked.

"Yeah, but I don't like Santiago," Patrick said shamelessly. "The Chilean police? Long story. Anyway, one more time!"

"You are a terrible man!" I was laughing hard enough that I thought my next shot went off, but I heard the light *'thunk!'* again.

"Ah, there you go!"

He untied my blindfold and I blinked twice. "Paris? Yes!" I clapped my hands, "I've always wanted to go to Paris! Definitely more than Santiago," I added, enjoying his sheepish grin.

"This is... Sweet baby Jesus this is grand!" I said, leaning over the balcony of our suite.

The Hôtel Raphael was the closest five-star hotel to the Eiffel Tower, and I was in love. The gracious old hotel was timeless, with its walnut wainscoting, amber-shaded lamps, and an exquisite canopied bed lording over the master bedroom.

"Did you know that Marlon Brando stayed here?" I said reverently, "So did Ava Gardner and Cary Grant. Oh! And Audrey Hepburn. I love Audrey Hepburn!"

"There's a fresco painted on the ceiling of the bathroom," Patrick strolled out to stand beside me. "I think it's the 'Birth of Venus' where she comes strolling out of the sea in that massive clamshell?"

I laughed at the thought of soaking in the big tub while the Goddess of Love and all her little cherubs stared down at me. It was late afternoon, and lights were winking on around the city like fireflies.

My wonderful, thoughtful husband checked his watch - a big, chunky Phillippe Patek I'd given him for his birthday last week - and put his arm around my shoulders.

"Watch the tower, *mo stór.*"

The Eiffel Tower burst into a blaze of a million golden lights, illuminating the structure and adding a glow that bounced off the massive windows of the hotel, turning it golden too for a moment.

I watched with tears in my eyes, thinking of all the times I added images and notes, places I wanted to go and scenes I was dying to paint, to my secret computer file. They were dreams and adventures that the sensible part of me knew could never happen.

"Are you happy, my beautiful wife?" Patrick wrapped his arms around me as we watched the tower sparkle.

"So much, my sweetheart, I just..." My throat closed up. He nuzzled between my neck and shoulder.

"I hate to rush you, darlin' but we are on a schedule," he said, "we have reservations at the Jules Verne for dinner."

"We do?" I gasped.

He kissed the tip of my nose. "I've put a dress on the bed that I'd like you to wear for me tonight. I'll get ready in the other bedroom to give you a little space."

Can any man be more perfect?

The dress was a long silk sheath dress, a gorgeous cream color that set off the blonde highlights in my hair. I was struggling with the zipper when Patrick strolled back in, buttoning his shirt cuffs.

"Jesus, Mary and Joseph..." he circled around me, admiring the view from all angles before zipping me up and pausing with his hands on my shoulders. "You are the most beautiful woman in Paris."

I smoothed down the skirt of the dress, hiding my grin. "Oh, stop, ya big softie." I walked over to pick up his suit jacket, holding it up for him.

"Thank you, darlin' *aahh!*" He yanked his arm back out of the sleeve, flapping it wildly and sending the little stuffed rat flying onto the bed. "Really?" He put his hands on his hips and glared at me. "Are you trying to kill me, woman? What the- *fine.* I'm goin' with it."

He stomped over and snatched up the little rat, putting it in his jacket pocket where one would usually have a pocket square. Hands held out dramatically, he asked, "How do I look, then?"

Struggling not to laugh, which I'm pretty sure would put me into a spanking rather quickly, I nodded solemnly. "So very handsome. Distinguished."

"We're going," he sighed, grabbing my hand and dragging me from the suite.

I was buzzing with excitement as the glass-fronted lift carries us higher in the Tower to the Jules Verne. When the doors opened, I looked around, frowning a little. "Is it closed?" The lobby was empty, aside from a smiling blonde hostess.

"Not at all," she said with an enchanting French accent that made me feel like a *Culchie* clomping in with mud on my boots. "If you'll come with me, Mr. and Mrs. Doyle?"

Looking up at a carefully expressionless Patrick, I narrowed my eyes, which just made him widen his innocently back at me. The dining room was empty, just the spectacular view of Paris and...

"Surprise!"

Bridget and the kids were there, along with Yevgeniy, who was carrying Finn.

Ella and Tania competed over who got to squeeze me first. "I told you, if it's a Bratva wedding, you totally get a do-over," Tania gloated. Maksim and Yuri nodded to me, smiling before heading over to shake hands with Patrick. And Lydia was... sitting on the lap of my mountainous bodyguard Jack, and he was holding Doris' leash.

"Go away outta that!" I laughed, "What the- how did you manage this?" I asked.

"Yer man over there," Bridget nodded her head at Patrick. "All his idea."

His vivid blue eyes met mine, glowing with love and maybe a bit of a smug for managing to surprise me.

Getting down on one knee, he pulled my wedding ring off as I laughed, and held it up. "Beautiful, beloved Aisling. Will you marry me properly? As two people who love each other might?"

"Of course," I said, "as the woman who loves you forever and always."

There was a little chorus of "ahhhs," except for Lydia, who made a slight gagging noise. A smiling official with a very strong

French accent had us speak our vows and this time, when I said "I do," I lunged forward to kiss Patrick before the chuckling officiant could say, "You may kiss the bride."

Holding the lapels of his jacket, I let him cup my face in his big, rough hands and kiss me again, thoroughly, with tongue and lips and teeth and much cheering from our little wedding party. "That's for missing my chance to kiss you the first time we got married," he whispered.

Then, there was cake - at least the bit I could wrestle away from Ella - and dancing with Bridget and Zoe, much drinking, and laughter. Some time later, I sat on Patrick's lap, laying my head on his shoulder.

"Are you getting tired?" He put his arm around me, holding me close.

"Mmm…" I hummed, "A little. But I don't want to go yet. Life is short, and I want to squeeze every second of happiness from this moment that I can."

"I love you, *mo stór*," he said with a smile so beautiful it made my heart hurt.

"A love that gives strength to endure all things," I whisper back.

What happens after Happily Ever After?

Life in the Doyle Mob is always complicated, so what happens *after* Happily Ever After for Patrick and Aisling?

Read the next chapter of their story - set two years later - in the extended epilogue here.

A Favor, Please?

If you enjoyed Patrick and Aisling's story, can I trouble you to leave a rating or even a review? Reviews are the lifeblood of an independently published book and often mean the difference between success or failure. Thank you for your time!

Free Books!

Join my email list to keep up with new releases and giveaways. If you love the Mafia bad boys and the women who (sort of) redeem them, I'll have a free book - *The Reluctant Spy: A Dark Mafia Romance* - to thank you for joining us.

The next story in the Morozov Bratva Saga is **Deceptive** - Giovanni Toscano and Ekaterina Morozov's arranged marriage - live on Amazon in July 2023.

The Morozov Bratva Saga

Arranged marriages are nothing new in the dark world of Russian organized crime. But arranged marriages in the Morozov Bratva seem to spiral wildly out of control. In the hottest possible way.

Mistaken - An Arranged Marriage Bratva Romance

What happens after a mistaken identity, a kidnapping, and a terrifying chase through the woods?
Something much worse. Marriage.
Maksim Morozov is the billionaire Bratva King of New York City. He takes what he wants. Unfortunately, that includes me. That's what happens when you're in the wrong place at the right time.

He thinks he will keep me locked up in his penthouse like a princess in a tower. He thinks I'm a commodity to be used, like the other women raised in his world.

What's worse? Maksim Morozov wants to own me, body and soul.

So, in the weeks between a Christmas wedding and Valentine's Day, he's about to find out that owning me is not going to be that easy.

Mistaken - An Arranged Marriage Bratva Romance contains dark themes and is for 18+ readers only.

Bedazzled - An Arranged Marriage Bratva Romance

I wanted Tania. She was light. She was the lynchpin that kept me from flying into madness.

My father taught Maksim and me with fists and cruelty that we were not allowed to want anything more than the life we were born into.

Tania showed me there could be more for me. But when I was kidnapped and tortured by a rival mob, I came out of it a different man.

I was a fool. I'm covered in scars and now I truly see my place in the Morozov Bratva. There's no room there for happiness. There's no room there for her. But I can't let her go.

Hellion - An Arranged Marriage Bratva Romance

How could I marry the granddaughter of the monster who murdered my entire family?

After I took my revenge on the patriarch of the O'Connell mob, there was only one choice. Marry Aisling O'Connell and solidify my new empire. Even if I have to drag her kicking and screaming to the altar. And after seeing the rage and hate in her green eyes, I know that's exactly how this is going to turn out.

She has every reason to hate me. But she's still going to be mine.

Books By This Author

The Reluctant Bride - A Dark Mafia Romance

Wait. What do you mean, my dad gave me to you?

I was ready for a fresh start in England, a career with the London Symphony Orchestra. But my father's "underperforming" company is bought out by The Corporation. Suddenly, I'm being told I'm marrying the tall and terrifying Thomas Williams, because dad would rather trade me to keep control of his company. Thomas tells me that it "looks better" to be a married man as his organized crime empire starts a partnership with the Russian Bratva Syndicate.

Really?

I'm a wife. I have a giant diamond ring to prove it... and a husband who can be kind in one moment and scary in the next. And there's car chases, and assassination attempts. There's a body in my cello case! Who has a marriage like this?

But by the time we're in St. Petersburg and surrounded by new friends and old enemies, my gorgeous, terrifying husband might just need me.

The Reluctant Bride is a Dark Mafia Romance and is 18+ only. It can be read as a stand-alone with no cheating and a HEA.

The Reluctant Spy - A Dark Mafia Romance

Maura MacLaren - mousey, dowdy, and very, very good with technology - is a perfect Corporation employee. Brilliant at her job, smart enough to know to keep her head down, and in debt to the criminal enterprise that gave her a chance when her past left her with nowhere to turn. But this puts her under the watchful eye of the Corporation's diabolical, gorgeous, and utterly unforgiving Second in Command, James Pine.

Pine has been sent by the head office in London to be sure nothing will go wrong with the Corporation's largest deal to date. The last thing a man in his dangerous position needs are feelings, or surprises. Especially feelings for a nerdy underling who is turning out to be full of surprises, including a sensually submissive nature that Pine finds too compelling to resist. But Pine is as cold-hearted as he is handsome and he never denies himself what he wants.

But when Maura's darkest secret puts her life and Pine's deal in danger, they both find themselves shocked at the sensual depths he will drag her to for revenge. And the lengths he will go to in order to save her life.

The Reluctant Spy can be read as a stand-alone with a HEA and no cheating. It is a dark romance meant for 18+ readers only.

Blood Brothers - Captive Blood One

"It'll be good for you," he said. "The stalker will never find you there." My agent sends me to stay on an Oregon mountaintop, cared for by a surly handyman named Steve, who looks like a supermodel ... lumberjack ... Greek God sort of guy.
I'm supposed to feel safe here? I keep having all these dreams ... dreams where Lumberjack Steve is biting me. Now, I'm losing

time. Losing blood.
And I think it's possible my stalker is closer than I thought.

The Birdcage - Captive Blood Two

Black Heart keeps me in the Birdcage, high above the blasted remains of the earth after the Night Brethren plunged us into darkness. At the gate of his mansion, the Shadows wait to tear screaming humans into pieces of blood and bone. In the Birdcage, the vampire who keeps me is growing impatient. What does he want? My blood? My soul? I don't have long to decide whether to take my chances with the Shadows or find out what Black Heart intends to do.

To make it worse? He's not the only monster who wants me.
The Birdcage is a dark romance meant for 18+ readers only.

I Love The Way You Lie - Loki, The God Of Lies & Mischief - A Dark Romance

A nameless princess: innocent, damaged and very lethal. A ruthless king with the power of a god. And trouble, lots of it.
When King Loki of Asgard takes the daughter of the Dark Elven Queen captive, he not only strips an enemy of a powerful weapon, but gains for himself a wife. Now the newly named and wed Queen Ingrid must learn to survive the perils of court life, the wages of war, and most dangerous of all, her seductive husband's bed.
"I Love the Way You Lie" is a Dark Loki romance for 18+ readers only.

Mr. And Mrs. Ari Levinsky Invite You To... The Worst Wedding Ever

Heather's given to Mafia King Ari Levinsky in an arranged

marriage to create an alliance with her terrible mobster dad. She's supposed to be touring Europe after graduating from college, but before she can blink she's standing at the altar trying to read her vows in... Aramaic? Heather's new husband is gigantic; tall, muscled, terrifying, and loud. And she doesn't even get to pick out her own wedding dress! Then, it's on to a romantic beach honeymoon, with so much double-crossing, and she finds the only way to outsmart her scary, ridiculously hot husband... is to out-sex him.

Mr. and Mrs. Ari Levinsky Invite You to... the Worst Wedding Ever is for 18+ readers only.

About The Author

Arianna Fraser

Working as an entertainment reporter gives Arianna Fraser plenty of fuel for her imagination when writing tales about current-day romance-suspense stories.

There will always be an infuriatingly stubborn heroine, an unfairly handsome and cunning hero - or anti-hero - romance, shameless smut, danger, and something will explode or catch on fire. She is clearly a terrible firebug, and her husband has sixteen fire extinguishers stashed throughout the house. She is also very fond of snakes.

When she's not interviewing superheroes and villains, Arianna lives in the western US with her twin boys, obstreperous little daughter, and sleep-deprived husband.

Join her email newsletter to keep up with new releases

and she'll bribe you shamelessly with a free book! https://dl.bookfunnel.com/4cnao7l0mg

Have a thought? Wanna share? ariannafraser88@gmail.com

Find her on Tumblr: https://www.tumblr.com/blog/view/ariannafraserwrites

On Goodreads: http://bit.ly/ariannafrasergoodreads

Printed in Great Britain
by Amazon

24537468R00145